Finding Angels

A Heartfelt Collection

of

Love, Laughter, and Hope

Finding Angels

A Heartfelt Collection

Of

Love, Laughter, and Hope

Rhett DeVane

Finding Angels
A Heartfelt Collection of Love, Laughter, and Hope
© 2025 Harriet DeVane
All rights reserved

Date of first publication: August 18, 2025
Published by Writers4Higher
Tallahassee, Florida, USA

Cover design by Elizabeth Babski, Babski Creative Studios
Cover photographs by Rhett DeVane

ISBN: 979-8-9992705-1-1

Library of Congress Control Number: 2025912910

Printed in the United States of America

The following are included by permission:

"The Traveler"/Forever Travels 2010. Mandinam Press.
"A Good Year for Blueberries"/Seven Hills Review 2016.
"Monkey Bars"/ Seven Hills Review 2017.
"When I am Old and Curled"/Seven Hills Review 2024.

Dedication

In honor of the angels,
human and animal, natural and mystical,
who have touched my life.

Acknowledgements

Rhett wishes to thank the following:

My blood family and heart family.
My friends, far and wide, old and new.
My beta readers, Donna Anderson and Jan Daly.
My cherished readers, who inspire and nudge me to continue.
My muses, who continue to hang out with me even when I am whiny.
My various dogs and cats over the years, loyal guardians.
Elizabeth Babski for her excellent graphic design skills and friendship.

And to God and this majestic planet I call home.

A Special Note From The Author

Recently, the weight of the world settled onto my shoulders. Like so many saddened by the turmoil and division in our world, I wondered how to move forward with my writing. A series of mystical events nudged the creation of the lead short story and urged me to continue the work. Who am I to question the reason I was placed on this earth at this critical juncture?

As I reviewed the numerous short pieces and poetry I had penned over the years, I spotted silken threads that knit them together. Joy. Sadness. Forgiveness. Kindness. Trust.

By honoring these common human experiences, we grasp the ways we are the same instead of focusing on differences.

It is my sincere wish that this collection shines forth a beacon of hope, like the one that had aimed in my direction.

In tribute to several cherished people, I have included these poems:

The Best I Know — for someone close

Wait for You — in memory of Steve Reker

Kris — in memory of Kris Knab

Perspective — in memory of Danny Henderson

When I Am Old and Curled — in memory of Theresa DeVane

1: Finding Angels

The woman waltzes to where Lou walks from the cramped, grassy parking lot, wedged into a spot she may later regret. Her silver hair floats, cape-like, behind her.

"Hi. Are you from around here? Do you know if it's all right for me to park by the road?"

"Not sure. I'm down from Tallahassee, about an hour from here. From what I read online, they only warned against parking along the main highway."

The woman flashes a wide, genuine smile. "I'm new to this area. Angelisa. Actually, I go by Angel."

The name fits. She has an otherworldly glow.

"I'm Lou. Real name's Loo Rain. Not Lorraine. But Loo plus Rain. My mother named me after what they call a restroom in the UK and the weather the afternoon I was born."

Lou marvels how she told a complete stranger her seriously guarded, embarrassing given name and the story behind it. Shall she hand over the sign-in codes for her bank and phone, too? Maybe this is the sign of early onset dementia. Fine. Add that to a mile-long worry list. Something to ponder at three in the morning when she should be sleeping. Along with climate change and global warmongering and the fact everyone on the dang planet views Americans as illiterate, mean, and bat-crap crazy. And ready to pull out a gun and shoot your head off, how could she forget that?

"I've never met anyone named after a bathroom," Angel says with a tiny chuckle.

"I've never met an angel."

"So we're even. That's a sound start."

They fall into companionable step on the narrow sidewalk, parting to allow others to pass as necessary, chatting like two old high school chums on an outing. Too soon, they reach the main entrance to the Worm Grunting Festival. Twin police cruisers block the way and the officers scan the passing crowds. Lou nods and smiles. Glad for their presence. No telling when someone with a firearm and a beef may decide to cut loose on innocent bystanders. The scent of hot grease sets the tone. None of the local festivals are known for health food.

Angel stops and pivots, searching the line of food trucks in one direction and vendor booths in the other. "I'm meeting a friend at the beer garden, wherever that is."

"Ask anyone. This town is not that big." Lou checks the text message she had received before parking. "I'm heading down this way to my publisher's tent."

After Angel asks one of the officers for information, she flashes that high wattage smile and floats away. Probably for the best. Before Lou leaves her all of her worldly possessions, which aren't grand or plentiful.

Lou's mother would be shocked about how easily Lou had warmed to Angel. Mother was the easy-going, never-met-a-stranger type, not Lou. Never. Mother had more friends and lovers at half Lou's age than Lou will manage if she lives to be a hundred.

Loo Rain had decided to come into Victoria O'Reilly's life at the end of her 39th year, a transition baby bracketed by hot flashes and mood swings. Though her mother could've coaxed the sperm donor for assistance, she did not. Loo Rain was her *darling girl*, the universe's gift meant only for her. As a traveling nurse, Victoria had paused long enough to give birth. For the first year, the new mother/daughter team remained in Colorado. After that, Victoria shifted her usual pattern, remaining in place for a year at a time before seeking the next opportunity. Through Lou's teen years, the two had been in step. Safe harbors for one another. Lou was never in one spot long enough to form lasting friendships, the one drawback.

Even when Lou attended college, her mother had shifted from facility to facility, yet always within close proximity. After Lou graduated, they struck out again, bouncing to wherever their hearts desired and the weather proved pleasant. The pandemic had stalled them for three years in North Dakota before Victoria accepted a position at a memory care facility in Tallahassee, Florida. Money wasn't a draw.

2

Nurses were in short supply and the money had always been more than adequate. Victoria O'Reilly bluntly refused to desert her profession. For her, retirement equaled stagnation.

Until the diagnosis forced both of them to remain in one place.

But Mom is gone now. At thirty-five, Lou should have reasonable wisdom about the meaning of life, and how she fit in. Even the tiny voices in her head can't manage to get the answers to their repetitive questions. Their three favorites play like one of her mother's old vinyl records when the needle got hung up. *If you could, would you want to be someone else? What do you really want? Why do you push people away?*

Lou can't take time to deep dive at the moment. She dodges packs of shoppers. A lady pushing a stroller nearly mows her over and doesn't bother to apologize. Lou spots the teal tent of the publisher and sidesteps through a family with four kids and two leashed dogs, ducking into the shade of the tent with a relieved puff of exhaled air.

"Good morn!" Her publisher clears a spot to set down bags.

"Glad I decided to come early. I scored a decent parking spot." Lou unfolds the portable chair. "Equally happy it's not raining or ghastly hot."

"I've already sold one of your books and two others. This event is always a good one for me. And it helps sales when the author is here to sign books."

The event works in both of their best interests. It's another thirty minutes to the small coastal town where Lou's rented a condo. She'll cut out before the sugar-buzzed, greased-up masses clog the narrow backroads and make it in time to check in and nab some fresh seafood for dinner.

Lou flops into the chair. The two women chatter between watching the ongoing conga line of interesting characters parading by the booths lining either side of the narrow walkway. People-watching was her Mom's delight, one she passed on to Lou. Every time Lou talks herself into getting out around humanity, she takes mental notes on details to sprinkle into future novels. People are endlessly fascinating, as long as you don't get too close.

The next couple of mornings, Lou savors a solitary scarlet sunrise, sipping strong coffee on a screened balcony overlooking Scipio Creek. The third floor Apalachicola condo is perfect for her needs. Small kitchen. Comfy bed. A view of the spot where the Apalachicola River and Scipio Creek blend to flow together into the bay.

Unlike the city, this place feels safe, with a lovely, slow rhythm. The commercial fishing vessels parade from their toils toward the marina to offload their catch. Seagulls and pelicans trail them overhead. Redwing blackbirds flit in the dried marsh grass. An occasional fish decides to try its luck at flight, jumping skyward then splatting into the creek. A gator guards its territory. Only the tip of its nose and the raised brow line show above the water's surface. To an untrained eye, it would look like a drifting log. Lou knows better than to challenge a full-grown alligator. It's down there. She is far above.

Lou breathes the salt-tinged air. Stored tension from the past few months seeps from her body with each exhalation. Maybe she should sell the modest house she and her mother purchased less than a year ago, buy a tiny condo on this creek, and become a dedicated hermit. A writer can work from anyplace.

After a quick breakfast of a toasted bagel and sliced pineapple, Lou walks the short distance to a small city park. This early on a weekday, she's alone. The grass is green, the park well-maintained. A few early flowers show pink and yellow faces. Funny how nature can bring joy when humans often cannot.

As she rounds a gradual curve, a solitary female runner passes, acknowledging Lou with a nod and flicked smile. Bad things can happen anywhere these days. Surely the woman is less likely to get jumped here.

A figure tucked into a shady corner snatches Lou's attention away from worrying about the runner and she leaves the paved sidewalk to investigate. What the heck is it? A mermaid? With the face of a crone and a stern countenance, it stands five feet tall, carved from what looks to be a tree trunk. Probably created by one of the local chainsaw artists. The way the wood surrounding its upper body has cracked, the mermaid appears to have two folded wings. Huh. A crone mermaid angel. How about that? Lou lowers to sit cross-legged on the dew-dampened grass. *Take time to notice,* her mother always urged her. *Really see, not just glance, my darling girl.*

Lou's mother would love this weird mermaid, as she had adored angels. Victoria O'Reilly hadn't belonged to a specific religion or denomination. After visiting nearly every country on the planet, she loosely adhered to a cobbled-together spirituality. Kindness. Giving. Respecting people. If you did all of that, who cared what version of God you worshipped?

"Many paths to God," she often said. It was one of the last mumbled statements of truth during Victoria Claire O'Reilly's parting hours. "The body dies, darling girl. The spirit does not. Celebrate me, for I will find release into a place of joy and peace."

Joy and peace: two commodities in short supply on Earth.

Lou had put together the farewell party to her mother's specifications, held the past weekend. She used her mother's long list of contacts to invite people she'd befriended over the years. Amazing how many took the time and trouble to fly in or drive to the Florida panhandle for the celebration. It was surely one to remember. Live jazz band. Dancing. Open bar. Catered food piled high on long tables. A mic for folks to relay how her mother had touched their lives. Picture after picture of Lou's mother, a woman who had embraced life and squeezed every drop of experience that presented itself. Even dying.

The one belief Victoria had held above all others was the protection and advice of angels.

Lou smiles, remembering her mother's take on the heavenly hierarchy. The Universal Spirit was far too busy with big issues to handle billions of pleas and prayers. So He, She, or It delegated such to a fleet of angels. Need inspiration for a project? Call on the Angel of Productivity. Taking a trip? Invite the Angel of Safe Travels to come along. The Angel of Lost Things stood at the ready to locate misplaced items. Any human endeavor or concern was passed along to the corresponding angel department. Even parking. Lou had asked the Angel of Good Parking Spots for assistance before she pulled into the small town.

The angels were there to help. All you had to do was remember to ask.

Other times, the flow worked in reverse. If they appeared in multiples— Victoria claimed the mystical number *three*, for some reason— angels carried an important message. It was up to the clueless, befuddled human to figure out the meaning.

A woman named Angel. Number one. Now a mermaid angel. Number two.

Lou lifts to her feet and makes three loops of the garden, taking time to note the way early light dapples the ornamental grass blades and the tight buds promising future flowers. Instead of noisy passing traffic or the clamor of neighbors mowing lawns and yelling at rowdy children, Lou hears the gentle whoosh of the breeze and the calls of crows. She stops to admire a painted box turtle and stand in the middle of a filigreed white gazebo, imagining the couples who had stood in the very spot vowing to be together forever.

She returns to the condo, answers email, and works until well after lunch editing the next novel in line. Every experience drops crumbs. If she follows them, a short story, poem, or novel will present itself. Writing provides income. More important, it offers a haven from the whirling mess of humanity.

Near nightfall, Lou sits on the screened balcony, decaf coffee in hand, watching the parade of boats returning to the marina, their coolers filled with grouper and shrimp. The freshest food, straight from Apalachicola Bay and the Gulf. Less than an hour prior, Lou had relished a skewer of pan-seared shrimp, gooey cheese grits, and cole-slaw. Tomorrow, she'll try out one of the other waterfront eateries for a grilled grouper sandwich thick with tartar sauce.

The swish of waves announces the boats before they come into view. One shrimp trawler enters the mouth of the creek with its twin outriggers extended like wings. Then it folds them with metallic groans and the diesel engine pushes it up the creek. The boat isn't shiny and impressive-new, like one of the few pleasure vessels she's seen, out for a day's joyride. Its stained and marred hull attests to the brutal work of culling a living from the sea. As it passes, Lou reads the faded name scripted on the side of the bow and stern: Flying Angel.

A sense of wonder circles her heart center. Angel number one: an effervescent human. Angel number two: a wooden crone mermaid. Angel number three: an aging shrimp boat? Seriously?

The universe has a wicked sense of humor. No doubt.

If you could, would you want to be someone else? The voice says. Maybe it's the Angel of Important Questions. If Lou doesn't answer, she'll just keep asking.

Lou takes a moment to consider. Sips coffee. Stares out across the water.

"No, I wouldn't want to be anyone else," she states aloud. "I like myself, for the most part. I can be messy and moody at times. But I enjoy my own company and the way I find humor in nearly every situation."

What do you really want?

Oh good. Lou must've satisfied the Angel of Important Questions with her answer. Time to try for another win.

"I want the same things mother wanted. Joy and peace."

Hadn't Lou found tiny bits of both these past couple of days? The soft pink of a buttercup flower. The way the rising sun shimmered the water. The sugared scent of wild honeysuckle. Why yes, she certainly had. Perhaps joy and peace were like salt and pepper: spices meant to sprinkle a tad here and there instead of things to squirt on like too much catsup.

Why do you push people away?

Lou pumps one fist in victory. She's managed to nail two from the Angel of Important Questions. Time to reach for a triple-header!

Before she can ponder this most soul-searching of the three, the phone trills. Lou glances at the caller ID. Selena. The nurse she and Mom had met through the oncologist's office. Mother claimed Selena's presence eased her when nothing else could. Selena was two years older than Lou, with the same gentle countenance as Victoria O'Reilly. Their tentative bond had taken seed the first time Selena stepped into the consultation room at the oncologist's office. A recent widow and no stranger to grief, Selena had remained beside Lou after Victoria's death, urging Lou to eat and rest, helping her finalize details for the celebration party.

"Hey, Lou. Hope I'm not interrupting your literary flow."

Hearing Selena's voice soothes the profound loneliness that had wedged into Lou's body the moment her mother exhaled for the final time. "Nope. Done with work for the day. I'm watching the boat parade. Glad you told me about this place."

"Knew you'd like it. I am *so* not a fan of theme parks. Much rather go somewhere that still looks like Florida before the invasion."

"I heard that. Same."

Selena chatters about nothing for a couple of minutes before Lou's silence becomes awkward.

"I'll let you go," Selena says. "Just wanted to check in. Make sure you're doing okay. I'm off work tomorrow, so I have a list of to-dos to put together. I should ring off now."

Why do you push people away? The voice nudges.

Why does she? Casual acquaintances are easy. She's long been a pro at them. Loose bonds don't snap and scar when broken.

Mother had filled in the void, until she didn't. Victoria urged, no *pleaded*, with Lou to open her heart. Not to the world. But to at least a chosen few.

"Forget the to-do list, Selena. Come join me here for the next couple of days. This condo has two bedrooms and a view to die for, as you are well aware. We can shop and eat amazing seafood and head out to the beach at St. George if you'd like. I found this tiny café that has the best buttermilk biscuits I've had in ages, and stellar coffee. What say?"

After Lou hits the icon to end the call, she leans back in the chair with a smile, cradling the coffee mug in both hands. A pelican swoops by, the last in line heading to the night roost.

2: Final Leg

A woman twice Nate's age and girth tucks herself into 33B, middle seat of his row. He's in 33A/WST, his personal nomenclature for the *window, seriously trapped* position.

One look into her rheumy eyes and Nate knows. Going to be a long, short hop from Atlanta to Tallahassee.

Not that I don't like people, or don't care, Nathaniel Hawthorne Johns thinks.

Nathaniel Hawthorne for the author his late mother wished Nate would've become. Johns for the father he barely recalls, thank you for nothing Vietnam.

"She was my only sister, my Barbara." The woman buckles her seat belt with help from Nate.

Oh good. Emotional trauma.

His shoulders uncramp.

Better than physical issues.

The first leg of his trip, SEATAC (Seattle) to ATL (Atlanta Hartsfield), Nate sat in seat B, wedged between the agonizing hemorrhoid surgery in 19A and the uneven boob lift in 19C. For an hour and a half, he endured the stereo monologues of his two row mates. Nate managed to introduce them, and one shifted seats with him to better compare health disaster notes with the other.

After that, Nate enjoyed most of the inflight movie.

Heaven. Better than two weeks in Tahiti. Better than sex, almost.

"I'm Katherine Hodges." The woman digs in an oversized handbag and offers up a stick of Juicy Fruit gum.

Wow. Didn't know they still made that. He accepts, unwraps the foil, and the tropical scent calls to mind a shadowy memory. A large, tanned hand holding his. He looks down at scuffed, boy-sized cowboy boots kicking up puffs of North Florida dirt.

The flight attendant passes, silently counting heads before the main cabin door snaps shut.

"Reckon we're not gonna get another seatmate," the old woman states.

"Most Fridays, this flight is full." Good thing it isn't today. Sometimes flying standby pays off. Otherwise, he would still be pacing the shiny terminals of Delta's southern hub.

Nate slips the gum into his mouth. Citrus and mango bathe his tongue. He closes his eyes and another memory surfaces. A wooden boat. The fishy scent of river water.

He opens his eyes. The woman, Katherine, watches him. "Oh. Sorry. My name's Nathaniel Hawthorne Johns. Nate." Oh no. Why did he have to elaborate? It invites dialogue.

She gives a quick nod. "Pleased."

His iPad idles in his lap with four downloaded novels desperate for his spare time.

"I've been up in Ohio for Barbara's service. Stayed on an extra week to help with family affairs. My niece just fell to pieces, bless her heart. Hard to suffer a loss, especially so close to the holidays." Katherine's eyes water. She blinks, takes a breath. "Toledo, you ever been there?"

"No Ma'am." Most everywhere else in the States, yes. Happens when you're in marketing, though virtual meetings occur more and more. Good thing too. Nate is convinced that airline food causes memory loss. Or maybe he wishes it would.

No way he can "un-hear" some of those tidbits of human interaction. Like the randy bedroom theatrics of one redhead's ex-boyfriend. Or the Texan's lanced boil that "shot hot pus like a Yosemite geyser." That one's still good for a stomach lurch.

Forget undercover air marshal. Nate figures Delta owes him hours of back pay for being the inflight counselor, hand-holder, and medical consultant.

"She looked so peaceful," Katherine continues, "but they painted up her lips way too much. Made her look like a common streetwalker."

Nate offers a slight smile. What makes him, Mr. Traveling Nobody, everyone's new best friend and trusted confidant? Maybe *by all means, tell me about your oozing rash* flashes across his forehead like a neon beacon.

"You have one of them kind faces," Katherine says, as if she can read his mind. "My eldest son Timothy was the same way. He passed two years back. Liver cancer. Drank like a cat with bad kidneys."

Nate folds his features into what feels like compassionate concern.

Katherine warms to her monologue.

Forty minutes pass. The plane's engines change pitch.

Nate starts his mental countdown. Fifteen minutes to wheels on the ground. He can almost set a watch by the sound of the jet turbines.

"And now Jessica's knocked up with baby number six, and God only knows how she's gonna feed 'em all, what with that no-account husband laid off from yet another job."

"Hmm," Nate acknowledges. He has the family history down pat, even the second cousins Jolene and Joanna who live in Chipley, but hardly speak to each other anymore on account of some falling out over a diamond dinner ring their grandma left Jolene, or was it Joanna?

The gum has long since lost its juiciness. Nate flattens it across his lower right molars, balls it up with his tongue, starts the process on the left molars.

"Lookie there!" Katherine leans over him and points out the window. "There's the Florida Capitol." She winks. "Don't look so much like a man's privates from up here. Not like when you see it a-risin' at the top of that hill on Apalachee Parkway." She laughs. Pillowed bosoms bounce.

The capitol building *is* known for its phallic shape and the twin domed buildings on either side don't help. Hearing such from a white-haired, Southern granny-type sets Nate back a bit.

The plane lands. Smooth. No stirred-up, summer thunderstorm air to perplex the pilot. Only cloudless, late November blue skies.

Nate helps Katherine unfasten her seat belt as soon as the all-clear icon lights up.

"Been a pleasure, Nathaniel." She extends a fleshy hand. He shakes it, surprised by the strength of her grip.

"Yes Ma'am."

Others step aside, allowing her to exit the plane. Nate trails her by several passengers.

Forgotten now.

He knows the drill. They walk off, all of them: those hordes of trusted aerial allies. He's grown used to it over the years.

She will probably round the corner to running hugs. Will her grown children Tommy or Susan come? How many of the grandkids? Maybe the whole lot of them will show to welcome her home. Katherine's been away for two weeks and Thanksgiving is coming up. Makes folks sentimental.

Nate too. He'd be talking turkey and the fixin's if he had family. At least he can watch marathon football games after his Swanson dinner. Not as satisfying as it used to be, since they switched the baked apple dessert to that other gooey crap.

Nate walks past a long wall where local artists' paintings hang. *Southern Fall Attitude*, the exhibit title reads.

He spies Katherine in a Hodges' cluster near luggage claims. A petite blonde woman wearing crop pants stands next to her. Has to be Susan. A man waits by the conveyor belt, angling for the suitcase. Three kids of various ages clamber around her. He can't hear what they are saying, but all are talking at once.

Nate shrugs his messenger bag over his shoulder and pulls the wheeled carry-on behind him, his faithful, battered companion. The used gum, he pitches into a trash can.

He's nearly to the double sliding doors when he hears Katherine calling, "Yoo-hoo! Nathanial Hawthorne!"

Nate swivels around. The old woman trundles toward him, face flushed from the effort.

"Whew." She stops a few feet away and holds one hand to her chest. "I got so caught up, I near to let you get off without saying a

12

proper goodbye." She holds out a piece of paper. "My kids tell me I get too familiar with strangers, and I reckon I do."

Nate accepts the note. Looks down. Up again.

"I know you probably have people, and it's fine if you bring a loved one or two, but I'd be honored if you'd join us for Thanksgiving dinner."

"I . . ."

"You don't have to bring a thing but a smile and an appetite. My house is easy to find, no more than fifteen miles south of Tallahassee. Call that number if you get turned around. Or stop and ask anybody you happen upon. They'll tell you where Miz K lives."

Katherine steps over, gives Nate a hug. The bosom pillows mush against him.

"Mama!" The blonde-haired woman motions her mother back into the safety of their numbers.

"Lawd. That gal's got the patience of a fruit fly." Katherine chuckles. Gives Nate a head nod and wink. Turns to walk away.

"We eat at one sharp," she calls back over one shoulder. "I don't abide tardiness."

3: The Hug

The witch woman in the fancy electric car zips in front of her and pulls into the parking spot she'd hoped to claim. Delilah hits the brake so hard, she's surprised the defective air bag doesn't deploy.

That would top off the day. A shard of metal flying through her face.

Yep, her car was on *that* recall list. It could happen, they said on the national news just that very morning. Chances went up if you lived in a hot climate. Factoring in the Florida heat *and* humidity, the safety device could go nutso and blow like a bad tire. Since the AC had wheezed its last wind two days ago, Delilah figures the car's inside temperature to be at least a gazillion degrees.

She puffs a hank of sweat-streaked hair from her left eye. *Guess I'll have to cancel the haircut next week. No extra money since I quit my job an hour ago.*

Wouldn't be the first time she had to hack her bangs with the kitchen shears. These days, didn't most hairdos look like a battle with a weed whacker anyway?

Witch woman gets out of her vehicle. Hits the automatic lock. Flashes a quick look Delilah's way. Lifts her chin and struts toward the grocery store entrance. Long hair swinging free. Tight, twenty-something butt.

For a moment, Delilah envisions a scenario. Shades of Kathy Bates, what was that movie? Oh yes. *Fried Green Tomatoes.*

Put the car into park. Drag the witch woman back to her lime green, gas-efficient subcompact and threaten to snatch every chemically treated hair from her head if she doesn't vacate that spot, the one right-fully belonging to one pissed-off, middle-aged, unemployed female who has had quite enough crap for one day, thank you very much.

Instead, Delilah breathes out a sigh so exaggerated, it amazes even her.

Two rows over, a parking spot opens up. Miles from the front door. By the time Delilah steps into the blessed arctic grocery store, sweat trickles down her cleavage and joins the holding pond at the base of her bra. One of her sandals is flapping in a strange way. Another shoe sole melted by the asphalt.

The grocery list, she pares down to six essentials: Bread. Mayonnaise. Cat food. Milk. Eggs. Wine.

Technically, wine is not an essential. But it's on sale. Doesn't she deserve a small respite from the crap storm? Not like she has a drinking issue. People make notes on calendars on the rare occasion she has so much as a lite beer.

Think happy. Act happy. Be happy. Her deceased mother's words pop into her mind.

In the short time it takes to pick the "hot six," plus that one bag of chocolate, the less-than-ten-item aisles are crammed full. She steps into a regular line behind a man who is stocking up for the end of times. Piles of meat. Fresh vegetables. Bakery goodies. Sushi. Must be nice.

Her turn. The cashier smiles. They could be an artist's study in opposites. Delilah with her translucent, freckled Irish face and red hair. The cashier with brown eyes and skin the shade of rich coffee.

"Good afternoon. Did you find everything you need today?"

Need versus want. Two separate things. Not this lady's fault. Be nice. "Yes. Thank you."

The cashier's gaze rests on the wine. Eyes lift to survey Delilah's face. She passes the bottle over the scanner.

"Too bad you didn't ask for my photo ID," Delilah manages to joke. "I would've come across this counter and given you a hug." Humor helps anything. Right?

The cashier's lips curl up. Delilah returns the grin. Been forever and a day since either one of them had to prove she was over legal drinking age.

"I will still give you a hug," the cashier says.

Delilah chuckles. Swipes her debit card.

15

A young man loads her tattered, reusable grocery bag. Doesn't ask if she needs help to her car. No need, not with one parcel.

"Wait." The cashier steps from her station, circles the checkout counter. "Still want that hug?"

Delilah shrugs. Steps into the embrace. Like two friends reuniting after years of battle. People around them pause. Watch. Smile. Is this one of those hidden camera moments?

They pull apart. "You have a good day now, you hear?" The cashier nods. Steps back to help the next shopper.

"I will. I surely will."

4: The Traveler

A hammock is the closest thing on earth to resting in the arms of God.

Patience White knows this for a pure-un-tee fact. Here it is, just three short days from Thanksgiving. She should be inside the cramped kitchen attending to her pumpkin, chess, and pecan pies. Lawd knows, they're not going to cook themselves. She still has three turkeys, two hams, and a passel of side dishes to prepare.

Sweetbay Jones left a bushel basket full of fresh turnips, their purple and cream roots clotted with dark garden soil. It will take four or five vigorous washings to rid the grit from those greens. But they are free and given with an open heart, those and the mound of sweet potatoes waiting on the sideboard. Though Patience pays for most of the food with money earned hard, more appears at her front door each year, gifts from neighbors toward a good cause. Patience's Stray Cat Thanksgiving Dinner is as much a staple of fall celebrations as carved pumpkins and children with sticky-candy rings around their lips.

The harder the times, the more they come: homeless loners, widows and widowers without their familiar tethers, children of deceased parents who long for the sound of human voices, and odds-and-ends people from just about anywhere imaginable. In the thirty years she has hosted the dinner, Patience has seen and heard it all. Sometimes, more than her heart can hold.

The gentle swaying of the rope hammock reminds her of something long forgotten, rocking in her mother's womb. She wonders if others feel this same melancholy longing from a time before adult concerns.

"Get your lazy butt up and get to cooking!" she chides herself.

No room or time for slacking around or sulking over past slights. Too many souls depend on her to provide the warmth of welcome, even if for just one meal.

A pottery plaque the circumference of a teacup hangs beside her front door. Roughly drawn in the blue glaze is a line drawing of a cat. Someone gave Patience the little plaque years back at one of the earlier meals. She can't recall if it was Thanksgiving, Christmas, or Easter, or who took a nail and tacked it on the frame of the front door. She does remember the little legend behind it.

In years past, when times were even harder than current days, leagues of homeless folk traveled the railways, camping out in the dark woods between purloined boxcar rides. Sometimes, as they passed the simple wooden houses along the way, the sign of a smiling cat hung on a shingle by the road signaled the home of a kind woman, a female soul who would give a hungry traveler a piece of ham on a biscuit and a drink of cold spring water. Some might even trade work around her place for a shed to sleep out of the weather and the promise of a good meal.

Patience likes the idea that she is thought of as a kind woman. Some days, she wakes up on the wrong side of herself and isn't fit company for man nor beast. She isn't a saint unless saints periodically fly off the handle like an ax blade too loose in its wedging, zooming off in an unplanned direction and God help who it zeros in on.

Good thing those dark spells didn't come along real often. Not with knives and big heavy pots and boiling broths as potential ammunition.

Patience throws light things. Pillows. Socks. Dishtowels. Bags of marshmallows. If anyone's hurt, it's their feelings. Once, she pitched a hot mushy sweet potato at a stray old man who had the audacity to ask if her cooking was from scratch or from a box. Godly kind woman aside, Patience reared back with that butter-oiled potato and sent it spinning like some kind of underworld arrow weapon straight at the offender's face. When it made contact, the mushy pink pulp hung on his nose for a moment before sliding in slow motion down his white dress shirt, over his pants on one side, and all the way down to smear the spit shine on his shoes.

"You'll know better than to ask next time, I'm thinking." Patience lay back her kerchief-wrapped head and bellowed laughter.

She howled like a dog, hooted like an owl, then settled into a set of hiccups.

She threw him a damp towel. "Here. Clean up. I'll not have you at my table looking like that."

No one ever questioned Patience's culinary skills after that. She could feed them dried cow manure with lumpy black gravy and they would lap it up and like it.

A matted yellow Tomcat ambles through the grass and pauses to regard her with almond-shaped amber eyes. The battle-scarred feline is a stray, one of many that have passed through Patience's life. The others appear for a day or a week. Some, pregnant with their bellies hanging down like wet wash from their starving frames. Others, young or old, hungry and lost. Patience often wonders if there is a blinking sign hovering over her house; if you are lost, tired, or hungry (human, or not), this is the place to come.

Most of the cats move on after a time. If she can successfully corral them into a sturdy cardboard box with air holes poked in the sides and top, she carts them to the vet for a check-over. Patience sees this as her mission, along with providing water and a bowl of food.

This cat she named Hobo comes and goes, as if her house is some kind of way station. Sometimes he stays for a single meal. Lately he has lingered longer than usual. Maybe whatever created the new notch in his right ear gives him reason to slow his wanderings for a bit.

"Hobo, what you about, old man?" She reaches down and scratches behind his ears and he trills appreciation. "Wish you could cook. Sure could use the help."

Patience swings her legs over the side of the hammock and stands. More often than not, her joints ache and complain. A good damp spell sends them to pounding, the bone music of advancing age.

"I'm about as no-good as you are anymore, Hobo."

The tip of the butterscotch tabby's tale twitches as he walks toward the house. He is one of the few Patience has ever let inside. She didn't make the decision. Hobo insisted and she couldn't find a good enough reason to deny him. Besides, he's good company, seldom talks back in an angry fashion, and respects the sanctity of her kitchen. No matter how simple the equipment, Patience turns out a meal fit for any gourmet, but she won't tolerate cat hair as a seasoning. No sir.

Hobo nibbles on a handful of dry cat food before retiring to a soft cushion on the floor just beyond the kitchen door. For a few minutes, he watches Patience's sure movements as she dances from the kitchen counter to the tiny cupboard to the stove and back. He yawns and snuggles his face into his curled body. The tiger stripes expand and contract with rhythmic breathing.

Patience hums low in her throat. Music never makes a hard job easier, but it sets a positive tone. She has sung and worked most of her life. She cleans after other people. Does the chores they find distasteful. Performs honest work for little pay. No one has ever given her a thing.

She sees the results of having too little, and those of having too much. Pricey toys end up scattered on the manicured lawn in the rain and searing sun. Women dripping with diamonds drink themselves into numbness. How having the world as one's oyster is never enough; even the pearl inside chips like dime store dishes.

Patience stands, her hands propped on her slender hips. "How many mouths you reckon we gonna feed this year?"

Hobo lifts his head, blinks sleepily, and meows.

Patience smiles. "You say thirty? That your guess?"

The cat answers, the main reason he's her favorite. Anytime Hobo is around, she has a living thing to talk to, one that talks back.

"I'd guess forty. Been a hard year for a lot of folks 'round here. Lot out of work." She points her finger in the cat's direction. "Why don't we fix for fifty or so. If we have leftovers, we can always send some home with folks what needs them."

A stack of clean butter tubs stands on a shelf in the cupboard, ready for sharing.

"Always shut-ins to think about, Hobo. You can't eat all the turkey giblets."

She hears rapping at the door, dries her hands, and moves through the narrow sitting room to answer it. The man standing at Patience's front door looks as if he has traveled more miles than the sum of all the vagabonds who have stopped on her porch. His jacket is so pocked with holes, it looks like military camouflage mesh. Beneath the layers of dirt, he appears to be a man of about forty years, though his soft brown eyes seem millennia older. The hair on his head stretches far below his shoulders, blending in front with untidy curls of a beard.

"Can you spare a meal for a poor traveler, Ma'am?"

His voice echoes kindness. Patience immediately relaxes. Everyone tells her she is too easy, that her gullible ways will someday end her life. Serial killers seem nice too, and full of honesty.

Patience unlatches the screened door and holds it open.

"I'm in the middle of cooking for Thanksgiving. If you'da come here in a couple of days, I'd have a feast fitting for royalty. Now I do have some sausage and eggs." She pulls on her chin in a gesture that helps her think. "If you don't mind breakfast food, I could drum up something, I reckon."

His gaze rests on her face. He smiles. "That would suffice. But only if you can spare the time."

Patience motions toward the kitchen. "There's a little wash-room off the back of the house. You'll find soap, washcloths, and towels. You go clean yourself up a little and I'll see what I can throw together. I don't abide road dirt in my kitchen. I got to have a few rules."

When the man smiles, his face glows. Patience holds her breath as he passes by, in awe as much as to avoid the body odor.

"If you'll look on the shelves by the sink, you'll find a stack of shirts, a few pants, and socks. You can help yourself to anything back there you can find to fit."

He nods and ambles to the rear of the house. Patience returns to the kitchen and removes a few links of country sausage and three eggs from the refrigerator.

"One of these days, I'm gonna have to buy a bigger refrigerator. Lordy! I don't know how I'm going to keep all I need to cram into this one."

She turns and busies herself at the stove. By the time she has the cooked sausage links draining grease on a paper towel, the man stands at the kitchen threshold.

"Well, now. That was fast."

The man drops a small bag onto the floor and kicks it out of the way with one foot. With the layers of road dirt removed, his face echoes traces of many nationalities. He is not exactly white, yet his skin isn't of a dark shade. His eyes are slightly tilted and almond-shaped, his lips full and expressive. Like her, the man would be hard to plug into any one slot.

He's a mutt like me, she thinks.

The man smiles. "I thank you for the bath and clothing."

"Ain't that something? They fit so well, that shirt and pants could've been bought for you."

He nods.

"My name's Patience White. You got a name?"

"I've gone by many names."

Patience considers. Running from something, or *someone*, more than likely. "What can I call you? Hate to cook for someone and call him *hey you*."

He chuckles. Patience joins him. One thing she notices about this stranger: no matter what emotion he emits, she feels it in waves.

"I'll leave that up to you."

Patience points to the small Formica and aluminum table. "Have a seat. How do you like your eggs cooked?"

"Most any way. I'm not choosy."

"Sunny-side-up, then. I do like the looks of an egg sunny-side-up. Something cheerful about it."

She takes great pains not to shatter the yolks as she shovels the cooked eggs onto a chipped plate. She adds a generous portion of sausage and a warmed-over biscuit from breakfast.

"There you go, Counselor." She slides the plate in front of him with utensils and a paper napkin. "Salt and pepper if you like. I add a little when it's cooking. Don't like to get too carried away with seasoning. You can always add it later, but it's hard to take it away once you've overdone it. Would you fancy some honey for your biscuit? One of my neighbors keeps bees, so I got the real deal."

"Yes, thank you."

He digs into the food with gusto. One thing Patience loves to see is a man who enjoys his food. Too many picky, skinny people anymore for her liking. In a few minutes, he finishes and sops the grease and streaks of yolk from the plate with a crumb of biscuit. He saves the last few bites of biscuit and slathers honey across them.

"Lordy be! I forgot to give you something to wash it down with. I must be losing my ever-loving mind. I don't usually fail as a hostess. I guess I've been so busy with my holiday baking and such that I got a little harebrained."

Patience sets a mug in front of him and pours coffee from a percolator. So many of her friends have drip brewers, but she hangs onto the old silver electric pot.

"Might be a bit strong, by now. I keep a pot going when I'm hard at it in the kitchen. I suppose if they ever tell me I have to give up my coffee, I'll just go ahead and shuffle off this mortal earth. Sugar and creamer are in those two little crocks. Help yourself."

The man sits back and wipes his mouth free of crumbs. "I thank you, Mrs. White. That was the best food I've had in as long as I can recall."

"You are welcome."

After he takes a few sips of coffee, he tilts his head to one side and studies her. "Why did you call me Counselor?"

Patience shrugs. "Just seemed to fit. You got that look about you. Like you might be able to sit and listen a spell, maybe provide some advice."

"And what would you have to say, if I was, Mrs. White?"

"First of all, my mama was Mrs. White. I never officially married. Not that I didn't have my share of times living with a man. Call me Patience. Everyone does. It's my name."

His brown eyes sparkle as if he enjoys the conversation. "Okay, Patience. Tell me. What would you say to me?"

"I'd say . . . I'm doing fine, but thanks for asking. I could use a bigger stove and refrigerator, though. Guess that doesn't count as needing advice, now does it?"

"You cook well with the one you have."

"I do, at that," she agrees. "Reckon I only wish for better at the holidays. I have my stray cat dinners, you see. Folks come from miles around. Folks in need of each other more than my cooking. I've been making meals in this little kitchen for going on thirty years. Suppose I will keep on doing it, too. Maybe my grumbling is as much a tradition as the turkey."

When Patience laughs, she puts her whole body into it. The man joins her with a hearty laugh.

"I'll see what I can do," he says when Patience's mirth fades.

"You do that, Counselor. You just do that."

She imagines the man finding a discarded stove and refrigerator beside the road in some Godforsaken, dot-on-the-map town. He will flag down a trucker and cart it back to her door. That and monkeys will do backflips from her behind. She has seen it before, many times. The less a person has, the harder they dream.

"Suppose I'll be getting along now." He stands and walks over to retrieve his worn pack. Hobo, who has passed the time deep in sleep, opens one eye, regards the stranger, stretches, and snuggles in for another nap. "I can pay a little for the shirt and pants."

"You'll do no such. Folks drop off clothes here like they do food around the holidays. Someone always needing. Those belong to you now."

He smiles, dips his head, and touches the tips of his fingers on one hand to the center of his forehead in a manner that reminds Patience of a priest starting the sign of the cross.

"You have to be tired, Counselor. I don't object at all if you want to crawl up on the couch in the front room and rest awhile. I'll be back here in the kitchen most of the day. Don't pay no mind to the door opening and closing. Folks stop by with whatever they have to spare for my meal. They don't tend to knock, just walk in and make a beeline to my kitchen. No one will bother you. Don't worry."

"You are most kind, Patience. Why do you do this?"

"I remember what it is like to wonder where your next meal will come from, or if you'll even get one. I know what it's like to feel the heat baking your skin or the cold scratching down your backside. This little scrap of a house isn't much, but it's a mansion in my eyes. Besides, I'd hope someone would do the same for me, if I was to be a traveler, like yourself."

Before he leaves the kitchen, he turns back and smiles. "We are all travelers, Patience."

The strays start to file in at noon on Thanksgiving Day. A steady stream, they shuffle through on their way outside to buffet tables fashioned from old doors and concrete blocks draped with clean white sheets. The few chairs in the sitting room await the elders too feeble or sick to eat standing. The table next to the back door holds jugs of sweet tea, pop, and water. A dinged chrome coffee urn borrowed from the Morningside A.M.E. church pipes coffee into waiting Styrofoam cups. Packets of sugar and powdered creamer rest nearby in a pottery bowl.

Patience moves between the outdoor tables and kitchen, checking and refilling, stopping to pat one on the back, hug another. She does not eat. Her appetite disappears beneath a heap of concern for her guests. Like the loaves and fishes of Biblical lore, the food somehow stretches until the line thins to a trickle an hour and a half later. Some leave as soon as their stomachs fill. Others mill around the dirt-packed back yard, forming loose conversation groups that change as quickly as they gel.

The man appears just as the last of the guests waves goodbye from the porch.

"Counselor! I wondered if you might stop back by."

He smiles. "How could I miss eating from your kitchen once again?"

She stands aside, motioning him in. "Ain't much left to choose from. Looks like a pack of vultures passed through. Let's see if we can make you a plate of what's left."

A few greens, a corner of cornbread, a small dollop of cold mashed potatoes, one slice of ham and turkey, and half a sweet potato sit on his paper plate.

"I hate that you missed out on the good stuff, Counselor. My strays surely do know how to clean me out."

"This is ample, Patience. Thank you."

When he starts toward the back door, she raises her palm.

"I'd surely like some company if you wouldn't mind. I hardly ever touch a bite when I'm in the midst of things. I always end up here, eating the scraps by myself."

She clears off a spot for them on the kitchen table and transfers a stack of empty bowls into the sink. A mound of litter and dirty pots form a teetering tower.

"You are left to clean up," he comments.

"Don't worry about all of this, Counselor. Gives me something to do with the rest of the day. I don't abide football games. Wouldn't watch them even if I owned a television. Most everyone else is holed up with their families after the meal, so it's no use to go looking for anyone to natter with."

Patience motions to the back door. "After I finish up in here, if the sun manages to come out and warm things up a little, I plan to spend some time in my hammock. That's my idea of Heaven, that hammock."

He nods. "I shall make a note of that."

Patience breaks off a piece of cold cornbread, dips it into the pool of juice surrounding her greens, and chews. "Don't forget my stove and refrigerator, if you're making a list."

A couple of days later, Patience answers the door. Two men in coveralls stand on her porch, one holding a clipboard.

"Patience White?" one man asks.

She looks past them to a large delivery truck idling at the curb. "Depends on who's asking."

"We have a delivery for Patience White."

"I didn't order anything." She narrows her eyes. "Must be some kind of mistake. I didn't pay for anything, either."

The man consults his clipboard. "This is your address and you are Patience White. Correct?"

She cranes her neck to read the invoice heading. "That's me, all right."

"This order has been paid in full. I don't take the orders, Ma'am. I just get paid to deliver the goods."

Her brows collide in the middle. "What exactly are you trying to deliver?"

"Two new appliances."

Patience glances to the van and back to the delivery men. "Two?"

He taps a pen on the clipboard. "One stove and one deluxe refrigerator."

5: A Rock

Charlene stares at the small creek. Prettiest spot in the lower 48. Okay, maybe Bright Angel Trail in Zion National Park. And that creek in Yellowstone. Or Acadia in Maine.

My, this is a divine country. And it's mine. About the only thing that is, except for the secondhand motorhome. A few clothes. And Hippie Freak, the wiry terrier mix she picked up south of Albuquerque.

Nothing to hold her down now, other than her promise to show up at the next camp host spot. A far cry from that twenty-room monstrosity, that Greek Revival turkey with all the trimmings. Husband number three, the poop for brains, had the nerve to die crack-deep in debt. Barely enough to liquidate and buy the used motorhome. And get the heck away from the Deep South.

She picks up a lump of green granite, or at least that's what she thinks it is. She'd know if she was a rock collector. But after chasing figurines, coins, heirloom jewelry, and vintage purses until they mocked her, Charlene doesn't collect anything now.

Hippie Freak taps by, sniffing the bushes, anointing every other one with two drops of pee. Good thing she loves that mutt. Ugly as a full set of demons. But loyal. That counts for something.

A faded pick-up eases into the small parking area. There goes the neighborhood. Anymore, people fracture her and it takes a few days of solitude to gather the shards.

A woman gets out.

Relief seeps up Charlene's chest and her breathing eases. At sixty-five, Charlene's not a looker like she used to be, but the knee-jerk to a lone male in a deserted place is a habit instilled from inception. He'll get you. You'll end up bleached-out bones, happened upon by some hunter. Or locked in a kitchen and forced to cook. She'd been there, earned the badge. At least husband number three had come with a chef and full staff. For five years, she knew what living large felt like. Pampered. Elite. Yet somehow devoid of joy once the blush faded.

Charlene watches the woman gather a walking stick and small belt pack from the pick-up. Like Charlene, she isn't dressed in high-end gear crisp from a catalog. Another good omen. She won't come jabbering stupid questions: *is there a gift shop?* or *what's the Native American legend surrounding that mountain?* One of the many reasons Charlene visits popular spots in off-season: fewer tourist morons, those *tour-ons.*

When you look trail-worn, Charlene figures, you must have the answer to anything. A living information search engine.

The woman picks her way across the rocks, stopping to bend over and finger through a pile, occasionally slipping a stone into the pack. It's against the rules to take even a twig from a national park, but this spot isn't that. Lot of rocks to plunder. If you were prone to collect. Which Charlene is not.

"Morning," the woman says as soon as she's within ear range.

"Morning," Charlene replies. Her voice comes out straggly, unused. Hippie Freak appears. Snuffles the woman's shoes and pants legs. The woman leans down and offers the back of one hand for his inspection. He sniffs. Licks. Wags.

Okay. She's not a serial killer. Females can be that too. Though they usually snuff out men. But dogs *know.* Hippie Freak is adept at detecting bad humans. His time as a drifter, Charlene surmises.

"Aren't these grand?" The woman holds out a palm of pebbles, identical to the thousands lining the creek. "Each has a personality." She flicks a pink round one with her finger. "This spidery line looks like a varicose vein with a question mark at one end. See?"

Only another woman near her age would come up with that reference. Charlene nods.

"Here. You can have it. I think it would like to go with you." She hands over the pink stone.

Never turn down a gift. Another thing instilled from inception, along with that distrust of strange lone men in deserted places.

Be polite when someone gives you something. You can pitch it later. Re-gift it. Or haul it off to charity like poop-brain's overpriced golf sweaters. Or she can add it back into the acres of rocks as soon as the woman is out of view.

"Thank you."

"I can't help myself," the woman says. "I've collected rocks since I was knee-high to a flea. The only thing I carry with me, these days."

"Don't they weigh you down?"

Hope that didn't hurt her feelings. The trouble with not talking to many folks: the filters wear thin and everything oozes out.

"Oh no. They're what keep me from floating off."

The woman bends and scratches Hippie Freak between the ears. More tail wagging. She uprights. Smiles. Nods. Walks away.

Charlene holds the pink pebble a moment before dropping it into a pocket.

Now she has a dog *and* a rock.

6: Battle of the Bands

The light turns red.

Vernell slows the aging Lincoln and queues up with the clot of motorists stopped by the signal. Lawd, how she used to loathe the early morning traffic in Tallahassee, back when she was working for the State.

"Must've been out of my ever-loving mind to make an eight o'clock dental appointment." Could've gone any other time. Retirement afforded such luxury.

A late model sedan with dark windows idles in the next lane. Pounding bass jars her windows. Sets her teeth on edge. A few more minutes of this noise and she won't have to worry about that dental appointment. She'll clench them all down to pearly dust.

"How do those young hoodlums listen to that rappity-tap-tap?" Vernell flips through her leather CD wallet. "Ah, this ought to do."

She slips a disc into the slot, mashes the volume control button, and rolls down the driver's side window. Old speakers might not be a match for this goofball's, but by golly, it's the principle that counts.

In the Mood blasts from all corners of her car's inner compartment. Sounds like Vernell is in the concert hall with the band. Horns scream out the melody, joined by enough bold beats to make her point.

The big band music overcomes her as it always does. She bounces, throws up her hands. If she could get out of the Lincoln fast enough, she'd dance a jig around the car. But the walker is cumbersome and she'd have to hold onto the car to balance.

She rocks her head side to side, catching a glimpse of the sedan's passenger window slipping down.

"Oh no, Vernell. You've done it now."

She'll end up shot in the head for sure. Dead as a doornail, middle of West Tennessee Street. On the midday news or the evening broadcast at least. Splashed all over the Internet for the world to see. It's that road rage she's heard about.

Might as well look the hoodlum full in the face. She pivots.

A young man studies her. Sunglasses hide his eyes. He extends one hand.

Oh here it goes. He's reaching for a gun.

Glenn Miller's orchestra swirls magic around her. At least she'll die happy, listening to her favorite tune, one she and Fred used to cut a rug to, back in the day, before the stroke stole his boogie shoes.

The man trills his fingers across something on the sedan's dash. The booming bass stops. He stares at Vernell with no expression. Her mouth goes dry as coffin dust.

His head bobs to the beat. Barely at first, then enough for Vernell to see for certain. He smiles. She fires back her grin.

Vernell lowers the volume after the final blast of horns. Nods to the man.

He trills the dash again and a fresh rash of beats sounds, a rapper calling loud strings of words.

Vernell lifts one hand. Snaps her fingers. The pacing ain't half bad. No matter she can't understand most of the words, and there doesn't seem to be a background tune. She bobs her head to the beat. He bobs his head. He smiles big, flashing even, white teeth any dentist would love. Vernell chuckles.

He lowers the volume. Vernell reaches over, turns her music up a smidge. She dips her head once. He dips his. Rolls up his window. Vernell can barely hear the thump of his music.

The light turns green.

7: Broadcast

"Good morning, neighbors 'n' gators!"

Hard to shove enthusiasm into the six a.m. show with the scent of wood smoke seeping through every crevice.

"Now I know most of you are feeling a bit coltish, what with the Apalachicola Forest ablaze." Robert Brown, "Bob Beetle" on-air, takes a breath to keep fear from closing his throat.

It's like talking a jumper down from a wooden bridge. Muddy water churning below. Charred supports promising to end it for him and the other poor sap. No rescue vehicles wailing in the distance.

He and the jumper are going down, no matter how sweet his words.

"Doug over at the Chevron called me yesterday. Said he still has a few sturdy boxes, free to anyone who needs them. He's leaving them by the front door. For those of you wanting to pack up."

Not that anyone remains now, not even Doug. But Bob Beetle is here.

Oh sweet heavens, help me.

"Okay, here's a little tune to break up those blues."

Robert flips levers on a jury-rigged console, slides off the padded headset. He leans back from the mic and the rolling office chair complains.

Could sit in silence. A light will cue him when the song ends. He needs uplifting bad as the next guy. He slides the volume lever. A Willie Nelson tune crowds the muffled noises from the outside. That'll do it.

What's to become of his studio? Not much to brag on, a shack moved from an old plant nursery filled with components cobbled together. Folks hereabouts look to him to spread the news, good and bad. Not many radio station broadcasts reach here. On a cloudy day, spits of sound might make it through the cypress swamp.

Margaret depends on his hobby too. Keeps him occupied and from idling next to her. He knows that look his wife fires at him, has seen it often enough before he slapped this studio together.

Reaching his eighties ain't all it's cracked up to be.

The light flashes. Bob Beetle doesn't interrupt the flow of music. What's left to say? The first licks of the oldie goldie sound. He jerks upright. The chair squawks. Two lever flips switch the broadcast to a prerecorded announcement from the emergency people. Second time in half an hour, but it's important for those just tuning in.

Besides, he needs to double-check the song line-up. *Smoke Gets in Your Eyes*. Not a good selection, given the circumstances.

Robert sneezes and wipes the nose water with his shirtsleeve. Margaret hates that. He'd catch holy Hades if she was here and not at her sister's in Tallahassee.

He tears off a strip of duct tape to cover a tiny slit between two boards. The larger gaps around the door were easy to find. Stuffed them with damp rags. It's these pinholes no bigger than a rat's anus where the stench of wildfire sneaks in.

Won't be long before the flames slip through too.

8: A Good Year for Blueberries

Marie turns right off Woodville highway. No need to follow the small blue and white signs.

George used to drive. She was the navigator. Good thing too. For all of her late husband's shining qualities, a reliable sense of direction wasn't in the mix. Poor man couldn't find his way out of an open paper sack.

The candy-apple red sports car in front of her turns left. She follows. Marie glances in the rearview mirror. The sedan behind her falls in behind them. And here she thought she'd be the first one here at eight a.m. on a Friday.

It's like this every year in early June. For several years, she's made the trek from Tallahassee. Except for last year during what she calls the "year of firsts."

First Halloween. First Thanksgiving. First Christmas. First blueberry season without George.

The caravan turns left again, onto an unpaved drive lined by pine and hardwoods. Oh look. The owner has spread gravel over the dirt. That'll keep her car from wearing a layer of white dust.

When Marie spots the parking area, her shoulders sag. So much for solitude.

Gatherings of people bruise her. No shopping malls, no parades, definitely no FSU football games. Always someone she knows, asking how she is. Marie has learned to offer a thin smile, tell them what they want to hear. Somewhere she read people expect grief to end after six months. Poof. Just like that, and you're carefree and happy once more.

"Mom, seriously. You hardly leave the house." Molly, her daughter. Such the mother hen. George taught her well. Marie never was one to coddle. Caring for him those last months stretched her caretaking abilities until they snapped.

The red sports car man parks and gets out. He's alone too. Wonder about his story. Maybe he's what her mother used to call a "confirmed bachelor." Maybe his wife, or partner—isn't that the correct term —is dead too.

The sedan pulls beside her on the other side. Young couple, early twenties, probably students. They step from the car and reach for each other's hand. Sweet.

The blueberry bushes spread out in long, precise rows. Even from a distance, Marie can tell they are heavy with fruit.

Other pickers leave their cars, chatting, laughing. Feels like a festival. Marie falls in behind a family cluster and they all move toward a walk-through structure. *Saladino's Red Barn Farm*, the overhead sign reads, *Home of the Blueberry*.

Marie spots one of the owners, the wife, busy weighing and dumping loaded buckets into plastic bags. Cash or checks, no credit cards. The woman smiles, makes small talk. Her husband greets the pickers. "Welcome. Have you picked before?" He asks and then gives a two-sentence in-service. "Remember, pick only the blue ones. Bushes in the far back are loaded." He motions.

Marie ducks her head, pulls her hat over her face, and grabs a four-quart bucket laced with a woven neck strap. She slips past the rookie trainees.

She pauses at the ends of the first few rows, judging. Finally, she chooses one deep in the patch. Shaded, at least for a while. Beyond the first line of bushes where the majority of the pickers loiter.

All of the bushes aren't the same. Every other bush holds a larger variety of berry. Someone who's a veteran at Saladino's knows such. Even the smaller berries are sweet.

Of course, she could fill a quarter of the bucket from a couple of bushes. Where's the challenge of that? George would pick in that fashion, stalled in a single row for an hour while Marie flitted from one row to the next like a demented, indigo-fingered fairy.

Marie selects a tall bush, loops the strap around her neck so that the bucket rests mid-body, level with her waist. Two free hands.

There's an art to blueberry picking. Find a ripe cluster, cup a hand beneath, and tease the stems with her fingertips until the ripe fruit gives up its grip. Marie has perfected this. Rarely drops a berry.

Sounds echo through the half-acre plot. A child's giggled words. "Look! Here're some big ones!" Another young voice sings some childhood ditty. A clutch of children round the corner and barrel down her row. Marie takes a breath. They scoot by, empty buckets banging against suntanned legs. George would've delighted in seeing them, pointing out the best spots where low branches waited for tiny picker hands. He was like that with people.

Used to take forever in the grocery store whenever he tagged along. He'd discuss how to choose the ripest cantaloupe or the tender cuts of meat with some random person, all while Marie filled the shopping cart with what they needed. Marie, six aisles and the bakery. George, stuck in produce with a white-haired senior, pontificating the merits of organic romaine.

"Don't eat a lot of 'em," a towheaded boy of about eight calls out to the bunch of kids, "you'll get die-ahhh-reee-yah!"

Marie chuckles. The sound startles her. Not flat like the laughter she's pushed out toward well-meaning others over the past few months.

The children's babble fades. She can still pick out the same blond boy ordering the rest. There's one in every group.

Marie stretches to capture a prime cluster of fat berries. They cascade into her open palm, pebbled rain. She lowers her hand to appreciate their dusty blue-gray color before dropping them into the bucket. She lifts one fat berry to her mouth and smashes it with her tongue. It tastes of sun and dew.

Too little time passes. The four-quart bucket is full. No green berries. No leaves. No bugs. No stems. Gosh, she's good. If Molly lived closer, she'd pick enough for her too. North Carolina's too far. Besides, her daughter probably has her own favorite U-Pick farms up there.

"I'm introducing you to Woodville's finest," Marie hears a woman say. She leans toward the conversation, somewhere through the maze of leaves.

"We're so lucky, you know?" another woman answers. "To have this close-by, and organic too. No chemicals. Love that."

"I picked blackberries yesterday. Four pints. Place near here on highway sixty-one."

"Do they freeze well?"

"No. Not like blueberries. They get mushy."

"What cha doing with yours?"

Marie continues to pick, listening to the pleasant banter.

"Think I'll make a cobbler."

Thinking of cobbler, Marie's mouth waters. Warm, sugared goodness, topped with soft dumplings. Vanilla ice cream drippling on top.

Wow. Laughter and an appetite in one morning. Write that one down on the calendar. Maybe she could gain a pound or two. Give Molly one less thing to worry about.

Her fingers trill the berries in her bucket, rolling them like soft marbles. She looks up. Skies the color of Paul Newman's eyes, the shade she imagines as God's own eye color, should He, or She, have eyes. The warm air feels silken on her skin. A slight breeze lifts the fuzz on her forearms. Marie closes her eyes and allows the morning sun to touch her cheeks.

The check and weigh station is five deep. She waits. No hurry. The owner lifts the laden bucket from Marie's extended hands.

"Well, hello." The woman's gaze rests on Marie. "I didn't see you pass by earlier. Good to see you again."

Marie nods. The woman dumps the berries into a plastic bag and centers it on the scale.

"Five pounds. That's light." She ties off the bag and taps on a calculator.

"Don't need much. Just for me."

The woman glances up. Something wisps between them, a knowing quiet as a husband's ghost. "Ah." She passes the bag to Marie without asking *that* question. "You chose the perfect time to stop by. It's a lovely morning."

"Yes." Marie hands over a couple of bills and accepts her change. "It is."

Marie detours a few miles to Wakulla Springs. She tiptoes into crystal water the shade of peridot. Her skin tingles. A trio of egrets fly over. A great blue heron perches on one leg on the far bank near a log where turtles bask.

In the water, a manatee and her calf bob to the surface, staunching the steady splat of kids from the two-tier diving platform. The manatees drift downstream. The lifeguard gives the all-clear. *Kaboosh. Kaboosh.* The kids jump and squeal, jump and squeal. Two snorkelers keep a safe distance.

In her pocket, Marie's cell phone trills.

Text message from Molly: *Hey, Mom. What r u doing?*

Marie watches a toddler trench the white sand with an orange shovel. Teenaged girls next to her flip their hair, busy being noticed while trying to act as if they don't care.

Mom? The next text insists.

Keep it simple and short. Can't send an epistle. *Standing with feet ice cold in spring.*

The answer comes: *You ok?*

Marie pauses, taps the keypad. *It's a good year for blueberries.*

9: Licky

Like she needs another critter. One hairy neurotic Goldie-mix and a senile tabby aren't enough?

"Sweet baby," Laurel coos to the black and white kitten. Barely weaned, if that. Found it huddled in the grocery store parking lot next to the back tire. Shivering. Plain pitiful.

Tuxedo cat. Perfectly dressed for any occasion. And those tiny yellow eyes.

Straight to the vet. Forget the milk and eggs. And the list of errands as long as God's arm.

The kitten is healthy, and a female, and someone has to care for it until a home is available. Laurel takes it to her house. But only for a few days.

She won't give it a name. Attachment is too easy.

The first morning, the kitten spots her through the sliding glass doors that separate the sun porch from the living room. Can't hear the yowls, but the mouth opens and shuts, opens and shuts. Cinnamon brushes against her leg, wagging her blonde flag of a tail.

"No, sugar. It's a baby. You can't have it."

Hate to leave it in the sunroom. But her aging cat Mr. Big sleeps on the bed and her Goldie-mix Cinnamon guards the rest of the house. Litter box, water and food bowls, and a pillow. Best Laurel can do in a snap. The new owner, whoever she or he might be, will provide suitable digs and some toys. Kitties simply must have toys.

Laurel pours a cup of coffee and manages to keep Cinnamon from pushing past her. The rescue dog has only been with her for three months, a one-year-old. No telling if the Goldie tolerates all cats. One as tiny as the tuxedo might look like a bobbing chew toy. Mr. Big, forget him sharing the love. She'd seen him burr up at his own reflection. He puts up with the dog, as long as Cinnamon doesn't try to get too cozy.

When she steps into the sunroom, the kitten climbs her pants legs almost to the thigh before Laurel can unpin its claws. Amazing how sharp they are.

A movement on the other side of the glass door catches her attention. Mr. Big has joined Cinnamon. Two sets of wide eyes watch.

The kitten scrabbles in her arms, burrows beneath her robe and pushes its nose against her neck. Searching. Poor thing. No mama.

She opens the door that leads to the kitchen. Cinnamon and Mr. Big meet her. The cat twirls in circles, looking up. The dog stands on her hind legs. Laurel dances between them, from the counter to the refrigerator. Eyedropper. Cup of warmed goat's milk.

She shuffles back to the sunroom, balancing the cup and kitten on one side, taming the animal guard with the other. If she can't find a new owner soon, her pets will have to meet this one nose to nose. Just not yet.

The kitten pulls at the tip of the dropper, suckling milk. Its front paws pulse against her hand. She studies its tiny face. Black head and ears. White across the nose and chin, except for one little dollop of black beneath the lips. Laurel feeds it until it no longer accepts the offering. It curls up against her, purring. Closes its eyes.

So sweet. Someone is going to have a nice pet. How had it ended up in the middle of a parking lot?

The phone rings. She slips the kitten from her arms and tucks it into the feather pillow bed. Steps inside. The next-door neighbor, calling to fill her in on last night's homeowners' meeting. Every dang detail.

Twelve minutes later, Laurel manages to exit the conversation. The sunroom door stands ajar. She hears squeaks and shuffling noises.

"Goodness!"

She pushes the door open. Steels herself to see blood.

Cinnamon's head hangs low, the kitten's head hidden in her mouth. Mr. Big perches on one of the chairs, eyes wide.

"Cinnamon." Laurel keeps her voice even, though she wants to shout. "Drop it."

The Goldie pivots her head toward Laurel. Big butterscotch eyes appeal. Not *look what I got, Mom*. More, *help me, Mom*.

The tiny black rump wiggles. Thank you Great Spirit. It's still alive.

Then Laurel notices how Cinnamon holds her maw steady, not clamped. The kitten's head appears. Clawed front paws dig into Cinnamon's muzzle. The dog gives a soft whimper. The kitten latches onto the Goldie's lower lip, swinging free like a circus acrobat in formal attire.

Laurel waits. No sudden movements.

The kitten claws and chews its way around the dog's lower lip. Cinnamon lowers her head toward the tile floor, until the kitten's hind legs touch. One small flick of the tongue, and the kitten lets go. It stares up at the dog. Mews. Cinnamon gives its head a slobbery dog kiss.

Mr. Big jumps down and strolls over. Looks at the Goldie. Looks at the kitten. Turns and ambles into the kitchen.

Laurel scoops up the newest member of the family. Names her Licker Lip, Licky for short.

10: Pledge of Trust

I really wish you would reconsider, Harry." Dorie hands her father two plastic drinking straws.

Harry Nichols smiles as he always does when his eldest daughter refers to him by his first name. "I can't let them down, Dorie."

"But—"

"No arguments. I don't have the time or energy." He sticks out his left forearm. "Cut this dang thing off, will you?"

Dorie shakes her head and frowns, then snips the hospital patient identification band from her father's wrist.

"Ah, better. Thank you."

"See? That's my point. You haven't even been out of the hospital long enough to remove your I.D. bracelet."

"I've made up my mind." Harry inserts one straw into each nostril, swirls a two-inch-wide paint brush in a bowl of thick bleaching cream, sections off a small hank of beard, and watches his reflection slather on the mixture. The chemical process will turn his thick mustache and long curly beard from patchy yellowed gray to brilliant winter white.

Dorie watches. "The fumes can't be good for your lungs, either." She shifts position in the cramped bathroom. A dollop of bleaching paste plops onto the tile.

Harry's gaze moves from his work to his daughter. "That's the purpose of the straws crammed up my nose. You know that. I've mastered this over the years. And these bendy straws are even better than the old straight kind, as they bring in air from the sides instead of below. Besides, my lungs are doomed anyway. What's one more insult?"

Pulmonary Fibrosis, the diagnosis. Payback for smoking all those years ago.

Harry tries to imagine his lungs as that doctor had described: two wispy, deflated balloons whose linings look like hardening concrete. Soon, air won't pass through, and he will cease to breathe.

How long, days, months? It doesn't matter. As long as he can bleach his thinning hair, mustache, and beard, don the custom-sewn suit, and carry a portable oxygen generator for a few puffs before and after his engagements, Harry is satisfied.

It is Christmas. And he is Santa.

As soon as he enters the double glass doors of the town's small city hall, Harry notices the little tow-haired boy, about six years old. The child is conspicuous because of his stillness. For a brief moment, their gazes connect across the crowd. The expression on the boy's face brings to mind one word: haunted. What burden does the child carry? Imminent divorce of his parents? Death of someone close? Some grave physical ailment? Too young to bare such.

Filling the cramped room, the children and haggard parents stand in a ragged, snaking line. Except for the one boy, the little ones bounce, rock, and tug on the adults' coat sleeves for attention. Santa has arrived in the passenger seat of the shiny red fire truck, exciting enough by itself. Now, the jolly elf who holds the solution to their every wish is in the very room.

The Chief of Police welcomes Harry with a handshake and a hearty pat on the back. He guides Harry/Santa past the yearning faces to a high-backed, dark red, upholstered throne festooned with tinsel and silk poinsettias.

Over the nearly thirty years he has posed as Santa, Harry has seen every type of child from well-behaved and polite, to boisterous and ill-mannered. He has been slobbered on, urinated on, pinched, screamed at, and hugged so tightly he could barely breathe, even before the lung issues. He has long lost count of the numerous times some child yanked his beard to see if it was real or fake. Most children come with well-rehearsed lists of toys and games, easy for Harry to repeat loudly for the attending adult. Others wish for things even the magical embodiment of the spirit of giving would be hard-pressed to provide. *Bring my daddy home from overseas. I want a new baby brother. Please, make my mommy well.*

Several minutes pass before the child he noted earlier stands next in line. The woman gives the boy's shoulder a slight shove. "Go on, Kyle."

The boy's gaze flicks up briefly, then back down to his dirty, worn sneakers.

"I ain't dragged you all the way into town to talk to Santa for you to act this way."

Harry notes the woman's stringy, overdyed hair and skinny, starved frame. When she kneels in front of her son, her red sweater is ripe with tiny wear-pills.

Years of dealing with shy, frightened children have taught Harry the art of gentling. He takes a long, even breath and wills his body to reflect peace and stillness.

The boy inches forward. Stops. His mother gives him a nudge. Without looking up, the child climbs onto Harry's lap.

"There now, Master Kyle. That wasn't so bad, eh?" Harry uses his cheeriest Santa voice.

The child's chest rises and falls in staccato bursts. His slight body trembles.

"What can Santa do for you, young man?"

The boy picks at the raw edge of a thumb cuticle until a bead of bright red blood appears. All of his nails have been chewed to the quick.

"Do you want to whisper in my ear? That way, it's between just me and you." Harry tilts his head down slightly, the movement slow.

The boy's brown eyes water. He studies Harry for a moment before cupping his hand in front of his mouth and stretching upward. "Make him stop hurting Mama," a pause, "and me." The words come out flat, the way wishes do after going so long without an answer.

Harry doesn't allow his face to betray emotion as he uprights. He looks down at the child and nods once. "All right, Master Kyle. Is there anything else?"

The boy moves his head from side to side.

Harry slips a red-striped candy cane from his coat pocket and hands it to the boy before helping him to the floor. As the mother and son walk toward the double doors, the boy stops once and gives Harry a final, serious look.

The next child bounces onto his lap. Harry forces a hearty Santa-chortle. The girl announces herself as Krystal and launches into a long list.

Harry sits, as he does most hours, in his worn, leather easy chair, his legs propped up to thwart the accumulation of fluid in his feet and calves. His middle daughter, drained from her three-week caretaking shift, kisses him on the top of his head before she makes her way to the guest bedroom. Between the Hospice workers, his three daughters, and the stream of friends and former co-workers, what he privately labels as his "final hoo-hah" is seldom lonely.

The soft whish of the oxygen generator sounds more and more like the gentle breaking of ocean wavelets on the shore. When he closes his eyes, he can almost smell the salt-laced air. His wife Jacqueline, dead now for ten years, stands at his side. She is smiling.

"Penny for your thoughts, Harry Nichols," she says in that sultry drawl he found so very intoxicating.

"I'm thinking that if I died right now at this very moment, I would die a happy man." When Jacqueline kisses him, Harry feels a brush like dragonfly wings on his cheek.

Then he rouses to the present. The beach, the surf, and his beloved are gone, leaving behind the white-noise of the apparatus that helps him breathe.

On channel six, the immense glowing ball drops in Times Square. Thousands of revelers celebrate the possibilities of a new year. He has visited many places, but not New York City. He and Jacqueline promised to slip it to the top of their vacation list but never did. Harry reaches for the remote and raises the volume to hear the crowd's cries.

How will that boy Kyle survive the New Year? What difference would it make if Harry took steps to grant that one wish? Kid might end up in a foster home in worse shape. Though well-meaning, the system is flawed and often harms more than helps. And his mother, what would become of her? The statistics brim with scores of women finally silenced by abusive spouses.

With one phone call, Harry can start the process. When does intervening become interfering?

Make him stop hurting Mama . . . and me.

Harry reaches for the phone and dials the Chief of Police's cell number. No need to worry over the late hour. The chief is on duty, watching over their small town as the world ages another year. "Hello my friend. Happy New Year to you."

"Harry? You okay?"

"As good as Santa can be. But something's troubling me, son. And I must enlist your professional aid."

"Anything I can do to help you, Harry. You know that. What's up?"

Harry feels the rightness in his heart. A wish to Santa is sacred, a pledge of trust.

"There's this little boy, you see . . ."

11: The Best I Know

The best I know
Were held by hands
And robbed of innocence
Yet they cradle pain
And spread empathy for others
Also held.

The best I know
Were bruised by words
And snubbed by promises
Yet they tamp sadness
And soft cushion the others
Also bruised.

The best I know
Were smeared by grief
And nailed by hate
Yet they create beauty
And share love with others
Always love.

12: Bird Chimes

Leslie entertains herself with different euphemisms for her late-term, hormone-driven state. *Mean as a cut snake. Ill as a hornet. Mad as a wet hen.* She leaves off the worn clichés, makes up a couple of her own: *stirred up as a cat caught in a blender, aggravated as a saint at a political convention.* Oh, that last one was exceptional.

She is so hateful, some days she can barely tolerate her own company.

And poor Stan. Poor beleaguered, long-suffering Stan. He learned early in the pregnancy to skim beneath her radar, careful to stay clear of his wife's unpredictable moods.

Baking! Of course. Baking! The aroma of warmed brown sugar and melting chocolate chips might soothe the edginess.

Leslie hoists her belly upward and manages to leave the recliner. She is no longer a slim size eight. She is no longer Leslie. Rather, she thinks of herself as an overblown gestation balloon: a tenement housing project bursting with far too much humanity.

Early on, it was easy to fall into expectant domesticity. Because of her initial boundless energy, the nursery stands ready with color-coordinated accessories. Disposable diaper boxes bulge from every closet. Stacks of baby-boy outfits line the chest of drawers.

In the final month, her legs swell to tree trunks, her bladder shrinks to the size of a white acre field pea, and her internal organs struggle to operate in a third of their normal space allotment. She can no longer tolerate working in her midtown office. Confined, sentenced really, to the small wooden frame house, she entertains the delightful, demented fantasy of using the bathroom plunger to suction the child from his watery domain. Was that the meanest thought she's ever had? But hey, it works on toilet clogs, so why not this?

Two weeks overdue. Normal for a first baby, her doctor reassures. How can *he* understand how *she* feels? He's a man. Sure, she values him as a doctor but despises him all the same.

Leslie removes her grandmother's chipped pottery bowl from the cabinet. Gathers the basic ingredients. No need for a recipe. She had learned to cook by feel. Same way the women have always cooked in her family. Pinch of this. Smidge of that. Mix until your touch or the drag on the spoon tells you it is just right. She could use the fancy electric mixer Stan gave her for Christmas, but no, right now she truly needs to *beat* something.

Tension slides from her shoulders as she creams butter and brown and white sugar in the large bowl. She adds the eggs, one at a time. She rummages in the spice cupboard for the vanilla. The flour comes after that and chocolate chips last, folded in.

"Well, crap!" The bottle holds two dang drops, the whisper-essence of the flavoring. "Now what?"

She thumbs through the mental list of nearby neighbors. Forget cramming behind the steering wheel for a trip to the grocery store. The tenement belly prohibits driving her tiny subcompact, and Stan won't be home for four hours.

Leslie wants cookies. *Now.*

Everyone within easy walking distance works, except for the witch-lady next door. Leslie has only seen the old woman twice since she and Stan moved in a few months back. She understands why the kids delighted in ringing the old lady's bell on Halloween. The crone has wild hair that sticks out in every direction, mostly silver with streaks of black. Reminds Leslie of the grade school science fair exhibit where she touched her hand to an electrified metal ball and the static turned her hair into a frizzy halo.

And for the love of Pete, let's not even talk about those cats! Leslie has given up on identifying and counting the number of felines that gravitate to the woman's house. More than once, she has awakened to the sound of caterwauling and robust mating outside of their bedroom window. Soon there're bound to be a few female cats with their own tenement bellies.

Strange noises emanate from the house next door, too. Since she is home in this latter stage of pregnancy, Leslie notes the consistent time of day: midafternoon. The discord rings out like out-of-tune

50

church pipes with no set rhythm. Is the old woman pounding on a progression of upturned aluminum pots?

The boy two doors down who mows their lawn assures Leslie that the clamor is the clash of human bones, some kind of satanic ritual. Part of her actually believes it.

Not exactly the kind of neighbor who welcomes borrowing unless it's eye of newt.

Leslie screws up her courage and grabs a small glass cup. No cookies equals no improvement in her mood. Better to risk the wrath of Hades than deprive herself, and her husband, of a peaceful evening.

The steep steps leading up to the old woman's front door cause Leslie to stop and suck in air. Where she once could bound up inclines in twos, she now struggles one step at a time to hoist the baby-luggage. Winded, she stands at the crest, cup in hand, and musters the energy and nerve to ring the bell.

The old woman answers on the second set of chimes. The house is semi-dark behind her, and her silhouette is one of an ancient black-magic sorceress. Leslie swallows around a lump of fear. Do they ever offer up pregnant women as sacrifices? No, just virgins. There's a relief.

"Yes?" The voice is gravelly, but friendly.

"Hi. I'm Leslie Hammerstrom. From next door. I know we haven't officially met, but . . . I was wondering if you might loan me some vanilla. Just a teaspoon. I'm trying to bake some cookies and discovered I'm out."

The baby boy kicks hard and Leslie sends a hand to rest on the side of her bulbous belly. Wow. Even the unborn senses the old woman's weirdness.

"Come in." The woman steps back and waves Leslie from the dark foyer into a front parlor.

The room reminds Leslie of her own grandmother's sitting room. A gilded mirror over a table covered with crocheted doilies. Sun peeping in from a high window over the door. Polished wooden floor. While Leslie assumed the house would reek of cat urine, she is surprised to detect a hint of lavender mixed with the chocolatey aroma of brewed coffee. Definitely not what she would expect from the dwelling of some cauldron-stirring crone.

"I'm Genevieve Calhoun." The old woman bobs her head once. "Call me Ginny."

Leslie stands for a moment, unsure of how to proceed, until her neighbor points to a high-back chair. "Why don't you take that one? The couch is hard as concrete. It was my late aunt's. Pretty to look at, but brutal on the back."

As much as her swollen feet throb, Leslie doesn't resist the offer. She trundles to the chair and manages to lower to the halfway point before freefalling the last few inches. Grace flew out the window two months ago.

The old woman smiles. "I've just brewed a fresh pot of coffee. It's decaffeinated, so it won't be bad for your little one. I can't drink the high-octane anymore. Makes my heart skip."

"Sure. Coffee would be nice."

Genevieve walks to the back of the house, her movements precise and quick for someone who appears to be well over eighty.

Leslie's gaze takes in the cozy room. Pastel shades of rose and blue dominate, with pots of African violets and philodendron lining the front picture window. Several antique tables and a sideboard of inlaid mahogany mix with the overstuffed chairs and couch. Family pictures punctuate the room, most with people caught mid-laughter.

"Here we are." Genevieve carries a carved wooden tray with a thermal coffee carafe, sugar and cream containers, and two delicate porcelain cups with matching saucers. A small plate holds an array of sugar cookies. "I know you said you were baking, but I just love a touch of sweetness with my coffee. These *aren't* homemade."

Genevieve fishes in her pocket and hands Leslie a small amber bottle. "Vanilla. Didn't want to forget to give you what you came after. Don't worry about replacing it. I have a spare in the cupboard. Besides, there're hardly a couple of teaspoons left in this bottle." The elder decants coffee into the cups.

Leslie adds cream and two sugars to hers. Sips the coffee. Perfect. "Thank you, Ginny."

"You are most welcome. I don't entertain many visitors, and I don't get out much anymore. Little outside of the house interests me enough to go to the trouble." She captures the wisp of silver that curls in front of her eyes and gathers it into a comb at her temple. "This hair of mine. You'd think it would do me the favor of thinning out at my age. Seems it gets bigger and more out of control every day. I'd twist it into a bun, but that makes me look older than a ghost granny's panties."

Leslie chuckles. A solid white Persian pads into the room, stops to skewer Leslie with disdain, and settles onto a pillowed ottoman.

"That's Liberace. You're in his seat," Genevieve says. "He's somewhat spoiled."

"I can't help but notice . . . you must like cats."

Genevieve shrugs. "Might as well. They like me. Keeps me busy and broke, what with the food and vet bills."

"How many do you have?"

"Lordy, I don't know. Twelve? Fifteen?" She bats the air with one hand. "I don't choose them; they choose me. Most are strays that show up for a free meal then go on about their business. A handful actually stay long enough for me to capture them and get them to the vet. Only three live in the house. Liberace, Tootsie, and Zsa Zsa."

Squawking echoes from the backyard. The old woman puts down her cup and jumps up. "Ah! Devil's spawn!"

Leslie watches the old woman skitter from the room. There had been a time when she was able to move that fast herself before the baby ballast. A ruckus sounds from somewhere deep in the house.

Genevieve reappears at the threshold. "Sorry for the interruption. Now, where were we?"

"I don't mean to pry but . . . what, exactly, was all that noise? I've heard it a number of times and sort of wondered."

Genevieve leans back her head and laughs, a sound so pure Leslie's spirit lifts. "I suppose it would make you ponder my sanity, eh?"

"No, I just—"

"It's those dang blackbirds. Every afternoon, they arrive in a fantastic swarm to light in my magnolia tree out back. I don't mind them passing through, so much as I mind the mess they leave behind. Droppings everywhere!" When Leslie crimps her brows together, the old woman pauses. "That noise is my clever invention. Want to see?"

Leslie lifts one shoulder, lets it fall. "Yeah, I guess."

"Come, then."

Leslie hoists the baby-luggage, stands, balances, and waddles behind Genevieve down a narrow hallway, through a galley kitchen, and onto a screened back porch overlooking a shady yard.

"Pipes. See?" Genevieve points high into the magnolia tree. "They're connected to a long rope that runs up and over a pulley, then to this handle. Had one of my nephews install it. When I give the handle a good yank, they clang like Lucifer breaking bad. Scares the bejabbers out of those birds, sends them on their way before they crap up my lawn furniture."

"Interesting." Leslie admires creative problem solving. She is the one at her office who always comes up with easy answers to difficult questions. Or she used to, before she became a human incubator.

"I can't tell you how much better it makes me feel to yank that rope." The crepe skin around the old woman's eyes crinkles when she smiles. "Appeals to me, something about being able to do something *so* simple to stop a thing I find *so* irritating. That doesn't happen very often in one's life."

"Really." Leslie nods. "Mind if I try it?"

"I've already run off the birds, but . . ." Genevieve opens the screened back door and unhooks the rope pull from its tether. "Don't see why not. Not illegal or immoral. And it won't cost you a thin dime."

Leslie grabs ahold of the wooden handle and tugs. The pipes rattle.

"Don't be timid, gal. Go ahead and snatch the fool out of it!"

Leslie pulls and releases for what seems a good five minutes before she stops. Her breath comes in puffs. Her cheeks sting. Baby boy kicks. Her hair must be as wild as the old woman's by now.

"Feels pretty darn good, eh?"

Leslie returns the rope handle to its hook. "Oh my yes! It certainly does."

"Well, honey. You can come over any old time and yank to your heart's content," Genevieve says. "Except at night. I've been told by a nice, young police officer that I should refrain from such."

Leslie notes how the smile changes the old woman's face. Even her hair looks less intimidating.

Genevieve rests a cool hand on Leslie's shoulder. "Shall we go and finish our coffee?"

"I have a better idea, Ginny." Leslie pushes on a foot-shaped lump until it smooths back into the round belly. If the kid doesn't come out soon, her skin will never be the same. "Why don't we pour our coffees into paper cups. You can come over to my house and we'll finish over there. That way, we can try my cookies straight from the oven while the chocolate's still gooey."

13: Baby Gift

Everyone calls the lady "Tee." Mama taught me to always call my elders by their proper full name, or else add a Mrs., Miss, or Mr., but Tee lets me call her just *Tee* like I am grown up, too. Her last name is *Hirt*, which is funny on account of she could never *hurt* anyone or anything. I have seen her scoop up a cockroach in a paper cup and tote it outside. That's the kind of gentle she is. I guess a person's name doesn't necessarily mean what it sounds like.

Tee and her husband, Homer, moved into our rental house just down the lane last year. I was seven then. I'm eight now. Out here in the country, time is still and hot, and no kids near my age live for miles. So, I set out to make friends with the new neighbors. A person can only watch so much television, my mama says. She runs me out of the house because I need the fresh air. I think it's because *she* needs it.

The rental house is not as big as ours. My daddy built them both with his bare hands. I don't remember it. I wasn't yet a glimmer in his eye is what he tells me. The little house is made from cinder block painted bright white with dark green shutters beside the front windows. The shutters don't do anything but make it look good. We have them on our house, too. The yard is big and thick with grass.

The most magical thing, ever, is the big oak tree that lives next to the house. A whole slew of wisteria vines run up the tree so far, it hurts my neck to look up. Daddy worries it will choke the life from the tree. How could a thing so pretty kill?

I love to walk under the canopy of wisteria flowers in the spring. The air is pure perfume. I would pour it over me if I could, or store it in a mason jar so that I could smell it all year 'round. The blooms look like bunches of grapes; that's how they're shaped. And you should see the bees! If I get a jar with a lid with holes poked in it, I can catch ten or twelve in no time flat. They are so drunk on nectar, they're sluggish and easy to hem into the jar. Mama won't let me keep them long. I have to let them go. Tee wouldn't much abide me harming the bees, either. It's just fun to get a bunch in a jar and watch them up close for a bit, all aggravated and kicking up a fuss.

Tee is in the cramped kitchen when I knock and push through the front door. My mama taught me manners. Tee calls out, "Come on in!" She has never told me to go away. Not once. And I know I can be a pill sometimes.

Tee's fingers are slick with cooking oil. She is mashing pizza dough onto a flat round pan, stretching as she pushes down and out.

"Yum pizza! My favorite!" I pull up an aluminum kitchen table chair and plop down. I love to watch Tee cook.

When she smiles, the skin around her blue eyes crinkles up and her eyes kind of twinkle. Even when her lips aren't smiling, she looks like she is. Tee has that kind of happy face.

"I'm making two. You want to eat supper with us?" She wipes her oily hands on a clean cotton dish towel before opening the can of pizza sauce.

"Do I ever!"

Tee laughs. "I'll call your mother and make sure it's all right."

"May I help?"

Tee nods and hands me the opened silver packet of grated parmesan cheese. I sprinkle it over the top of the red sauce she has spread evenly across the dough.

"You can fix us a glass of iced tea. We'll visit while the pizza cooks."

I rummage in the freezer for the aluminum ice trays. "Where's Homer?"

"He's still at work. He should be home shortly."

We take our tall glasses of sweet tea outside to a small wooden picnic table and sit down. Tee asks me questions about how I spent my day and I ask about hers. Besides Samantha on *Bewitched,* Tee is about the prettiest woman I have ever seen. Even my mama agrees, and she's pretty herself so she should know.

Tee tilts her head. "Marcie, do you recall when I told you Homer and I wanted to have a child?" Her eyes water slightly.

"Uh-huh."

Tee's tears frighten me, the way things do when they aren't normal. "Are you sad?"

She wipes away the moisture. "Oh no, honey. I'm happy!"

Adults are strange. They get things all mixed up and cry when they're happy and laugh when they're sad. At times, I'm at a loss to figure them out.

"We're going to adopt, Marcie. We've waited for almost a year, but finally, our baby girl is coming to live with us."

"Here?" I look around like a baby girl might just appear out of nothing.

"We'll be traveling to pick her up sometime in the next few days."

I take a long sip of tea, considering. The aftertaste of fresh crushed spearmint burns my tongue.

"You can be her big sister." Tee rests a hand over mine. "What do you think about that?"

Big sister. Quite a change from being the little sister I've always been. Maybe if I call my own sister, she'll give me a few pointers. Would I boss the baby around and tell her she's being a little pill? Do I babysit and make her go to bed before the sun goes down? Do I get all aggravated because she uses my favorite hair scarf for a play wedding veil?

"The whole thing is going to take some getting used to, is what I think."

Tee laughs in the tinkling way that makes her face go all soft and dimpled. "For all of us, my dear. For all of us."

For the first two days after the baby arrives at the little white house down the lane, Mama makes me stay home, to give them time to settle in before I go making a nuisance of myself.

By the third morning, I dance with anticipation. "Tee might need my help!" I tell her.

Mama is worn out trying to contain my growing urgency. "Go on down there, Marcie. Carry Tee these fresh-baked biscuits when you go. Come home when she tells you, you hear? Don't wear out your welcome."

I *yes ma'am* as the screened door slams behind me. Dodging between long rows of tall camellia bushes, I take turns skipping and running, careful not to dump the basket of biscuits on the ground.

I sit very still in the padded rocking chair, willing myself not to squirm. Tee glides into the cozy living room cradling a pink bundle. Homer walks behind her, a smile as wide as all get-out plastered on his face.

"Here she is!" Tee's voice is soft and musical. She bends down and carefully places the child into my cupped arms.

"Be sure to support her neck like this." Tee demonstrates. "She can't hold her little head up by herself, just yet. So it's important you do it for her."

The baby gazes up at me with bright, blue-green eyes. Her wispy hair is a deep shade of red. On one side of her face, a small raspberry-colored birthmark kisses her cheek.

Tee gestures toward us. "Marcie, meet Meredith. Meredith, this is Marcie."

"Meredith. Meredith." I practice saying her name. It suits her, a sunny kind of name.

A faint sweet scent fills my nose, and I lean down to snuffle her hair. New babies smell so good—puppies, kittens, and humans — before living makes them stale like old soda crackers.

Meredith's rosebud lips purse. Spit bubbles ooze from the corners.

"Oh look, Homer. Meredith likes Marcie already. She's flirting with her." Tee gives a little laugh. "Would you like to feed her?"

"Sure."

I worried that Tee wouldn't have time for me anymore. The baby would be much more important. I would be deserted, left to fend for myself all summer with nobody to talk to.

I tilt the warmed bottle to the baby's waiting mouth. Now I have the super special job of being a for-real big sister.

14: Light Feet

Dancing is infinitely more pleasurable than lovemaking; Sam Blount reaches this conclusion without a smattering of doubt. Even with his beloved wife, the consummation of marriage had seemed like an awkward and tawdry act, lacking in the over-the-top, grasping passion touted by Hollywood. He had loved Irene, yet the memories from their bedroom don't match the depth of his feelings for her. To dance is to consummate without defrocking or embarrassing noises.

Sam reaches to the passenger side and retrieves a gift box and a paper grocery sack, its top neatly crimped end over end. This year's contribution to the Annual Davis New Year's Bash is a slow-roasted pork loin, carved into thin slices with an apricot spread and crisp toast points made from his home-baked wheat bread. The wax paper-lined box holds his hostess gift: fluffy, cloud-white, sugary divinity peppered with pecan chips.

Big Sam Blount knows his way around a kitchen, a fact not overlooked by local society. Had he not been invited solely on the merits of his jovial, genial personality, his food offerings would surely prompt his name's addition to most guest lists.

He parks the Chevrolet, washed and polished to a high gloss, in the long row of vehicles lining the sandy lane. Big Sam whistles as he walks toward the Davis farmhouse. Inside, the lights glow. Laughter and music filter through the crisp New Year's Eve night.

Sam always carries a song in his head, as if he has one of those new-fangled transistor radios in his brain. Most of the time, he hears sultry, lady-singer-in-a-red-dress, nightclub melodies. Some mornings, as he sweeps the sidewalk in front of the Five and Dime, big band tunes flow through and he fights the urge to jitterbug, his push broom held like an adoring partner. Oh, but he wouldn't do such in public. Not on the street. He saves that for later in the privacy of his linoleum-tiled living room.

After Irene died, the formal front parlor stood idle, seldom visited or dusted. Little by little, it morphed. First, the sofa, mahogany coffee table, and two chairs were shoved to the walls to provide room for his impromptu solo dance. The hooked rug disappeared, rolled in plastic and retired to the hallway closet. Irene's glass animal menagerie vacated next. Finally, the twelve-by-fourteen room stood barren, save for one small occasional table topped with Sam's turntable and a teetering stack of records.

Tillie Davis opens the kitchen door after his second set of knocks. She stands on tiptoes to deliver an affectionate peck to his right cheek. "Happy New Year's Eve, Sam." Her eyes sparkle when she notes his packages. "What do we have this year?"

Sam hands the decorative box over first. "Sweets for the sweet. Starting with the hostess."

Tillie peeks into the box and squeals. "Your heavenly divinity! I'll have to find a place to hide this from Dan and the kids." She offers a conspiratorial wink.

Sam carefully removes the plastic-wrapped meat platter and locates a niche amidst the food offerings table.

Tillie grabs a plastic fork, stabs a small piece of pork loin, and pops it into her mouth. "Big Sam, you put all of the cooks in town to pure shame."

Sam glows with the compliment. "Try the apricot spread on a toast point. It brings out the flavors of the meat."

The spacious country kitchen teems with clusters of laughing, talking friends. On the end next to the fireplace, the food table strains under the weight of dishes: a turkey, a baked ham, platters of raw vegetables, deviled eggs, chips and dips, a relish tray, and an array of layered cakes. A second smaller table holds soft drinks, mixers, assorted liquors, a coffee tureen, ice, and cups.

Piddie Davis Longman, Tillie's sister-in-law, slides up next to Sam and gives his arm an affectionate squeeze. "Be sure to get a piece of my chocolate cake before it's all gone. I know how much you like it."

"Rest assured, Miz Piddie. Rest assured."

Hands down, Piddie Longman makes the best dang chocolate cake and icing Sam has ever tasted. And he has tasted a good number.

Dan Davis, host and fellow West Washington Street business owner, weaves through the crowd and pumps Sam's hand. "Big Sam. Glad you could make it out!"

"Remember, Sam," Tillie says as she turns to make her way back into the living room. "Take your shoes off when you go in to dance. I just waxed my floors and you'll leave black scuff marks if you don't. Everyone is putting their shoes by the back door." She throws a grin back over her shoulder before being swallowed into the crowd of revelers.

Piddie motions to the drink table. "Want me to mix you up a little hooch? Whiskey is considered mostly medicinal, you know."

When Big Sam laughs, his bulk heaves up and down with an internal rhythm of its own. "Think I might start off with a cup of coffee, Miz Piddie. Strong drink makes me lose my step on the dance floor."

Piddie smiles. "You're the exception to the rule, then. Takes most of these folks a good stiff belt or three before they loosen up a bit."

The opening strands of a Glenn Miller number sound from the living room stereo speakers.

Piddie grabs Sam's hand. "Forget that coffee. C'mon, Sam. Kick off those shoes. We're going to go cut a rug!"

Sam takes Piddie's hand and transfers it to the crook of his arm. The couple weaves through the kitchen and into the living room turned dance hall.

The music transforms him, as it always does. The pressure of his bulk falls away. The bass thump of the Glenn Miller Orchestra pulses and his feet move to the rhythm. He is no longer Big Sam Blount the fat man, owner of the Five and Dime. Piddie Longman is the perfect partner, head thrown back, eyes closed, grinning to beat the band.

Without glancing at the crowd, Sam senses the admiring female eyes watching him: lionesses stalking prey. Tonight he will not feel the press of loneliness. His dance card will be full, and the women will dance perfectly in time. He knows this. One by one, Sam has trained them all.

Big Sam recalls the second his life changed for the better. It began innocently, as many things do in adult life.

The brass bell tinkled when the heavy wooden door shut. A woman and a little boy stepped into the cool interior of the Five and Dime. Sam glanced up from the log book. "Morning, Miz Eva."

Eva Spenser nodded in his general direction. "Good morning." Then to her son, "One toy. Just one."

Eva meandered down the narrow aisles, picking up trinkets and inspecting them with feigned interest, occasionally glancing Sam's way.

"You looking for anything in particular, Miz Spenser?"

Her petite hand fluttered to her face. "No, not really."

She ambled toward the counter where he sat perched on a wooden stool. With every shift of his weight, the wood creaked in dismay.

"Stephen had a dental appointment this morning. He was very brave, so . . ."

"So you decided to reward him. Very good."

"Yes."

Spots of color rose high on her cheeks. Her gaze fell to the clutch purse gripped in her hands. "I . . . I wonder if I might ask something of you, Mr. Blount."

Eva glanced toward the rear of the store. Her son was engrossed in a display of toy soldiers.

"Of course. Ask away."

"Could you, I mean, *would* you consider giving me a dance lesson, or two?"

Sam sat in stunned silence. He could have been no more surprised had Eva Spenser asked for a recent copy of *Playboy* magazine.

"Dance lessons, Miz Eva?"

He noted how her long, feathery eyelashes fluttered over hazel eyes.

She waved a hand through the air. "It's silly. Never mind. Forget I asked."

Sam slid the accounting ledger aside. "No honest request is silly. Only, why?"

"Last year. At the Davis's annual party, then later at the hospital dances, I've noticed how good you and Miz Irene danced."

Sam involuntarily flinched at the sound of his deceased wife's name.

"I am so sorry, Sam. About Irene. The whole town is. Oh good heavens. And here I am troubling you."

"No harm done, Miz Eva. I'm doing fine. Really."

She searched his face before continuing. "I've always wanted to learn how to dance like that. My husband Earl doesn't care for it. But he might if he had a dance partner to help him. I could teach him, maybe, if I learned first."

"And you want *me* to teach you?"

"I will pay, of course. I simply can't drive to Tallahassee to take lessons. But Earl mustn't find out. It would hurt his pride."

Sam smiled. Eva's desires sounded more clandestine by the second.

"I suppose I could help you out, Miz Eva. And I do live outside of town toward the lake."

"Away from prying eyes."

"Exactly."

Eva's son rushed to the front of the store, a tin toy artillery tank clasped in his hands.

"Why don't you take that on out to the front sidewalk and take it for a test drive, Son? Your mama can pay me."

When the door closed, Eva said, "Every other Friday night, Earl plays poker with a group of his buddies." Her voice fell to a barely audible whisper, despite the empty store. "I'll come to your house at six-thirty."

Two hours beyond the start of the New Year, Big Sam joins a clutch of revelers exiting the party. The music still blares from within, but only a handful of diehard dancers remain. Soon Dan and Tillie will be forced to herd them to their cars or insist those too unstable to drive camp out on the floor.

In the car, he notes the throbbing burn in his feet, a sure sign of the evening's success. He watches couples arm-in-arm as they pick their way in the starlight toward their vehicles, as he and Irene had done, not that long ago. For a moment, a cloak of loneliness threatens to smother his mood.

Then Sam recalls the giddy sensation of dancing one after the other with lovely sequined ladies. The sadness abates.

15: Lake Share

Etta Dunkirk sits on a bench by Lake Ella in the warm early spring sun. In a few short weeks, when summer buckles sidewalks into pretzels and waves of heat shimmer from the asphalt, she will move to one of the benches in the shade of a moss-draped live oak. Or maybe that bench behind the American Legion Hall or one in the cluster next to the branches of the children's climbing tree on the opposite side of the park.

Life is just about as perfect as an eighty-seven-year-old woman can expect. Etta sits in the one spot on God's earth that she feels closest to Heaven. Lake Ella is not big or ostentatious. No speed boats break the shush of the spring breezes. No fancy houses surround it. But it's calm and active all at once, a place where an old woman can sit with a cup of good coffee from the Café and watch a parade of people.

Once Oscar passed, her only son Walt insisted that she leave her small town and move to the city of Tallahassee. Near him. He would've had her move in with the family, but she couldn't abide the notion. Never a peaceful moment in that house, what with three dogs, two cats, a bevy of hamsters, fish, birds, and three active children. Visits over a couple of hours wear her completely out, and her ears seem sore for days afterward. All that rampant energy running amok overpowers her nervous system.

"But, Mama. Where will you go? I'd prefer that you not live alone anymore."

Walt is a good son. He works like a dog, long hours. His wife Nancy is a teacher. She puts in a full day too. Then, it's kids to cart around to first one thing, then another. Busy. Busy. Busy.

Walt took her to visit assisted living facilities. She liked them okay, but most were too fancy for her simple tastes. She learned of a place that appealed. More of a large boarding house. A simple apartment with people nearby if she needed to scare up a bridge game or talk over old times. The clincher: easy walking distance to Lake Ella.

Etta sold the house and most of the belongings, what she didn't give to Walt. He's so sentimental. Everything his father ever touched becomes something to enshrine. Etta doesn't hold such attachments, a fact that makes some people believe she has no heart. Growing up in the time of Nazi Germany, she has long since learned to cling to memories as her dearest possessions. Trappings of life hold a person down.

Etta's room has a single bed, one bedside table, two lamps, a small desk, a good reading chair and ottoman, and a low rolling cart holding a small color television. One window holds her African violets. The efficiency has a sink, compact stove, and refrigerator, enough of a kitchen for her needs. A narrow bathroom with a shower, tub, and wash basin. A walk-in closet for a few clothes and shoes, and ample linens and towels for one person.

The grocery store is two blocks down. Though Walt insists on driving her once a week, Etta often walks the distance to meander down the long, clean aisles. She chooses fresh vegetables dripping with misted moisture and bakery bread still warm. She buys only enough to fill one mesh bag. In her younger days, she was a pack mule: strong and sure-footed. Now one hand is reserved for the cane.

If Walt suspected how many times a week she trundles across busy North Munroe, he would put his foot down. Poor dear. He's always doing that with her, putting his foot down. Makes no difference. She will go where she will go. When a woman's universe is reduced to five city blocks, only the Grim Reaper himself can stop her with a well-planted foot. Some days, Etta thinks the Reaper drives one of the many automobiles who threaten to send her flying. She has survived a war, marrying a service man from the Deep South, and moving to a country where she barely knew how to say hello. Still some days she wonders if one of the crazy drivers will do what all the rest had not. At least she won't die young.

Etta thinks about God. Often. Almost every day. She's researched the great religions of the world. Read up on the saints, the various messiahs and gurus, and done her fair share of talking to the occasional clergyman who wandered into her orbit.

All in all, Etta sees God as Santa with more clout. You ask for something. He keeps a list and checks it. You either get what you want, or not. Plus you can't really see either Santa or God, though representatives are everywhere. Both seem to care about what goes on but maintain a safe distance. If Etta was in such a position, she'd keep humanity at arms' length, too.

The coffee shop next to Lake Ella suits Etta. It's small, the floors are real wood aged by multitudes of shoes, and the help is friendly.

"Morning, Miz Etta," the young woman says.

"Two cups of joe, please."

Same order, day after day. Unless the wind is so cold it cuts straight through her or a hurricane blows from the Gulf, Etta appears at the coffee house. She had to school them those first few visits. The staff understands not to quiz her about lattes or fancy additives or prissy names. Just coffee.

"Yes Ma'am."

Etta smiles. No matter what else is said about the South, no one can deny the polite manners of the natives. She waits for the order, then steps over to the counter to put plenty of creamer and sugar in hers. The other, she leaves black. The lids take a little finagling with arthritic fingers, but she makes sure both are tight before she sets them into her cloth bag.

Outside, Etta spies the same man on the lakeside bench behind the American Legion Hall. Ripped and faded army fatigues. Beard. Bony like near death.

"I have an extra one of these," she says in a soft voice when she reaches the bench.

The veterans. The ones with haunted eyes. She knows to approach them as one would a spooked horse. No fast moves. Waiting for the invitation to enter their private space.

He grunts. Slides over until he hugs the far end of the bench. Etta lowers herself down.

"I take mine with heavy cream and a generous helping of white sugar. Not everyone does."

She digs in the pocket of her light jacket and leaves a pile of creamers and several packets of sugar on the bench beside the cup. "Suit yourself. I even brought a stirring stick."

Etta sips, taking in the line of ducklings trailing after their mother. Some say the ducks make a mess with their droppings. The city rounds them up from time to time and relocates them. No matter. Like the homeless and the wounded, they come back to sit by the lake.

The man cradles the cup with shaking hands. Etta takes note. This one uses no cream or sugar. Tomorrow, she might bring some cookies. Oatmeal. Even those who don't take to heavy sugar like cookies.

16: Contentment

Karen Price stops in front of the desk at the entrance to the long-term care wing of Magnolia Arms Nursing Facility. A woman in baby blue scrubs looks up and smiles.

"There you are. I figured you'd be by today."

"Afternoon, Francine. How is she?" Karen asks.

"She was a little more confused than usual before lunch. Been talking about all kinds of things that don't make half-sense. Bits and pieces about her brothers and sisters, like they were still alive. But she could be settled into reality by now. She's a flickering light bulb. On and off."

Karen shakes her head. "Bless her heart."

Francine jots notes in a wire-ring notebook. "She's still sweet, though. Sweet as sugar pie. Some get combative when they're heading into dementia."

Karen pulls a small stuffed animal, the likeness of a mocking-bird, from a shopping bag. "I found this over in Tallahassee at Native Nurseries. Listen." She presses a plastic spot on the cloth bird's belly and the recorded birdsong sounds. "Think she'll like it?"

Francine flits one hand in the air. "Uh-huh, I reckon she will. Days she can get up, she near 'bout runs the aides crazy to get out in the garden. Doesn't matter if it's a hundred degrees in the shade; she pitches a conniption fit if we don't roll her out for a few minutes. There're a couple of doves that come up. We try to keep a little seed around, so Birdie will have it to cast on the ground for them. They're not the kind to eat from a feeder, you know, as they'll walk around and peck rather than perch."

"You sound like someone who's been around Birdie Bidwell a little."

"Can't help but learn about birds if you hang around her for more than five minutes. I was helping her to a bath, couple of nights back, and she told me all about how two male hummingbirds will scrap with each other over the nectar feeder. Said it would sound like you were caught up in the middle of a helicopter fight if you sat nearby."

Karen nods. "She had two of those red glass feeders. One on either end of her porch. And, yes. If you sat there, you got buzzed. For such small things, hummers can make a loud noise. Especially when they zoom by just inches from your head."

The charge nurse gathers a handful of charts and stands. "Don't let it upset you, Karen, if Miz Birdie doesn't know who you are. She thought I was a long-lost cousin from Mississippi this morning. Not that I wouldn't love to call her kin. She's a sight sweeter than some of my own. But her skin is a bit too fair to be one of mine."

Karen grins. Moves away from the nursing hub. She taps on the door to room twelve and enters. Birdie's eyes are closed. An uneasy sensation shoots through Karen's middle until she sees the withered old woman's chest rise and fall.

She stands at the threshold for a moment, considering their unlikely friendship. Karen, at fifty. Birdie at ninety. The age difference falls away and they are just two people sharing stories. Birdie insists she isn't really older than Karen; she just got here first.

The second bed in the narrow room is unoccupied. For now. The last roommate, a bellicose woman in her late eighties who tried everyone's patience, even Birdie's, had been carted off to the hospital a week back. Though Birdie would never let on, she was relieved to see the cantankerous old geezer go. Hopefully, the next resident will be less of a grouch.

Karen smiles, remembering Birdie's statement: *I'm sure she's still living. On account of, Heaven doesn't want her and Hell is full.*

Birdie's eyelids flicker and open. When she focuses on Karen, the corners of her lips curl up. "Thought you'd forgotten me."

Karen's spirit sinks. At least twice a week, she visits. Birdie exists so much in the present, she can't hold as much of the past.

"Forget my best across-the-street neighbor? Now why would I go and do a thing like that?"

"K.P.? It *is* K.P., isn't it?"

The old woman calls Karen by her initials for two reasons. One: she once knew a lady with the same name who she didn't care for. A woman who thought feeding the birds was a waste of time and wouldn't put a bell on her murderous old Tomcat for love nor money. Second: Birdie knows Karen's not one much for cooking, and it's just plain funny to refer to her by the old military lingo associated with kitchen duty.

"It's me, Miz Birdie. How are you feeling this afternoon?"

"Like someone slipped in here and beat me senseless during the night." She lifts a bony hand. "Could you raise the head of my bed? And shift my pillow. I got a crick in my neck."

Karen sets the shopping bag down and works the hospital bed's controls. Birdie settles back into the freshly plumped pillows.

"What do you have there?" Birdie motions to the plastic bag.

Karen hands it over. "I brought you a surprise."

Birdie's blue eyes widen. With her tiny shriveled frame, wispy white hair, and gingham gown, she looks like a porcelain doll. Childhood comes twice in life if a person is lucky. Birdie is rocking hers.

"Ain't this sweet?" The old woman lifts the gray, black, and white stuffed bird from the bag and turns it in several directions. "Pretty true to form, too."

"Press the button," Karen says.

The old woman does and the distinctive warble, chirp, and whistle recording plays.

"Pretty close to what one sounds like, too." She cradles the toy in her arms. "I love just about any kind of bird. You know, we have that in common. But I have always had a soft spot for mockingbirds. I like to try to pick out the different calls and figure out where they've been to hear them. What all have they seen? How many miles have they traveled to bring their list of songs back to me?"

Karen drags a chair to the bedside and sits. "I think I like robins the best. Just when I think cold weather is never going to leave, that winter is going to go on forever, I see a robin. Then, a few more. Pretty soon, they gather up in big groups beside the roadways and in yards.

When I don't notice them around anymore, I know they've left to fly north, and spring is right around the corner."

Birdie nods. "And chickadees! They flock to my feeders, the greedy little buggers. Them, and the purple finches. I don't know why they call them purple, on account of their little heads look orange to me."

Karen kicks off her shoes. Settles in for the visit. The talk will center around birds. It always does. That, and the end of life.

"I think today might be the day, K.P.," Birdie states.

"Why today?"

"I just feel like it might be."

Every time Karen stops by, Birdie repeats the words.

"Are you not feeling well?" Karen asks.

"No, dear. Not particularly bad. Just not particularly good. I'm ninety. I have to die sometime. Everything dies, K.P."

"Yep, Miz Birdie."

"You know, it isn't always bad. Just think, if that woman hadn't died and left all those precocious children for the handsome Captain Von Trapp to care for, then Maria would never have left the convent to be their governess."

"Good point."

Karen Price and Birdie Bidwell share more than a love for nature and birds. Between them, they've watched *The Sound of Music* over fifty times. The videotaped recording Karen had bought her former neighbor several years back had been played so often, it finally snapped. No problem. Last Christmas, Karen provided one of her extra DVD players and the classic musical on disc. The two had been known to sing *The Lonely Goatherd* together, yodeling at the top of their lungs like neither possessed good sense. Or they would tear up Karen's favorite, *Edelweiss*. Birdie was tone deaf and couldn't carry a tune in a bucket, and Karen was only confident in the shower. What they lacked in talent they made up for with enthusiasm.

Too bad Karen can't get the old woman interested in watching *Star Trek, The Next Generation*. The relationship would truly go beyond any age confines. But Birdie isn't one much for space adventures, and she can't bear the sight of a Klingon. Birdie says the waffle-forehead aliens give her nightmares.

"Pull the shades up, will you?" Birdie asks. "The nurses never let enough light in here. And I can't see my birds."

The view from Birdie Bidwell's window looks out over the parking lot. Not a sign of a live bird in sight. Only the avian images frozen in slips of color.

"I love that stained glass you made me better than life itself," Birdie says. "Every time I look at it, I pick out something different. The way the bluebird looks like it's smiling. The way the mockingbird looks like he's thinking of all the places he'll visit and all the songs he'll take to heart. The way that bright red on the cardinal's back is richer than any king's cloak. You are just pure talented, my gal. Just pure talented. I told your mama when you were born that you would be something special. I've known you since you were just a twinkle in your parents' eyes, and I know these things."

Karen feels the color rise in her cheeks. Compliments have never been easy to take, even if they are true.

The piece measures three-by-four feet, small compared to many of Karen's other commissioned works. Unlike some pieces using a commercially-prepared template, Birdie's gift, a piece the old woman calls her *bird's-eye view*, Karen had created from pure imagination. She used her most favorite, intense colors: jewel tones in emerald, lapis, ruby, and sapphire. In the intricate design, birds flew, perched, or preened on branches curling with lush greenery. All, knit together carefully with copper foil treated to foster the appearance of an aged patina.

Karen recalls the feeling: the intense rush of muses looking over her shoulders as she worked. National Public Radio played in the background. Both cats— usually twirling at her feet or batting important pieces of polished glass onto the floor— had been unnaturally sedate, happy to curl up on the nearby computer desk. She remembers eating handfuls of buttered popcorn and sipping sweet tea as she cut the glass shards to shape.

Birdie glances from the stained glass window to Karen. "The nurses hope I'll leave this piece to the home when I pass. They want to hang it in the lobby so everyone can see it when they come in."

"It is yours, Miz Birdie. I reckon you can do whatever you want with it." Karen rests one hand over her elderly friend's. "But let's not talk about that. You aren't going anywhere anytime soon. It's almost time for the stone crabs to come in. I have already ordered twenty pounds for the freezer. As soon as they arrive, I'll steam up a batch and bring you some."

"With melted dipping butter?" Birdie asks.

"Of course. I can use the microwave in the nurse's lounge so it's nice and warm."

Birdie holds up her arthritis-deformed hands. "I can't crack the shells anymore."

"I'll do that before I bring them. No worries. All you'll have to do is eat."

Birdie grins. The thin skin wrinkles around her eyes. "You'll have hell to pay with the nurses. All that richness will tear up my stomach, for sure."

Karen tilts her head to one side. Considers. "So, I'll bring you a big box of Depends. That way, you won't mess up the sheets."

"You could find a way around the devil himself, K.P."

Karen nods. "Probably."

Birdie's gaze drifts to the stained glass again. "I don't have much left that means anything to me. That's what happens. You spend all of your life toiling to get stuff, then you get old and decrepit, and you have to give it all up. Then, to beat all of that, you up and die and you can't take any of it with you!"

Karen laughs. "You are so profound, Miz Birdie."

"Don't fault your mama for her ways, K.P. She loved you all the same."

"Okay . . ." Birdie shifts subjects so quickly, Karen often struggles to keep up.

Birdie shakes a finger in Karen's direction. "Your mama was so tied in to her brand of religion, she couldn't open her mind enough to understand that love is love no matter who a person falls for. Still, she was proud of you. Told me more than once."

"Miz Birdie . . ."

"Let me finish. That's one of your faults at times, K.P. You interrupt. Now, your lady friend is one of the nicest humans on God's green earth. Don't you let nobody go judging you. You hear?"

Karen nods. Her voice is stuck behind a lump.

"You bring her around to see me, next time. She's a pretty little thing, and she makes me laugh."

"Yes, Miz Birdie. I will. She works over in Tallahassee, so she doesn't get home most days until after you've already dressed for bed."

"Then I'll visit in my night gown. No matter. It doesn't have any holes in it. Bring her one evening soon."

"I will."

Birdie stares at the window for a few moments. Her expression darkens. "Figure me a way, K.P."

Karen studies her friend. "A way for what?"

"When I pass. And, I'm telling you, it's coming up sooner than later. Figure a way I can have my bird's-eye view with me." Birdie pauses. Moves her head from side to side. "It'd be a crying shame to tear up my piece. I'd love to leave it whole for folks here to enjoy. But, maybe you could run me a paper copy, somehow. You know, I'll be cremated, so it'll burn with me. I like the thought of that."

"I'll make it happen, Miz Birdie. I promise." Karen stands. "I have to run into town for a few groceries. If you'd like, I can pick up some ice cream and come back."

"I suppose I could force myself to eat a bowl."

"Good."

Birdie makes a sour face. "Long as it's not raspberry. I've never been one much for them."

Karen nods. "Got it."

As Karen turns the small pick-up truck from the parking lot, she sings the first few lines of *My Favorite Things*.

A list from a self-help book comes to mind. Three things required for contentment: something to do, someone to love, and something to look forward to.

The way Karen feels, she has all three.

17: Wait for You

I will wait for you
in spring breezes dusted yellow
and we'll soar with cloaks of gold.
I will wait for you
by springs crystal and deep
and we'll float with faces to the sun.

I will wait for you
in moss-draped oaks
and we'll chase squirrels branch to branch.
I will wait for you
down summer-hot lanes
and we'll dance sugared sand between our toes.

I will wait for you
in flowered pastures
and we'll make a bed of sedge and clover.
I will wait for you
by salt-tipped surf
and we'll hear angels in echoes of shells.

I will wait for you
'neath scores of stars
and we'll grasp hands to touch each one.
I will wait for you
with each breath, touch, and scent
and you'll trust I wait for you.

18: Truck Stop

Lucille perches on the edge of the truck stop's cranberry-red, puffy-vinyl booth seat. She checks her watch for the third time in less than five minutes. *Soon.* She clucks disapproval of her sloppiness and mops a ring of spilled cream from beneath a coffee mug.

Even at the late hour, the restaurant bustles with activity. Steam from a hot food bar mingles with the mixed aromas of brewed coffee and road grime. People push through the double glass doors, as varied as the trucks lined up in the parking lot. Some head to the pay-showers; others meander through the mini market. Most end up in the series of booths and tables, their plates piled high with gut-sticking Southern cooking. The room is ripe with ideas, and Lucille chides herself for forgetting to bring a yellow legal-sized writing pad.

No matter how many times she rendezvous with her chat room friend, Wandering Elf, Lucille always feels the same level of giddy anticipation.

"First of all, I can't fathom you meeting someone on a computer," her best friend Sara Beth told her, "but to actually plan to meet in person in this day and age of serial killers and such is just plain-out foolishness!"

"Wandering Elf is no stranger. She is a fellow writer and I have talked to her over and over. I've even spoken to her on the phone, besides in the chat room. And this isn't the first time we've met. Besides, her husband is with her. They're fine people."

Sara Beth huffed in the way she did when she heard anything she didn't cotton to. "No telling if she really is a writer. How do you know for sure? It could be some kind of crime ring just sucking innocent, law-abiding folks in. You haven't written anything but a few paragraphs for the church bulletin. How does that make you a writer, exactly?"

No one really understands an author. Not in a small town where everyone knows each other's business, and why write it down anyway? If you publish a romance novel, you might claim some fame in their eyes but forget poetry. Poetry is for long-haired hippie types and folks with nothing better to do with their time. And certainly not something a seventy-year-old widow and church secretary would claim as a hobby.

Lucille plays with words. Loves the feel of them as they scatter from her mind onto paper. Glows with the way she trims the sentences down to just the right amount of phrases to conjure an image or evoke an emotion. Lucille's poems reach out from her soul and grab her. She has no choice but to give them wings. The only people who truly empathize are her chat room writer buddies.

"I should go with you," Sara Beth told her.

"We talk about our writing. You would be bored stiff."

"You need protection."

Lucille had stifled a snicker over that one. Soaking wet, Sara Beth did good to weigh ninety pounds. Unless she packed heat, her best friend couldn't protect a fly from a swatter.

"Tell you what, I'll take my cell phone and call you when I get there and again when I start home."

"If you insist. But I will sit by the phone until I hear from you. And if I don't, I *will* call the law."

Lucille pops back to the present. A woman stands by her table.

"Hiya, Mad. Been waiting long?"

"Elf!" Lucille bounces up, gives her friend a hug. "Not long at all. Ten or fifteen minutes, tops."

Though they know each other's true names of Lucille and Marie, the two prefer to reference their online titles: *Wandering Elf* and *Madhatter*— *Elf* and *Mad*.

Lucille glances around. "Where's the hubby? You're not driving that big old rig by your lonesome this time, are you?"

They slide into the booth across from each other. A waitress appears and Marie orders iced water with extra lemon and coffee for herself and her husband.

"Abel headed to the showers. He needs one. Trust me."

Lucille grins. Each time she meets with Marie, she marvels at how much the younger woman resembles her online title. Marie would not be out of place in the midst of a primeval forest, perched on a stump, her pointed ears peaking from beneath dark wisps of wavy hair. Even when her lips aren't curled upward, her expressive green eyes seem to smile as if she knows the hidden secrets most mortals seek.

"I'm so glad you called me on your way through. Where are you headed today?"

"Just south of Orlando by tonight. Then, up to Wisconsin."

Lucille wiggles in the seat, eager for details. Other than a few road trips to south Georgia to visit her late husband's relatives, she has never been out of the state of Florida. She keeps up with Marie's travels as if they are hers, following the routes on a United States road map that hangs on a cork board in her kitchen. Places like Fishkill, New York. She probes for details. What does it look like? Are there mountains or flatlands? What is the temperature? What kind of things do you see by the roadside as you pass by? What kind of people do you meet? What are you hauling?

"We would have more time to visit, if the truck hadn't blown an alternator in Louisiana." Marie takes a long drink of water. "That took us most of last night and this morning to get it repaired. If we'd have gotten here when we planned, I was going to ask you to take us to Whataburger. Abel loves that place, and we don't have them in Nevada."

Lucille taps her chin. "I think there's one not far from here off the next Interstate exit, on into Tallahassee. I'd be glad to run y'all in. I like a good fast food burger myself from time to time. I think most of those places stay open pretty late, what with the college students and all."

"Maybe next time we're through here. We have enough time to eat and refuel, and then we have to hit the road again."

The conversation moves to writing. Marie's upcoming young adult fantasy novel release. Lucille's poetry.

"I can't wait until your first book comes out," Lucille says. "You must be positively giddy."

81

Marie shrugs. "It's kind of like being ten months pregnant. It seems like it will never happen." She narrows her gaze. "And, what about you? Have you given any more thought to actually trying to get your stuff published?"

Lucille's mouth draws into a thin line. "I don't know, Elf. I don't think my writing is good enough."

Marie reaches over and rests her hand on Lucille's for a moment. "I've read some of your poems. Trust me. You are good. Please, please give it a try."

A tall man dressed in jeans and a T-shirt slides into the booth beside Marie. "Evening, Mad. How's it going?"

Abel is the kind of man who instantly enables serenity, the perfect balance to his wife's electric energy.

"Besides the fact you could fry up a dozen eggs and a slab of bacon on the asphalt, even at this late hour, life is good." Lucille studies the menu. "Let's order, shall we? I know you two have to put the pedal to the metal."

Marie and Abel exchange amused glances. "Some old trucker sayings never quite seem to die," Abel says.

"Want to see the new truck?" Marie asks as she lines up to pay the cashier.

"It's not the white one you had last time?"

"Nope. Wait 'til you see it. It's a beauty."

Marie and Abel lead the way through the thick cluster of automobiles choking the front fuel pumps to the expansive side parking lot. Trucks parked in neat rows circle the periphery. Others wait in line to reach one of a series of covered fuel lanes.

When they near a shiny dark green truck, Marie waves one hand through the air. "There she is. What cha think?"

Lucille circles the massive truck, studies the fancy script writing on the door panels and airbrushed fantasy scenes that start on the sides and climb upward toward the hood. "Isn't this something!

Whoever did all this artwork surely was talented. Looks all the world like little elves and fairy people are frolicking all over the place."

"It suits us better than that plain old white one. Want to take a look inside?"

Lucille glances up. The cab towers a good five feet over her head. "Lordy be. I don't know if I can climb up there."

"Mad, you act like you are a million years old. You can climb a ladder, can't you?"

"You forget I'm in my early seventies, Elf. And sure, I can still climb a ladder."

"This is no different. I'll show you the handholds. Piece of cake."

Lucille hoists herself up and up, finally landing in the soft cushioned passenger-side seat. Abel and Marie enter from the opposite door. Marie plops onto the lower sleeping berth and Abel settles into the driver's seat.

"So give me the specs."

Abel ducks his head to hide a grin. Lucille reckons he loves it when novices talk shop.

Marie spreads her hands like a game show hostess. "It is a Freightliner Columbia, condo double sleeper. It's got a 515 hp Detroit Diesel engine series 60. It's a 10 speed auto shift. It has two, 140-gallon fuel tanks, for a total capacity of 280 gallons. We have an AM/FM CD player, CB, XM satellite radio, microwave, coffeemaker, and fridge. Only the fridge and AM/FM CD player came with the truck. Oh and the radio and CB have weather band."

She pauses, then continues. "It has a built-in inverter, not sure of wattage. But it lets me plug in the laptop, coffeemaker, coffee grinder, etc. It has air ride suspension and the seats have lumbar support."

Lucille whistles low. "It must weigh a million pounds." Her gaze roams across the dash controls. In her little Honda, she's doing good just to check the speedometer and gas gauges. The truck's instrument panel looks as foreign as the cockpit of a jetliner.

Abel says, "All tractor trailers, unless they get special permits, have a maximum weight allowance of 80,000 on the US highways."

"And the most important thing: it's green. Green is the best color for a truck." Marie grins. "Any elf will attest to that."

A small silver chime charm in the shape of a kneeling elf dangles above the driver's side door. Lucille smiles. The truck feels as if the little people protect it.

"And you live in here, weeks on end? That is purely amazing." Lucille turns to study the lower bunk. Marie's laptop rests at one end. "How long can you go before you have to stop somewhere?"

Marie glances toward her husband.

Lucille shrugs. "Listen to me. I ask way too many questions. It's just so interesting. I see these big ole trucks flying past me on the Interstate, and I wonder . . ."

When Marie smiles, the dimples deepen at the corners of her mouth. "No problem, Mad. I don't mind. We stop from time to time to eat and take bathroom breaks, like you would do in a passenger car. Our truck gets around seven miles per gallon, which is pretty darn good if you do the math. We can go about 1,500 miles pretty easily, before we become concerned about driving on fumes. We usually will not let it get beneath a quarter of a tank, because it isn't smart to let it get that low."

Abel adds, "The D.O.T., the Department of Transportation and our lord and master, says we can't drive more than eleven hours a day and must be off ten hours. Eight of those hours must be in the sleeper. So generally Marie and I take turns driving ten-hour shifts. I usually drive day hours and she drives nights. We both prefer it that way."

"I love night driving," Marie says. "I got the inspiration for my first fantasy novel, *A Bridge in the Forest*, when I was driving through some thick woods one night. It was a full moon and breathtakingly beautiful."

"Sounds like you love your job."

Marie nods. "I can't imagine doing anything else. Well, besides being a famous author one day. I get paid to roam the country. How many jobs let you do that?"

"I know you've seen some pretty parts of the country." Lucille sighs.

As Marie talks, she counts on her outstretched fingers. "Willamette and Deschutes National Forests on OR 58 in Oregon. Snoqualmie and Wenatchee National Forests on I-90 in Washington. The Columbia River Gorge along I-84 between Oregon and Washington. Coconino National Forest south of Flagstaff, Arizona, on I-17. Arches National Park on US 191 near Moab, Utah. The list is much longer, but those are the first places that come to mind."

Abel nods. "Coldest memory: State line I-94 Fargo, North Dakota, and Moorhead, Minnesota. I think it must have been January. That was where we saw the sundog when the sun rose that morning. Beautiful! Amazing phenomenon! But freaking cold!"

Lucille's eyes glisten. Other than the half-inch of powder back in the early sixties, it rarely snows in North Florida. She recalls rolling up half the front yard to make a snowman barely a foot tall. Even then, it melted by midafternoon.

"Sundog? What in the world is that?"

Marie explains, "It is this really cool thing that happens when conditions are right. When the sun rises, you have mirror images, one on either side. It looks as if there are three suns on the horizon. It has to be really, really cold. Something about ice crystals in the air reflecting the sun's rays. I have a picture of the one we saw on my website."

Abel checks his watch.

"I know you have to be going," Lucille says. "I've kept you way too long with my yapping."

Abel motions toward the fueling deck. "We need to go ahead and pull up while there's not a long line at the pumps."

Lucille reaches for the door handle.

"Wait, Mad. Stay. You can ride up to the pumps with us. I'll walk you to your car after we finish."

Lucille's eyes widen. "Really?"

This is the part that will eat Sara Beth alive when Lucille relates the story later, where the husband and wife serial killer team abducts her and takes off to parts unknown. Later, the authorities will find her faded old blue Honda Civic in the side parking lot. No trace of foul play. No trace of Lucille Becker.

"For sure." Marie grins.

Abel slips the truck from its space and circles to the fueling arena where he whips the steering wheel back and forth to bring the big rig into perfect, straight alignment between the banks of pumps. The ease of his movements astounds Lucille. She can barely back from the garage without hitting the mailbox.

"I'm going for ice cream. Want one?" Abel asks.

"Nah. I'm good." Marie darts a questioning look to her friend.

"None for me, thank you. Sweets keep me awake."

Not that she will sleep later. Home is only a twenty-minute drive west on the Interstate, but seeing her writer buddy always charges her word-batteries, and she will be lucky to fall asleep at all. The start of a poem lingers in her brain like the aura preceding a migraine.

Lucille scales down from the truck easier than she ascended. She could get used to this trucking business. She stands back, awestruck as her petite friend handles the large diesel pumps, one on either side of the truck.

"Must take a long time to fill up these tanks."

Marie swipes the company fuel card, then uses a black rubber strap to lash down one of the fuel handles. "Not really. Probably faster than you take for your little car. It pumps around sixty gallons a minute. That's why I secure the handles with straps. If one pops off, diesel goes everywhere and we pay for it. Pumping that fast, it adds up."

Lucille eyes the side of the truck. "Must be a heck of a gauge to check those tires, too."

Marie opens the driver's side door and pulls out a long, clubbed stick. "You won't believe this." She motions for Lucille to follow as she strikes the tires one by one. "I can tell by the sound it makes whether the air is low."

"Kind of like thumping a watermelon to tell if it's ripe?"

One of Marie's dark eyebrows shoots up. "I guess so. Sort of."

After Marie removes both fuel pumps and tightens the tank caps, Lucille stares at the meter, her mouth ajar. "Is that right? Lawd help!"

Marie chuckles. "Kind of makes your gas bill seem tiny, eh?"

"That would pay my bill for a couple of years!"

Abel walks over, an ice cream sundae cone dripping melted chocolate onto his fist. "Ready to go?"

Marie slips the heavy leather gloves into a compartment and snaps the door closed. "I'll walk Mad to her car."

The two friends stand beside Lucille's Honda. Snarls of people and cars dot the parking lot. Waves of heat left over from hours of cloudless sunshine boil from the blacktop. Lucille feels a trickle of sweat dribble between her breasts where it settles into the already damp elastic band.

"I'll be glad to be heading back up north, for sure," Marie says. "This heat wave stretches across the country, but we may catch a break in Wisconsin. I hope."

Lucille unlocks the car door and pitches her purse onto the floorboard. "So I guess you're driving now?"

"All the way to Mouse Land." Marie shakes her head. "Not to put down your state, Mad, but I could do without ever going through Orlando again. The part we see is ugly and seedy, and downright scary at night. Definitely not the lily-white touristy part of town."

"As far as I'm concerned, the Panhandle is the best."

"Promise me you'll at least think about submitting your poetry." Marie gives Lucille a goodbye hug.

Lucille sits in the car long after she watches Marie walk across to the rig and climb inside. The Honda's air conditioner struggles against the humidity and bottled-up heat.

In the bright fluorescent lights, the green truck eases from the fueling arena and inches behind a line of semis toward the traffic signal.

Trimmed by the moon's illumination and the yellow-orange glow of running lights, the Wandering Elf's rig pushes forward toward the Interstate. One last glimpse of brake lights. Then, it turns and disappears.

Lucille ponders friendship. Two people from the opposite ends of a vast country. Both united in the sometimes lonely act of creating images from a string of carefully pruned words. Two people separated by over thirty years in age.

She thinks about comings and goings. Her return to a small town in a compact car. Marie, back to a boundless world in a behemoth truck. In two or three months, maybe more, Lucille's phone will trill and she will drive to talk again, the universe willing. In the meantime, friendship will survive through a series of small moments strung together by the magic of computers.

The title for her poetry collection pops to awareness, a gift from the muses. If she had her laptop, she might sit all night long in a booth inside the truck stop. It's late, almost the witching hour. Lucille taps the cell phone to speed dial Sara Beth.

No need for the police to get involved.

19: Word Lesson

Summer of 1964

The Calhoun boys stand at the edge of the three-acre cornfield behind the farmhouse. Hattie waves. Who is that little girl with them? Hattie glances over her shoulder at the house before tearing off toward the group. She reaches them in no time flat. Good runner. Better than any ole boy.

"What. Y'all. Doing?" she manages to squeak between gasps for breath. Air thick as cane syrup crowds her skin.

Stevie, the oldest at twelve, stands a head taller than Hattie, with brown eyes and a mop of tangled hair the same color. He rolls a green, sweetgum twig from one side of his cracked lips to the other, spits before he answers. "We gonna walk down to your daddy's pond. Wanna come?"

"Can't." Hattie studies the spot where the phlegm landed, wondering if the dirt longed for moisture as much as the twisted corn plants. She motions toward the skinny girl with the stringy blonde hair. "Who are you?"

"Mavis." The girl wipes her nose on the sleeve of the faded, cotton print dress that hangs from her bony shoulders like wet laundry.

"Cousin from Alabama," Stevie says. "Why can't you come? It's *your* pond."

Hattie lifts her shoulders, lets them fall. "I'm not allowed to go into the woods unless an adult comes along."

"That's dumb," says Michael Jack, the younger Calhoun brother. He is Hattie's same age, eight, but shorter and bone-thin. His knobby, stick-out elbows remind Hattie of the legs on a scrawny water bird she once saw jabbing for frogs at the pond's edge. "You ain't goin' by yourself. Besides, Stevie's near to grown," he says, and jabs a dirt-crusted finger toward the house. "Go ask your ma."

"She's not home from teaching school yet."

Stevie rakes a hand through his hair. It rebels in greasy clumps. "Nobody home but you?"

"Just Julia Mae. Don't know if she'd let me go, neither."

"She's your help, ain't she?" Stevie's lip lifts on one side. Not in a smiley way.

Hattie digs the toe of her flip-flop under a clump of dried weeds and flicks it into the air. "She cleans for us. Cooks some, too."

Stevie raises one eyebrow and huffs. "I surely wouldn't kowtow to no . . . " Then he spits out that word Mama doesn't allow.

Hattie glares at the older boy. "I don't really *have* to answer to Julia Mae."

"Come on with us then." When Stevie smiles, Hattie notices the dark holes like termite trails between his front teeth, and how his gaze slides over her, kind of slick and oily.

"I got to get my sneakers on. I can't climb that hill by the pond in flip-flops."

The three Calhouns tag behind Hattie until they reach the back porch of the farmhouse.

"Wait here. I'll be right back." Hattie eases through the door and slips past Julia Mae in the den.

The old woman works her way through the week's ironing, clucking to herself over the crazy folks on her soap opera. "Miz Hattie? Where you going in such a tear?" she calls out.

Hattie ignores the question and races to her room. She dives into her small closet, flinging shoes and soiled clothes until she uncovers a threadbare pair of Red Ball sneakers. Already laced. All she has to do is wiggle them on.

She dashes back through the kitchen seconds later. Julia Mae yells after her, "Hattie? Hattie?" The woman props her hands on her ample hips and sighs. Hattie hears her say, "Lawd have mercy! That child." It's a mystery to Hattie, why her every move can summon a plea for mercy from the Almighty.

Hattie bangs the screened door shut and the group turns to leave the back porch. The door hinges screech behind them. Julia Mae leans out. "Where you off to, young'un?"

Hattie spins around, an easy move with the Red Balls. "I'm walking down to the pond with the Calhouns."

"You know your mama tole you to stay out of them woods 'less your daddy or brother comes along." Julia Mae takes a few waddling steps onto the wood plank porch. She shields her eyes from the intense sun with one plump hand and uses a rag in the other to mop the sweat beads from her face and neck.

"I'm *just* going to the pond. Besides, I'll be back long before Mama even gets home."

"Don't reckon that's up for disputin', Miz Hattie. Now either you stay close by, or you'll have to answer to Miz Tillie and Mr. Dan."

"You gone take that off the likes of *her*?" Stevie mutters, tipping his head toward the porch.

Hattie's gaze twitches between the portly black woman and the Calhouns. "I don't take orders from you. You're just a . . ." She spits the last word out, the ultimate of curses.

Julia Mae's soft features seem to curl in on themselves for a moment. She gathers her arms around her billowy bosoms and rocks back and forth, shaking her head, making a low humming noise.

Hattie feels remorse stab her. She faces the group. "Let's go."

Halfway down the long dirt lane leading to the edge of the woods, Michael Jack speaks up. "Don't reckon she'll tell your ma you sassed her, do ya?"

"Dunno." Hattie kicks up dust clouds with her shoes. "Don't much care if she does."

Stevie slaps her hard on the back. "After all, who's your ma gone believe? You, or some dumb ole . . ." That word again!

Hattie fights the dull ache lodged in the pit of her stomach but forgets it when she spies the sparkle of the pond water between the trees. The four dash down the earthen steps to the broad dirt dam. Deep in the pine and hardwood forest, the family's one-acre fishpond nestles in a natural depression where three springs converge. Dark green and cool, the small man-made lake harbors farm-raised catfish. A few— big, whiskered monsters that measure three inches between their round marble-like eyes— have a pull strong enough to land an eight-year-old girl in the water if she isn't paying good mind to her cane pole.

"Wow!" Mavis's dull green eyes open wide. "Is they really fish in there?"

"Shoot yeah. Tons of 'em." Hattie picks up a piece of lead pipe and clangs it on the side of an oil barrel turned fish food container. "That's like ringing the dinner bell for them. Watch and you'll get your eyes full."

Hattie slides the weighted lid off with a grunt and uses an empty coffee tin to gather a scoop of floating catfish food. Raring back, she swings her arm in a wide arc, spraying the pellets across the water's surface. She can throw better'n any ole boy.

The slap of fins cut the glassine stillness. Whiskered faces flash to the surface, open-mouthed to gather in pellets before flipping underwater. The feeding frenzy lasts for several minutes. A scattering of shiners, tiny silver-flanked minnows used mainly as bait, swirls the few remaining chips of food. The perfume of fish and muck hangs in the air. Hattie draws in a deep breath and sighs it out.

"Dang!" Stevie says. "Surely wish I had me a fishing pole!"

"Ain't never seen the likes of that before." Mavis smiles. Her teeth are no better than her cousin's. Kind of green at the gums. Bet her mama doesn't make her brush after every meal.

Hattie puffs out her chest. "My daddy's pulled them out of here that was this wide betwixt the eyes." She holds up her fingers to measure and warms to the boast. "And there's this one he catches and throws back that's an albino."

"What the heck's that?" Michael Jack asks.

Hattie scrunches her brows and narrows her eyes to slits. "He's solid white with creepy-looking pink, pig eyes."

Mavis's shoulders give an involuntary shudder. "Eww!"

"Hah! Rabbit run over your grave!" Michael Jack points and laughs.

"Did not!" The little girl tunes up to cry.

Stevie shoves his girl cousin on the back. "Shut up, Mavis. That's just something you say when a thing makes you shiver like you just done."

Mavis sniffles, wipes snot on her sleeve.

They gather handfuls of smooth pea gravel and take turns skipping the stones across the water. After a short time, the game grows dull and they sprawl on the wide bank, chewing on stalks of dried Bahia grass. The high clouds make shapes, barely moving in the blanched sky. The cicadas sing *see-see-see*, a new group starting up as soon as the others wind down. Reminds Hattie of "Row, Row, Row Your Boat." Later, the peeper frogs will take over the chorus. Hattie's heard them plenty of times, but they don't sing 'til near dark.

"Getting late," Hattie says. "I better get home before my mama does." She stands and whisks the dirt and dried grass from the seat of her shorts. "Y'all want to come on up to the house?"

"Naw," Stevie says. "We got to get on back. Aunt Sassy's comin' to pick up Mavis and carry her back to Alabama."

When they walk off, Hattie notices the dirt on Mavis's dress. Nobody bothers to brush it off, and it blends with the other stuff clinging to the cloth.

By the time Hattie reaches the farmhouse's back yard, she is out of breath from running. Sweat stings her eyes. Her mother's Pontiac station wagon hunkers beneath the covered cement carport, its engine tick-ticking as it cools.

"Oh rats."

When she enters the house, Julia Mae stands by the kitchen door, her cloth bag hanging from one meaty arm. Hattie's gaze falls to her own sand-speckled sneakers. She kicks them off and shoves them to one side, out of sight.

"Miz Hattie," Julia Mae says with a slight nod.

"Where's my mama?" Hattie's voice quivers.

"Up changin' out of her good clothes. She's fixin' to carry me on home."

"She been looking for me?"

"She asked where you was, yes."

A lump the size of Georgia forms in Hattie's throat. "You gonna tell her?"

"I'm studying on it. Ain't quite made up my mind yet." Julia Mae's voice sounds uncommonly stern.

Hattie chews on her bottom lip.

Tillie Davis bustles into the kitchen and grabs her purse and keys from the counter. "Hattie, stay here while I take Julia Mae home. I'm expecting a call from one of the parents, Darren Brown's mother. Take a message and tell her I'll phone her back in a few minutes."

Before Hattie can put in an impassioned plea to ride along and perhaps steer the conversation away from her recent backtalk, her mother and Julia Mae leave. She runs to the front plate glass window and watches until the car turns from their sandy lane onto the paved highway. The dust stream settles.

Armed with a bag of potato chips and a cold cola to float her sorrows, Hattie retreats to the safety of her bedroom.

The tantalizing aroma of Julia Mae's homemade chicken pot pie sluices through the farmhouse and into Hattie's room, drawing her from hiding.

"What's the matter with you, short stuff?" Her sixteen-year-old brother Bobby reaches across the dinner table and ruffles Hattie's clipped blonde hair. "Cat got your tongue?"

Hattie shrugs and bulldozes the last of the baked carrots to the edges of her plate, the only part of Julia Mae's pot pie she shuns.

Bobby holds the back of one hand against her forehead, checking for fever. "Must be sick, not to want to run your mouth."

"Leave her be." Their mother passes a basket of warm buttered dinner rolls across the table. "She's had an eventful afternoon, from what I understand."

Hattie meets her mother's intense gaze. So Julia Mae tattled on her. Might as well just die right now and get it over with.

Bobby grins. The tanned skin around his eyes crinkles. "Oh, don't tell me. Julia Mae made you clean up that pig sty of a room you live in."

"Eat your dinner, Son," Mama says. "This is between Hattie and me."

Her daddy looks at her mama with question-eyes but doesn't speak.

The possible punishments page through Hattie's mind. No Saturday cartoons for a year. No riding horses with Carol Anne down the lane. No chocolate cake for the rest of her natural born life. Hattie loses what little appetite she has. The carrots mock her like tiny mushy, round orange eyes.

"May I be excused, please?" Hattie folds her paper napkin and places it next to her plate.

"You've barely touched your food, gal," her father says. "Julia Mae made this special for you. She knows how much you love her chicken pie. Something's bad wrong when my little Hattie-butt doesn't eat chicken pie."

Even Daddy using his fun nickname for her fails to bring on the usual laughter.

"Go on to your room, Sister," her mother says. "I'll be back soon as I clear the dishes."

The gentle concern in her mother's voice sends Hattie's spirit to a new low. Hattie is pond scum. No. Worse than that even. She is the boggy mud, fish poop, and yuck-green slime at the bottom of the pond.

Hattie picks up her plate and utensils and carries them to the sink. As she slinks away from the family, the conversation shifts to Bobby's baseball triumphs.

Nobody cares about her and her suffering. Not at all.

A while passes before Hattie hears a tap at her bedroom door. Her mother enters. Hattie sits motionless, curled up on one end of the canopy bed with her sun-kissed arms cinched around a hot pink stuffed dog. The family tabby cat, Ena Belvedere, sleeps peacefully at her feet. At least somebody is happy in this room.

Her mother sits on the side of the bed. "Hear you took a little hike in the woods this afternoon. You want to tell me about it?"

"I went with the Calhouns and their cousin to the pond."

"I see." Her mother's lips draw into a thin line. "You know why I'm upset with you, don't you?"

Hattie hangs her head. "Yes Ma'am. I went into the woods without an adult."

Tillie swivels to sit cross-legged facing Hattie. "It's more than that, baby."

Oh no, here it comes. Mama hates the *N* word with a passion. Forbids it to be spoken anywhere near her.

Hattie is as good as dead. The smell of her own sweat makes her stomach roil.

"You disobeyed Julia Mae, didn't you?"

"Yes Ma'am."

"Hattie, do you know why your daddy and I work so hard? Why I took on teaching the extra classes during the summer at a time I should be, by all rights, on vacation?"

Ena Belvedere opens one eye to a slit, meows, closes it again.

Tears burn Hattie's eyes. She shakes her head *no*.

"To make enough money so we can afford to send you and your brother to college. An education is the one thing we can give you that no one can ever take away."

Her mother reaches over and cups one hand beneath Hattie's chin, lifts it so they look eye to eye. "I know you won't understand this until you're older and have to make your way in the world, but money doesn't grow on trees. You need clothes, shoes, and school supplies. You want to do fun things with your friends, and Bobby wants to play his sports and burn up gas in our car. It all has to be paid for, somehow."

Her mother remains silent for a moment. The clock on the dresser tick-ticks. "Julia Mae has worked for us since before you were born, Hattie. She looked after you and changed your diapers when you were just a baby. If it wasn't for Julia Mae, I wouldn't be able to teach school every day like I do. She's a member of our family after all of this time, and I greatly respect her and her hard work. She is my friend, and you will treat her with the same regard as you would me, or your father, or any other adult. Have I made myself clear?"

"Yes Ma'am."

Her mother holds out her arms. "Come here."

Hattie lunges into her mother's hug and cries. She rocks, gently cooing until Hattie's sobs change to hiccups.

"I love you. I just don't love what you *do*, sometimes." Her mother wipes the damp bangs away from Hattie's forehead and kisses it with a loud smack. "All actions have consequences. You chose to disobey Julia Mae. For the next three weeks, you are to come straight home after the summer school bus drops you off. No TV. No horseback rides. Straight to your room to your reading list. Understand?"

"Yes Mama."

"Another thing. I want you to speak to Julia Mae tomorrow and sincerely apologize. I can't abide you disrespecting her authority the way you did today."

The next afternoon, Hattie finds Julia Mae in the washroom sorting clothes. "Miz Julia Mae?"

The old woman stops her deep musical humming and glances up from the laundry basket. "There're fresh teacakes wrapped in some wax paper on the kitchen counter if you're hungry."

"I'm real sorry for what I did yesterday. Will you accept my 'pology? Pu-lease?" Hattie turns on her best begging face.

Julia Mae tucks a stray sprig of wiry gray hair beneath the faded bandana tied around her head. "Reckon I can. God likes a person what forgives."

Hattie lingers by the washroom door, shifting from one foot to the other.

"Somethin' else weighing on yo' mind, child?" Julia Mae pours a measured cup of soap powder into the washing machine and swishes the water around before adding the clothes.

"You didn't tell mama I said *that* word."

"No 'um. I didn't."

"Why not? I mean, I'm glad you didn't. Mama would've tore me up."

Julia Mae closes the washer lid and gives the control knob an experienced spin. "Figured that was between you and me. Now, as to disobeying your mama's wishes, I had to tell her that part. Rules your parents make are for good reason. Bad things can happen to a child going into the woods without an older person along." She pats Hattie on the shoulder. "Let's us talk it over with a glass of milk and a teacake. I can't yell over this old machine's racket."

Seated at the table across from Julia Mae, Hattie licks the milk mustache from her upper lip. The blend of sugar and vanilla coats her tongue. "I'm really, really glad you didn't tell Mama about me saying the N word."

"I knew you didn't mean it. You was just showing off for them Calhoun children. They's a low bunch of folks, them Calhouns. Older ones into drinkin' and stealin' and God knows what all. Always just this side of the law, from what I hear. Best you pick your friends a little more careful. Birds of a feather flock together."

Hattie wolfs down another teacake. "Mama and Daddy don't much like them neither, but there's nobody to play with, out here. I wish we lived in town."

Julia Mae nips off a piece of teacake and chews thoughtfully. "You ever give it much mind, what it might feel like to be called what you said to me?"

Hattie shakes her head.

"It's just a word, I'll grant you that, but words can cut into a person's heart of hearts worse than a sharp butcher knife." Julia Mae pats a spot dead center of her chest. "Terrible business happens when a person feels that kind of deep pain. You go off saying that word to someone who don't love you like I do, and they might just lash out and hurt you bad."

Julia Mae reaches over and pats Hattie's hand. "I want you to run back to the book shelf and get that big dictionary of your mama's."

Hattie jumps up. In a minute, she heaves up the massive reference and plunks it down on the table.

"Look up that word for me and read what it says." Julia Mae settles back, propping her crossed arms over her belly.

Hattie flips to the *N* tab, then trills her fingertip down and up several pages until she finds the word and its definition. "Here it is. Says *Negro. Taken to be offensive. A member of any dark-skinned race.*"

Julia Mae traces a finger over her muscled forearm. "Well, I am dark-skinned. I'll cotton to that. How about *offensive*? What do you reckon that means?"

Hattie's brows knit together. "I think it's something that stinks, or maybe something in football."

Julia Mae laughs, her large bosoms bouncing up and down beneath the flowered house dress. "Means more'n that, I believe. Go on and look it up."

Hattie flips the pages. "*Giving painful or unpleasant sensations,*" she reads. "*Causing displeasure or resentment.*"

Julia Mae nods. "That near 'bout sums it up."

"I didn't mean to hurt you, Miz Julia Mae."

"I know, young'un." Her eyes, soft brown like her skin, fix on Hattie. "You know what I want for you to do from now on?"

Hattie downs the rest of the milk and swipes the foam from her lips. "No Ma'am."

"Think about the words that pop into your mind before you let them slip past your tongue. My mama always told me to ask myself three things." She lifts fingers to count off the points. "Is it true? Is it necessary? Is it hurtful? If you hold up, just for one second, your heart will tell you what to say, or not to."

"I'll be better from now on. I promise."

"The Good Lawd knows we all fall short of His notions, Hattie. But it makes peace with Him when he looks down and sees us trying to do right."

When Hattie smiles, the teacake crumbs rain from her lips and sprinkle onto her lap.

"Always remember your Julia Mae, baby doll. She loves you like you was one of her own children."

Hattie jumps up and Julia Mae wraps her arms around her. Love gushes out in a warm, steady stream. Hattie feels her soul open up.

The old woman can hug better'n any ole body.

20: Proper Tinsel

Robbie can tell a lot about a person's character by the way they put icicle tinsel on a Christmas tree. She knew from the first time she saw her boyfriend Troy helping his future mother-in-law trim the family Fraser fir: this was the perfect man for her. Carefully, one by one, he eased the thin silver strips from his open palm where they lay like limp cooked spaghetti. One icicle per needle before moving to the next tiny branch of extended greenery. Perfect alignment of the real and the manmade.

She smiles now, drifting back to that Christmas long ago. How her younger brother Nathan had approached the same process.

"Nate! No!"

Robbie stood with her hands propped on her hips. She wore a green velvet dress trimmed in red embroidery. Her dark unruly curls, drawn back with a matching flocked ribbon.

The tinsel sat atop a branch in a tangled clump. Totally unacceptable.

"Why aren't you doing it like I showed you?" Robbie lifted the pile of wadded tinsel from the tree and extracted one long silver strand. "Watch me, again. Hang just a little of one end and let the long part dangle."

She tipped her head to one side. "See? Doesn't that look exactly like ice dripping from the tree?"

"Dumb. Just dumb. It takes too long." Nate's red flannel shirt was wrinkled, and one button was missing. The knees of his blue jeans were permanently pocked with dirt.

Once the lights were in place, as far as eight-year-old Nathan was concerned, the fun was over. The rest, ornament placement and garland measuring, proved far too demanding and time-consuming. Definitely, not interesting.

"It's not dumb! Do you want Santa to see our tree looking all messy?" She stomped one foot for emphasis. "Well, do you?"

Nathan shrugged. In contrast to his sister's sultry beauty, his tawny hair and green eyes made him seem as if he had been dropped into the wrong family, a kickback to their father's Irish lineage.

Nathan wrinkled his freckle-dusted nose. "It'll be way dark. He won't be able to even see your dumb old icicles, anyway."

Robbie narrowed her gaze until only a hint of her brown eyes were visible. "I'm going to tell Mom that you aren't being very helpful."

Their mother swept into the room, a tray laden with chocolate chip cookies in hand. She was a raven-haired woman, an older version of her daughter.

"I heard some sounds I didn't like in here. You two getting along?" Their mother looked from Robbie to Nathan.

"We're having artistic differences," Robbie stated.

Their mother's lips twitched the way they always did when she tried not to smile. "Artistic differences?"

Robbie waved one palm toward the tree. "Icicle tinsel should be carefully hung just so." She jabbed an accusing finger toward her little brother. "Nate hurls a big old wad at the tree with no care *where* or *how* it lands."

Their mother offered a warm cookie. "I see." She pressed a finger to her chin. "What if . . . you do it your way and let Nathan do it his?"

Robbie's lower lip poked out. "Mom! I—"

"Wait. Let me explain, please." She sat cross-legged on the floor and motioned for her children to join her.

"We don't have icicles and snow down here in Florida like we did where I grew up in Pennsylvania." She closed her eyes for a moment and a smile floated across her features. "It was so beautiful, especially this time of year."

Their mother opened her eyes and looked first at Robbie, then toward Nathan. "So what I'm going to tell you comes from direct experience. You are *both* correct."

Nathan stuck out his tongue and wagged it at his sister. Robbie huffed.

Their mother wiggled her fingers, painting a picture as she spoke. "The snow packs in little patches at the tips of the branches like a bunch of tinsel in a wad. When it melts a bit and the water drips off the end, the cold air causes the water to refreeze and it forms a little frozen spike. The combination of your two techniques is precisely, absolutely perfect."

Nathan grinned. The gap in his front teeth shone.

Robbie studied her mother's face for signs of insincerity. "You're not making this up?"

Their mother's left eyebrow shot up. "Not something as important as decorating a Christmas tree. This tree represents the love and care we show toward the season. I would never lie about such." She stood and brushed her pants clean of carpet lint. "Don't eat too many of these cookies, now. Save some for Santa's saucer."

Melted chocolate smeared the edges of Nathan's lips. Robbie dabbed hers free of crumbs with one corner of a folded Christmas napkin.

"You go first. Then I'll add mine," Robbie stated.

Nathan giggled as he hurled balls of tinsel at the branches. Adding one at a time, Robbie fell into pace behind.

The life inside her shifts and Robbie rests one hand on her stomach. She blinks back the mist in her eyes. The memory fades.

"Kicking again?" Troy asks. He adjusts the tree stand and steps back to see if the trunk is straight.

"He's going to be a little bruiser, this one." Robbie unwinds a strand of lights and plugs them in as a test.

"This time next month, he'll be here with us." Troy grins. "Hard to believe, isn't it?"

"I can hardly wait to make cookies and decorate the tree together next year. Just like Nate and I used to . . ." Robbie's voice falters.

Her husband glances up from tightening the braces around the tree's trunk. "I'm sorry."

"It's okay." Robbie brushes aside a tear. "I always get a little emotional this time of year."

Troy stands and gathers his pregnant wife into the circle of his arms, her belly a mountain between them. "You sure you're okay with having everyone over this year? It's a lot of work. I can help out, but I can't cook like you. Maybe we should eat out, or not—"

Robbie pushes back from his embrace. "I'm fine. Really. It wouldn't be Christmas without a houseful of people all talking at once and eating tons of food."

"But you'll rest some, too. Promise?"

She pecks him lightly on the lips, then traces the worry crease from between his brows. "I promise."

When Troy leaves to locate the box of heirloom ornaments, Robbie stands and stares at the empty green branches waiting to fulfill their joyful duty. She gazes at her segmented reflection in the front bay window, then beyond to the neighbors who are stringing lights in long loops through their hedges.

The baby is a boy. They will name him Nathan. And she will let him put the tinsel on the tree in any fashion he wishes.

21: Monkey Bars

Jeremy stalls beside the rust-pocked monkey bars. At least they look the same. Nothing else in this place does. The dirt dusts orange on his sneakers. Everything feels sluggish, heavy, even the air. The sunlight burns his eyes and freckles his pale skin, and people talk all syrupy, with words he can't understand. Not like in New Hampshire.

Mama didn't like the South. Said over and over how she'd never again set foot in "Ala-dang-bam-er." Jeremy had never been able to find that on any map. He didn't think it was a for-real place.

But now he lives in Ala-dang-bam-er. Though, his grandfather looked hard at him when he first called it that.

Jeremy doesn't know what to think about this slow, hot place where he landed after Mama got in that accident. "She's with the angels," is what Grandma says. Where is that? Jeremy might've caught sight of those angels in New Hampshire, and Mama too, if his grandparents hadn't taken him away. Besides, angels live in Heaven where it's pretty and perfect and probably not really hot. And isn't Hell the place his grandparents' preacher man said was full of eternal heat and fire and something called brimstone? Ala-dang-bam-er *is* hot enough, Jeremy figures. He's never seen brimstone and wonders if it might be red like the dirt here.

A tall boy walks up to the other end of the monkey bars. He holds up one hand and points a finger up, jabbing, talking in lazy grunts Jeremy can't decipher. Why is he looking at Jeremy so smiley-faced? Jeremy glances around the rutted playground. A swing set with broken chains. A volleyball court with a shredded net. One leaning basketball goal. Nobody here but him and the tall boy with leather skin and hair that looks like wet straw. Maybe the tall boy wants to go first. Maybe he figures Jeremy is so small, he can't reach. He's only six. And the tall boy is not.

Monkey bars are Jeremy's specialty. That's the way Mama said it, all proud and smiling, his "specialty."

Jeremy lunges up to grab a hold. He swings side to side, skips every other horizontal bar. He gets fancy and does it in reverse. Halfway back, he clamps his hands around the fat poles on the outside of the metal ladder rungs and whips his bent legs over them, turns upside down, then backflips onto the ground. Without falling.

The tall boy is gone.

22: Cap of Rainbow Colors

My friend Addie is sick.
Sometimes, when I see her she is angry.
We pretend our fingers shoot dart rays at the things
inside of her that make her feel so bad.
I play the part of the bad cell, clutching my throat,
falling on the floor with my feet kicking the air.
We laugh so hard and loud, her mother looks into the room
to see if we're okay.

I bring her pink and yellow balloons from my birthday party
because she can't be there.
I tell her stories about our friends at school
and give her cards of construction paper and curly ribbon.

Sometimes, she is too tired to play.
When the medicine that is trying to make her well
makes her feel worse and her mother says, "Maybe tomorrow."

When I see her, her eyes are weary and purple underneath.
Her brown hair falls out in clumps on her pillows.
I teach her to crochet like my mother taught me,
and we make a cap of rainbow colors.

Her stomach aches, and we eat dry crackers and sip water,
pretending we are silly-rich, having a party
with fancy biscuits from France and hot tea in silver cups.

Addie has a bruise where the medicine went in.
I paint around it with colored markers.
The bruise turns into a tall purple mountain
topped with clouds with the sun shining overhead.

She smiles because she loves the mountains
and dreams of going there when she feels better.

Addie tells me how nice the nurses are
and about the funny faces they make
that help her feel brighter.
We practice those faces and giggle.
Often, I feel helpless.
I want to make her well
Right away!

I talk to Addie each day and hold her hand when she's sad.
We shoot dart rays at the things inside her
that make her feel so bad.
And she wears a cap of rainbow colors.

23: Garden Partner

Kate McDonald read somewhere that life comes in segments, each distinct from one to the next. Others talk about it. How they grew up in one place, took school in another, married and moved to yet another, then settled in to live out the dregs at the end somewhere between the familiar and not.

Her life inches forward: childhood, young married woman, childless years with husband Warren, widow, to old lady in a bandana tending her flowers. Distinct parts, lived within the corral of a ten-mile radius. Once she visited Macon, Georgia, to see a first cousin. Like everyone else in town, she takes her share of day trips to Tallahassee and Marianna for shopping and doctor appointments. In the mid-sixties, she and Warren drove to central Florida one dreary humid weekend to watch bathing-suited mermaid beauties twirl in the crystal spring waters while sipping air through tiny bubbling tubes. The remainder of Kate's existence revolves around the town of Chattahoochee, with a slight overlap into the adjoining county west of the Apalachicola River. She knows most everyone, and everyone knows her. She saddens when she ponders on city-dwellers in high-rises who rarely creep from their rooms. People who know only a handful of others. Tragic. Just tragic.

Kate bends over a bed of narcissus, their white crepe blooms balanced atop stiff spindly dark green stems. A cherry-red scarf captures the wisps of long silver hair. A second cloth, a dampened paisley lime-green bandana, prevents the spring fog of pollen from clogging her nose and mouth.

The dark-haired boy lurks behind a bridal veil spirea bush. He thinks himself hidden. Like everything else in Kate McDonald's yard, he doesn't go unnoticed. Dark brown eyes the color of fertile loam watch Kate's every movement.

"You going to step out from behind that bush and introduce yourself, boy?" she asks in a soft voice. She knows the secret; a calm demeanor works best with all living things, people and plants.

The boy stands. Blinks. She judges his age to be five, maybe six.

"Step on over here so I can see you. My eyes aren't as keen as they once were." She gestures with a gloved hand.

"Are you a robber?" His voice quivers.

Kate pauses. Considers. Laughs and pulls the bandana down below her chin.

"Reckon I resemble one, now don't I?" She leans on a rake. "My name is Kate McDonald. You may call me Miz Kate. Do you have a name? Or should I just keep on calling you *boy*?"

"Harrison."

"Harrison. Fine name. President's name. Did you know that?"

He shakes his head slowly, then takes a step closer. "What are you doing?"

Kate gestures to the disturbed earth around the narcissus clumps. "Weeding. Dull, hard work, but necessary. If I don't keep up with it, this fine spring weather . . ." She chuffs. "Sometimes I think I should just pull up the flowers and let the weeds have their way. They are much hardier and don't need any bother from me."

The boy's gaze sweeps across the banks of azaleas. A few show the start of the hot-pink blooms that will soon blanket the bushes.

"You like my flowers?" she asks to no reply.

Kate slips the bandana up over her mouth and nose and sends the rake dancing through the bed, nimbly avoiding the clumps of narcissus. "You look like you could use something to occupy your time. That how it is, Mister Harrison?"

He shrugs. Nods.

Kate trundles to a rolling garden cart and riffles through the contents. "Here it is. Just your size." She holds up a hand tool, a petite version of the long-handled rake she uses. "C'mon over here and I'll point out the difference between the weeds and the wonders."

For three days, the boy comes. Sometimes he goes straight to the garden cart for a trowel or hand rake. Often Kate spots him darting between the moats of azaleas, a limb held in his hand like a sword. The bandana Kate gives him is at times a kerchief and at others, a miniature cape. He seldom speaks, and volunteers nothing.

"Where do you live, Mister Harrison?" Kate asks. She bends over a piece of turned earth, preparing the soil for the herbs that wait in pots in a small greenhouse beside the back stairs.

He pauses, points to the back of the lot. "Over there."

Kate smiles. "In a tree? In a bush? Or maybe, in a culvert?"

Harrison giggles, the first time Kate hears anything resembling merriment.

"No, silly. In a house."

"You must be new to town, then. I know just about everyone. You live with your parents?"

The glimmer behind his brown eyes dims.

Kate glances away from him. Sometimes looking sideways at a thing brings it closer into focus. "Oh I see. You must live with a troll who only lets you come out once a day."

"I stay with Aunt Nan."

"What about your mother and father?"

His eyes hold a deep sort of sadness. "I don't have a mama. Daddy travels."

Kate scans her memory of the neighbors. "Would your aunt be Nan Pease?"

Harrison nods.

"Well, now. I didn't know Nan had such a fine nephew. Doesn't she worry about you coming off by yourself like this to help me in my yard?"

He shuffles his feet, kicking up small clots of dew-moistened soil. "She sleeps a lot."

Kate drags the bandana from her neck and swipes perspiration from her face. Soon, the days will lengthen and her sweat will pour like tears. "I take it she has no notion that you aren't home."

Harrison's head drops forward.

"Hmm . . . Maybe we should tell her. I wouldn't want Aunt Nan waking from her nap to find you missing, one of these spring mornings."

Kate slips the dirt-caked cloth gloves from her hands. "I could surely use a break this morning. Why don't I go into the house and whip up some lemonade? I have some banana muffins I made just last night. I can wrap some up and we'll go see your aunt."

"I'm not in trouble, am I?"

Kate makes a harrumph noise. "Certainly not. I think it proper to speak with Nan so I can tell her about my intentions to hire you as my garden partner."

His eyes widen. "For real?"

"I could use the help. You could use something to occupy your time. Seems to me, we're a perfect match."

24: Glass Slipper

June of 1958

For Sabrina, every morning holds the potential of a marvelous day. A story lurks behind each azalea bush. Magic hides beneath the buckling sidewalks. Drama swirls around the trunks of the massive live oaks lining Main Street.

"You with me, or what?" Sabrina flips her pale blonde ponytail in a way she imagines alluring.

Kathleen, best friend from birth, curls her upper lip. "It is miles to the cemetery. It will take years to get there. Besides, it's off the main highway, and my mom will kill me if she finds out I rode my bike."

"Really, Kath. You worry too much. It's not that far. And besides, we can ride on the grass. We won't even be on the road."

Kathleen's Irish eyes study hers. "Let's ride up to Pickens' Pharmacy and get a soda float. Why the heck do you want to go to some creepy old cemetery, anyway?"

Sabrina considers. "Make you a deal. I will buy sodas for us on the way back if you will just go with me. It's research."

"Research? For what? School's not even in. It's summer, for crying out loud."

When you are twelve and think you are thirty, a friend's reasoning is exasperating and annoying. "For my stories, Kath. I need inspiration."

Kathleen's nose wrinkles. "From dead people?"

Sabrina snaps the metal kickstand horizontal and slings her leg over the pink and white bicycle. The wicker handlebar basket holds a spiral notebook and a wooden box filled with pencils and erasers.

"Just because they are dead, doesn't make them dull. My daddy always says the tombstones tell stories. I aim to get some of those stories. Because," she strikes a pose meant to be serious and glamorous. "I am going to be a world famous writer. You going, or not?"

Kathleen shrugs, sighs. "Only if we get back before two."

"What's at two?"

"My piano lesson. If I miss that, I'm toast."

"See? You're doing what you need to do to be a world famous pianist. So why can't I do what I need to do?"

Sabrina thinks of how she would describe the two of them. Friends who illustrate the meaning of opposites. She is lanky and lean with tanned skin, pale Nordic-blue eyes, and white-blonde hair. Kathleen's body suggests roundness and a future tendency toward weight problems, like her mother. Her friend's skin glows with ruddy health, dotted by freckles, and her thick auburn hair complements the shamrock green of her eyes. Kathleen is the voice of reason. Sabrina is the song of defiance.

Kathleen bounces aboard the rusted blue bike, a hand-me-down from her older brother, and balances on one foot. "Okay. But if we get into dutch over this, it's your fault."

"You're such a wet blanket sometimes, Kath. Good grief."

The girls pedal through town, past the city limits sign, then up a gradual incline that takes forever.

"I can't believe I let you talk me into this." Kathleen stops, dismounts, and pushes her bike. "This hill isn't this horrible in a car."

"What else do you have to do this morning? Besides, it's good exercise."

Sabrina stops to pick a small bouquet of wild blue phlox. In a couple of weeks, the roadside garden will wilt in the growing summer heat.

A half-hour passes before they spot the marker designating the entrance to Mount Hope Cemetery.

"Wish we'd brought some water." Kathleen wipes the beads of sweat from her upper lip and frowns at Sabrina.

"I'm sure there's a spigot somewhere. Don't worry. I won't let you perish."

Kathleen puffs out an exhausted comment. "If I die, at least I'll already be where you can plant me."

Sabrina rolls her eyes. "You can be so dramatic."

They park the bikes under the shade of a magnolia tree and plop down. A slight breeze licks away the sweat.

"Follow me." Sabrina gathers the notebook and a pencil and wanders into the first row of headstones.

"All of these are kind of dull. Just a lot of names and dates." Kathleen picks her way between the plots, careful not to step directly on a grave.

"The best ones are along the fencepost." Sabrina points. "My dad told me."

Beyond the more recent section of ornate marble markers, they enter the oldest section of Mount Hope Cemetery. Deep shadows from the adjoining woods fall across simple rounded slabs. They tilt as if skeletal hands pull them down. Kathleen shivers.

"You can barely read the writing on them." Kathleen squats beside a family of markers. "Hey, look at this. It's a little shoe." She hands a figurine up to Sabrina. "What do you suppose it's doing here?"

Sabrina turns the dirt-pocked glass in her palm. It's the startling blue of a robin's egg, the shade of calm Caribbean seas. "I don't know. But, I betcha there's a story behind it."

"Let's take it. It's pretty." Kathleen reaches for the glass slipper.

"No way! One, it's not ours. Two, it belongs here. That would be grave-robbing."

Kathleen snorts. "I do believe grave-robbing refers to actually stealing the body. And I have no intention of doing that."

Sabrina returns the shoe to the weedy grass at the base of the headstone. "It wouldn't be right. It stays."

They continue around the grounds, stopping periodically. Sabrina scribbles notes, dates, and names.

"The words on some of these crack me up," Kathleen says. "Like . . . *only sleeping.* I mean, who are they kidding?"

Sabrina smiles. "Really. Strange place to think you're just taking a nap."

When she turns to head back to the bicycles, Sabrina notices another visitor to the cemetery, an old man. She watches him trundle to the back row of graves.

"Look. He's stopped next to that one with the little shoe." Kathleen shields her eyes with one hand. The sun licks a red blush across her nose and cheeks. Her skin does not tan like Sabrina's. By August, freckles will march thick across her face and arms.

"I bet he'll know the story behind that shoe," Sabrina says.

Kathleen takes a step. "We should ask."

"No." Sabrina lowers one arm like the barricade across the railroad tracks in River Junction. "I don't want to interrupt him. It's bad luck."

Kathleen squints. "Who says?"

"It just is, okay?"

"You bumfuzzle me, Sabrina. We ride all the way out here for you to get inspiration, and you're too chicken to go after the story. What happens if you have to write for a big newspaper one day, huh? You going to shy away then?"

Sabrina stores her pencil and notepad and balances the bicycle while she snaps back the kickstand. "I'm not shying away, Kath. It's responsible journalism to understand boundaries."

Kathleen pulls up alongside her as they negotiate the packed dirt driveway leading to the highway. "Where'd you get all this stuff? I mean, about writing."

Sabrina pedals, careful to avoid patches of soft white sand that could send the wheels sliding sideways. "I read, Kath."

"So do I."

Sabrina glances over. "As if the teen magazines at Pickens' count."

Sabrina perches on one of the silver swivel stools lining the soda fountain counter of Pickens' Pharmacy, her long legs swinging in silent rhythm. A slick of white foam remains in the bottom of a vanilla shake glass. Kathleen is gone, off to trill scales on one of Nana Green's pianos. The tablet is open and she scribbles notes. At the end of the counter in one of three padded booths, the old man from the cemetery leans over a cup of coffee.

According to her parents, talking to strangers is number one on the seven deadly childhood sins list. Sabrina fidgets and weighs the certain consequences of her actions. If she follows her writer's instincts, someone will squeal. Nothing goes unnoticed in a town the size of theirs.

Sabrina slips the pencil from behind her ear, grabs the paper pad, and slides from the stool. She hesitates by the old man's booth.

His face seems to slide downward like melting candle wax. Old people look mean, sometimes. The weight of living and gravity tug their skin into permanent frowns. Sabrina notices the same expression on her grandparents.

"Excuse me, Mister," she says.

When the man glances up, his watery gaze rests on her. For a moment, she freezes.

"Yes?"

"You were just out at the cemetery."

The man nods. He uses a folded handkerchief to wipe the edges of his mouth.

"May I ask you something?"

His lips curl upward on one side. The other remains frozen in a scowl. "Seems, you already have."

"Suppose so." She motions to the red vinyl cushion across from him. "May I sit down?"

"Why?"

"I'm a writer *and* a reporter." Sabrina makes the statement with a slight uplift of her chin. She slides into the seat, aware with a quick backward glance that Mr. Pickens is drinking in the scene.

"I see." The man takes a long sip of coffee.

The interview process has to be easier than this. Since this is her first, the others will flow in a more natural, even fashion.

"I'm doing a piece on the cemetery. About the people buried there."

"Hard to get tales from the dead." He uses the edge of a paper napkin to wipe spilled coffee from beneath his cup, then uses it for a coaster.

117

"Not exactly what I have in mind." Sabrina consults her notes. "More like, something about the people who are buried there, but from other people who are . . . alive."

The old man nods. "I get the honor on account of I was the only living thing you saw out there this afternoon?"

Okay, so he was watching her, too. Sabrina purses her lips. Thinks. "Sort of."

"Didn't your mother and father warn you not to talk to strangers?" he asks.

"My name is Sabrina Humbolt. What is yours?"

"Bernie Hinson."

Sabrina scribbles his name. "Now we're officially *not* strangers."

He shakes his head. "You're determined enough to be a reporter, all right."

"So, Mr. Hinson. Who were you visiting today?" Sabrina's pencil hovers just over the paper's surface.

"What makes you think, little Miss Writer Lady, that I was visiting someone in particular."

"A writer must be observant. Like how you noticed me there. You stopped at one grave. The one with the little blue shoe."

"If you are so observant, tell me the name on the headstone." He taps his bony finger on the rim of the cup.

Sabrina's mind searches for an answer and comes up lacking. "I guess I don't remember."

"Marjorie Summers. Marjorie Hope Summers." His gaze falls to the table and his shoulders lower to more than their normal stoop. Sabrina wonders if he might cry.

She scribbles the feminine name beside his on the tablet and draws an arrow between them.

"I, *we*, saw a little blue shoe. My best friend Kathleen was the one with me."

"You really want to hear a story, then?"

Sabrina sits up taller at full attention. "Yes Sir. I do. If you don't mind me writing it down."

"First of all, what do you plan to do with this information?"

She presses her lips together, then twists them to one side. "I don't know yet."

"If you are going to be a good reporter, or whatever you do with this writing career you've enchanted yourself with, you must learn to protect your sources."

"Sir?"

He tips his head to one side. "That means, I will share my story with you as long as you never tell it was me. I have people I like to protect."

Sabrina inches forward on the booth seat. The conversation becomes more interesting by the second. "I won't tell a soul. Cross my heart, swear to die."

"Sounds like a good enough promise to me."

She holds her pencil at the ready.

"You've heard the fairy tale of Cinderella?"

"Well, yes. Who hasn't?"

"Don't get fresh with me. I never assume anything. Nor, as a writer, should you."

"I love the Cinderella story. Mama and Daddy took us all to the theatre to see it. It's not real."

He lifts one thin finger. "Ah! But it is a love story, and there are many of those."

Sabrina wonders if all writers have to go around in circles just to get started. "I suppose."

"You will know for yourself, one day." He offers a slight smile. "The pretty young lady who rests eternally in that grave with the little blue shoe on top was *my* Cinderella."

"Glass slipper. Now I get it. Only, was Cinderella's slipper blue?"

His brow creases. "Don't think the story ever said anything about the color of the shoe, just that it was glass."

Sabrina scribbles a note to research this later. "Right."

"Do you know much about history?"

She shrugs. "Some. I don't really like history. Too boring."

"Not so boring if you lived it." His eyes grow distant, as if he looks past her into another place. "I was in the First World War. Marjorie was my sweetheart. We were promised to each other and were to be married when I returned."

The old man shifts in his seat. "I won't tell you about all the horrors of war. You will learn about the inconceivable things people can do to each other soon enough. I held the image of Marjorie's face in my mind and heart. It gave me a reason to strive to come home in one piece."

He stops, takes a sip of coffee. Sabrina scratches down notes.

"My Marjorie died of the terrible flu that killed so many back in 1917." He stops long enough to make Sabrina wonder if he's forgotten she's sitting across from him. "I was the one whose life was in mortal danger. Bombs falling. Bullets singing in my ears. And my sweet Marjorie dies from something so small, the human eye can't see it."

Sabrina scribbles as fast as he talks. She glances up from the notepad. The old man is staring straight ahead.

"So about the shoe . . ."

His eyes refocus on her. "Right." He runs his fingers through thinning white hair. "She gave me a tiny charm of a shoe a couple of days before I left for overseas. I kept it pinned inside my uniform."

"Oh and you would bring the slipper back to her, like how Prince Charming did after Cinderella left it when she fled the ball?"

"You are a bright young lady. Yes, that was our plan. Kind of a magic trick to keep me safe. If I promised to return the slipper, I would have to live to come home to her. Then, she would wear the beautiful real slippers she was saving for our wedding."

Sabrina's eyes water. "That is so sad."

"Yes. And, unfair." He hesitates. "I still have that charm in a case back home. I couldn't bring myself to part with it. So, over the years, I've left first one shoe or the other beside her headstone. Blue was her favorite color, and I was happy when I found that little shoe you and your friend saw today."

"So you never loved again, and you come to visit her a lot."

The old man holds up one hand. "Life moves along, whether one feels like moving with it, or not. I met my wife of now fifty-two years that same year. I had not planned on ever giving my heart to anyone else, but Esther had her sights set on me. We have four grown children and nine grandchildren, so I suppose Esther knew better than I."

His face softens. "It is possible to love more than one person, Miss Sabrina the Writer. A man should be so lucky to ever catch the heart of one woman. I have been loved by two. I come to pay homage to Marjorie every few years. Esther knows it. I've never tried to hide it from her. Still, I don't throw it up to her. I have no need to make her feel like second place."

"I will protect you as my source, okay?"

"I would appreciate it."

Mr. Pickens studies them from behind the drug counter. Sabrina will catch holy heck when she gets home.

"Now I think I need to do something nice for you, since you have been so kind to listen to the ramblings of an old soldier." He waves to hail the druggist.

"What can I get you, Sir?" Mr. Pickens asks.

He holds up two fingers. "A fresh coffee for me and a cola for Miss Sabrina here."

Mr. Pickens returns shortly with the drink order. "You two know each other?"

"Not until today. I thought this young lady reminded me of someone from years ago when I lived in these parts. Turns out, she's Harold Humbolt's grandchild. Her grandfather and I knew each other when we were just boys."

The druggist nods. "Small world, isn't it?" He wipes his hands on a white cloth hanging from his belt. "Now if you'll excuse me, I have to get back behind the counter. My help is out sick this afternoon, so I'm doing double-duty."

After the druggist leaves, Sabrina asks, "Why did you tell him that?"

He leans forward and replies in a soft voice, "I didn't lie, if that's what you are implying. I *did* know your grandfather. I only stretched things a little. If I know one thing about small towns, it's that everyone looks out for each other. Somehow or the other, word will get back to your parents that you were seen having a soda with a strange man. No doubt, you will get into hot water over it, innocent as it is."

He sits back. "I don't condone someone your age taking up with strangers, don't get me wrong. A lot of people are no good, anymore. But you and I know why you came over here. I'm not a mean man, and you are not a stupid young girl. I merely planted a little seed that will grow and get you off the hook. Protecting my reporter."

"Gee. Thanks." It was sort of a lie, and sort of *not* a lie.

"Your curiosity is necessary if you are to be a writer, Miss Sabrina. But mark my words, from this point forward, think long and hard on your actions. Not everyone will be honest or have your best interests in mind. Am I clear?"

"Yes Sir, Mr. Hinson."

"Good enough, then." When he smiles, this time the emotion makes it to his eyes.

25: Kris

It rains for three hours,
two days after I lift.
Snaps of dazzle-light,
thrashing thunder goliaths.
The perfect way of a summer storm.

I dip low over pine tips
and live oak branches thick as giants' arms.
Moss waves hello and goodbye
in equal measure.

Through familiar rooms I float,
trilling fingertips across framed images of captured time,
evidence of the ripples I leave.
My children, family, so many friends, my pets,
that zippy Miata before the minivan rolled it to the back sales lot.
And you.

My reading chair waits,
its flowered cushion curled with my imprint.
An opened book, face down, Chapter Six, page forty-one.
I sense the plot, the author's intent, the tidy, hopeful ending,
as I understand my own questions and answers.
Who lied easy.
Who loved free.

I see you, my heart, painting your grief,
as we agreed you should.
The brush dips between muted blues and grays.
I tip your cheek with a kiss
and urge you to add a pop of yellow.

You stand, defiant, ready to tell me the reasons you shouldn't.
My gentle laughter pierces the glassine curtain between us.
I am here.
Your features soften. Your lips tremble, smiling.
You hear me. You always do.
You always will.

26: Yard Rats

The spring air is soft on Ellis Futch's skin. Soft like dark chocolate melting on his tongue, or like the down at the nape of his wife's neck. In a few weeks, the humidity will build on its steady victory march to summer; but for now, his skin registers the sensation of perfection.

He would enjoy it if he wasn't so dadgum aggravated.

Joyce, his wife of thirty years, peers from inside the house through a raised slat in the Venetian blinds. Though he can't make out her features in the dim light, Ellis knows her expression: bemused, with the addition of a slow head shake.

He stalks the prey with care. Raises the gun. Aims. Misses. The rotund gray squirrel stops its frantic scrabbling for a buried acorn and glances around, searching for the source of the light pinging noise in the dried leaves to its right.

"Dagnabbit!" Ellis snorts. Lowers the pellet gun.

Joyce appears at his side. "Really, Ellis. All you need is one of those silly caps with the ear flaps and you will look just like Elmer Fudd."

"I resent that, Joyce. I'm much taller than that particular cartoon character, and besides, I'm not bald."

Joyce reaches up and slips her fingers through his thinning brown hair. "Yet."

He shrugs off the minor insult. "I think the sights are off on this thing."

"Or yours." Joyce smiles. "I can't believe you are shooting at our squirrels."

Ellis's lips draw into a thin line. "You weren't singing their praises when they ate that emission system hose in your car, as I recall."

"True."

"And when you noticed they had nipped all of the buds off your hibiscus plants."

"Well."

Ellis points a finger toward the house. "Or when they chewed on the deck rail and ate the edges of the trim."

"Shooting them just seems so . . . harsh."

"No, harsh would be the flame thrower I'd like to aim at their fuzzy little butts. I'm just trying to scare them off, Joyce. It's not like I can start brandishing a .22 here in town. They'd cart me off." He glances down at the gun. "It's just a BB gun. Besides, at the rate I'm going, I'll be doing good to annoy them a little."

"Why don't you do something else for a while? Give it a rest. You'll run your blood pressure up."

Ellis heaves a sigh. "Maybe you're right. I'll go start the boat. Weather this nice, we'll want to take off down the river soon enough."

The combination fishing/pleasure boat glitters when the sun hits the paint. Besides his pick-up, the eighteen-foot Winner with its custom garnet and gold sparkly finish and 150 hp outboard motor is his baby. The teak shines with a layer of fresh oil, the rails glisten, and the seats glow, slick with protective spray. Though it sits beneath a custom-made shed, the craft is covered from bow to stern with a weather-resistant drape.

Throughout the winter, Ellis periodically starts the engine to keep the gasoline from turning into a goopy sludge in the valves. An orange extension cord snakes beneath the cover to a trickle charger that keeps the batteries fully operational.

He slides the cover up and over the motor and flips open the rear hatch that protects the gas tank, bilge pump, and twin marine batteries. When he reaches to release the charger's alligator clamps from the battery posts, his hands encounter a mass of wires. He lifts the bundle and stares. His mouth falls open as he glances down to check the lattice of chewed-up electrical connections. Not one wire is attached. Not one.

"Dadgum! Curse you all to Hell, every living one of you!" Ellis shouts. "This is war! I am here to tell you, all of you! This is war!"

"New yard art?' Joyce asks.

Ellis positions the two-foot-tall plastic owl figurine on one of the privacy fence's support posts. "Nope."

"Okay, so what?"

He gives the owl's head a gentle push and it pivots. Two eerie yellowish eyes stare into the space above their heads. "To scare the squirrels. I even paid ten bucks extra for the model with the head that rotates. Makes it look more lifelike."

Joyce cocks her head to one side. "It is kind of cute, in a plastic sort of way."

"Not meant to be cute. Supposed to instill fear into those little yard rats." He peers up into the canopy of oak leaves. Nothing living stirs in the breeze.

"Come inside, Ellis. Dinner's ready."

He lifts a forkful of salad toward his mouth. From the vantage of the kitchen nook table, the new yard sentinel is clearly visible. Ellis watches. Two squirrels sit on the railing close to the owl, their tails flitting back and forth. First one, then the other, take turns chattering.

Joyce shakes her head. "So much for that whole instilling-fear thing. Looks like they're flirting with it."

Ellis drops his fork onto the salad plate. "Well, I'll be doggoned."

Joyce chuckles. "Wonder what they are saying to it? Maybe, 'do you come here often, big boy?'"

A puff of unseen air causes the owl's head to turn. The yellow eyes stare through the kitchen nook window.

"Now that was creepy. It's like it heard us talking," Joyce says.

Unruffled by the movement, the squirrels continue to converse with the statue. A third joins the group. The next time Ellis glances up from his dinner, one of the rodents moves to a position on top of the plastic owl's head.

Sunday morning offers a sanctioned reprieve from Ellis's labor. The grass, clipped and edged, shines green with dew. Songbirds flit from the oaks and magnolia trees surrounding the backyard. Ellis sits at the bistro table on the screened porch, sipping coffee and reading the *Tallahassee Democrat* comics. Other than the sports section, the funny papers is the only segment he reads. The rest is too darn depressing. Too much talk of war. A person should be able to feel safe in his own home.

"Isn't it just perfect this morning?" Joyce asks. She stands, glancing out over the yard. "I love this time of year. In a few weeks, it will be so hot and humid, we won't so much as step outside."

Ellis nods. Lowers the paper. "Looks like you need to refill your birdfeeders."

Joyce squints in the direction of the rear right corner of the yard. "I can't believe they're empty again. I just filled them two days ago."

"Got to be the blasted squirrels."

"Ellis, you'd blame the national deficit on our squirrels."

He snaps the paper closed. "I've seen them, Joyce. You can't really believe the birds can eat that fast."

She sighs. Shrugs.

"I'm going to buy some of those baffle things to hang above and below the feeders. By golly, that will stop them. There are enough acorns in this yard to sink a battleship. They don't need your birdseed."

Joyce turns back toward the yard. "Maybe they just want variety."

Ellis's smile is wicked. "I'll give them variety."

Ellis stands back with his hands propped on his hips, admiring the two pole-supported birdfeeders. Above the top of the feeders hang shiny metal inverted cones. Below, the same configuration protects the bottoms. The theory: any varmint trying to access the seeds will flounder on their slick surface and plummet to the ground.

He grins and affects a south-of-the-border accent. "Game on, you sons of beeches."

The next morning, he sits on the porch before work. One squirrel, a large male he has dubbed *Bogart* because of a thin black streak of hair across his head, hunkers down at the base of one feeder pole. His thick tale flits. Ellis watches as Bogart scales the pole and encounters the lower baffle.

For the next half-hour, the spectacle beats any sitcom Ellis has ever watched. After a handful of attempts, Bogart calls in reinforcements. Four junior rodents appear. Each tries unsuccessfully to breach the lower baffle. Then, one scampers up the fence and flings his body at the top of the contraption, completely missing, sailing in an air-clawing arc, and thudding to the soft cedar-shaving bedding at the base of the pole.

Ellis chortles so hard, his sides ache. It is a silent type of laughter, the kind with both hands clamped over his mouth and tears streaming from his eyes.

The squirrel battalion increases in number as new recruits appear. A steady line forms at the crest of the fence. Ellis is reminded of school children queued up at the base of a diving board ladder, awaiting turns at belly-flops into the community pool. Most miss the tip of the upper baffle entirely. A few manage to land and scrabble on the slick downward-angled metal before falling. The pole lists a bit from the repeated attacks but holds steady.

Ellis smiles. The superior intellect of man overcomes the pea-brains of his animal foes.

That afternoon, he returns from work, anxious to revel in the victory. The poles lie on the ground. A smattering of seed spreads out like spilled blood: the aftermath of a jubilant feeding frenzy.

Joyce appears, still in her nursing scrubs. "What happened to the feeders?"

"Joyce, don't think ill of me. Things are going to get ugly."

Joyce hands Ellis a plastic bag. "This is for you. Don't ever say I didn't give you anything." She smiles as he opens it and peers inside.

The crease between his eyes deepens into a furrow. "Hair? You bought me a bagful of hair?"

Joyce nods. "Mandy at the Triple C was telling me about this. Seems, you can sprinkle human hair around the plants and the squirrels stay away. So when I started to leave, she swept up the clippings and gave them to me. Most of it is my hair, of course, but there're some from others mixed in, too."

"Bound to be worth a try."

Ellis rations the hair as if it is spun gold, circling the wisps around his wife's hibiscus plants and the potted ferns commonly attacked by Bogart and his mob of marauders.

Joyce hands over a tall glass of iced mint tea. "I hesitate to tell you what else Mandy said."

Ellis wipes the fine sheen of perspiration from his brow with a faded bandana. "At this point, I am open to any and all suggestions."

"She heard that they don't like the scent of human urine." Joyce pauses, waiting.

"That's something I can produce for free." Ellis grins.

"I was afraid you'd say that."

He waits until the last licks of orange sunset fade in the west before he acts. After a gallon of water and a diet soda, Ellis figures he can produce sufficient urine to sprinkle liberally around the yard. Joyce hides inside, periodically peeking out to follow the silhouette of her husband as he trots from one potted plant to the next like a honey bee to jasmine.

The next morning, the hair is gone.

"Well, that worked." Ellis shakes his head. "I should've known. They dragged every last piece to pad their nests. Surprised they didn't leave us a thank-you note. Between the hair and the shreds of rope they culled from my hammock, they ought to be sitting sweet."

Joyce fingers the remainder of a hibiscus bud. "Wonder what they get out of eating my flowers. Must taste good to them."

"Our yard smells like a urinal," Ellis says. "You just wait until I see Mandy Andrews. She should stick to cutting hair and leave off the gardening advice."

Two days later when the potted ferns and hibiscus turn brown, Ellis acknowledges that urine isn't the best choice of liquid nourishment for living things.

"Afternoon, neighbor," a voice calls from across the tall boxwood hedges.

"Hi, Ralph." Ellis hauls the last of six trash bags to the curb.

"You've been busy." Ralph's eyes search the pile of refuse. "Most of the leaves are down in my yard. You redoing mulch . . . or what?"

Ellis frowns. "Nope. These bags are full of Joyce's potted plants. Dead as a doornail."

"It's been pretty dry, all right. I have to water most every day. You must've forgotten, eh?"

"Oh I watered them, all right."

Ralph's eyebrows lift and lower as Ellis shares the stream of events leading to the genocide of Joyce's prized plantings.

"I've got just the thing for you, Ellis."

His neighbor leaves and returns shortly with a narrow metal cage.

"It's the humane way to get rid of squirrels, my friend. Just put a dollop of peanut butter on this little metal plate and set the pin. I guarantee you will have one trapped in no time. Then, you load him up and take him to a new home away from home."

Ellis studies the trap. "Joyce will like the idea. It's not like I'm hurting them."

Ralph smiles. "Squirrel relocation program. I toted off ten last year. You have to make sure you drive them far enough so they won't return. From what I heard, they have one heck of a homing instinct. I took mine down by the lake. Nice there. Plenty of trees."

"You need this back soon? I have a lot of them to deal with."

Ralph shakes his head. "You go right on and use it as long as you like."

"You don't have a problem with them?"

131

"Not anymore."

"What'd you do? Poison?"

"Rhonda feeds them now. Long as she doesn't cut off their corn, they leave my stuff alone."

Ellis snorts. "So, you gave up."

"I have better things to do, is all." He pauses, considers. "Like watch my next-door neighbor try to outwit the little suckers."

Ellis hears the commotion as soon as he steps from the back door, a loud metallic clanging peppered with short bursts of agitated squirrel chatter. A satisfied smile spreads across his face.

"Well, well, well," he says as he squats down to view the captive. "I'll be! Bogart! I would've thought you would have been too smart to fall for this."

Bogart peers at him with wide round eyes. His tail is fluffed to its fullest. If he hadn't been the focus of so much destruction, the rodent might have been considered beautiful.

Ellis uses the wire handle to lift the cage. Bogart freezes, his sides pulsing with quick breathing.

"Don't have a freakin' heart attack, old boy. You and me, we're going for a little ride." Ellis speaks the last line in a voice reminiscent of a hired-gun mafia thug.

For the six miles leading to the public landing on Lake Seminole, Ellis keeps up a running one-sided conversation. Bogart listens between bursts of frantic scrabbling in the confines of the cage. When he reaches a thick wooded area near Turkey Point, Ellis pulls onto the grass and kills the engine. Instead of dragging the cage across the pick-up's bench seat, he hops out and rounds the truck to open the passenger door. He gently picks up the cage, careful not to agitate Bogart, who at this point is reconciled to life in the metal prison.

Ellis turns the cage one way, then the other, searching for the latch. Both ends look similar.

"How the heck do I get the dang thing open, Bogart?"

He spots a long hook attached to one side and removes it from the mount.

"Here we go, buddy. I just stick this into this little hole and lift and presto! You are a free man in a new world brimming with opportunities."

One end of the cage ratchets open with a loud squeak. Bogart cowers in the closed side.

"Well don't just sit there. Take off!"

Ellis lifts the cage a couple of inches and gives it a little shake. Bogart darts out, jumps on the top of the cage, then scales Ellis's arm. When he reaches the top of Ellis's head, he swivels and claws his way down again. The squirrel vaults into the air, lands in the grass, and races to the safety of the first available pine tree.

At home, Ellis slams the door leading from the garage. Joyce looks up to see Ellis, small specks of dried blood dotting his arms, neck, and face. "What the . . .?"

Ellis closes his eyes a moment. Breathes a sigh so heavy, the air leaves the room. "Don't ask, Joyce. Don't even ask."

Two days later, Bogart sits on the top of the fence close to the owl yard art. He stops chewing an acorn when Ellis spots him. For a moment, the two share a staredown that would have made an itchy-trigger-finger gunslinger flinch.

Joyce stands with her hands on her hips, peering over her husband's left shoulder. "What is it?"

A four-inch-square metallic box sits on the bistro table.

"This," Ellis states, "is an ultrasonic rodent repellant."

Joyce leans down to study the device. "Looks like a little boom box."

Ellis nods. "A squirrel boom box. Yep. That's what this is, all right. Cost me $29.95 plus tax, but it is guaranteed to send the little varmints packing."

"It doesn't shock them, or anything?" Joyce's voice is soft with concern.

"Nope. It drives them batty. Seems, it sends out this noise we can't hear. Won't hurt birds or cats or dogs. Just rodents like mice and squirrels." He points to the illustration on the side of the box. "See? They're supposed to haul buggy when I plug this baby in."

"If you can't hear it, how do you know it's working?"

Ellis gathers the box and an extension cord. "Time will tell, Joyce. Time will tell. It only covers a short radius, so I will plug it in next to the boat shed. I can rig up something to set it up on so it will fan out across the boat. That'll fix their little red wagons."

The next afternoon, Ellis finds the little box drowning in the plastic bucket he left beside the boat after washing it two days before. In the bottom stands just enough water to short the device and trip the circuit breaker in the garage.

He feels a rush of pure, white-hot anger. It builds from his toes, ripples up through his trunk, and comes from his mouth in a string of curse words. He raises his fists to the trees, and the world goes black.

Three days later, Ellis opens his eyes. The pale green room is filled with filtered light, bouquets of flowers, mounds of cards, and clicking monitors. He fights to focus.

"Oh, you're awake."

He feels the brush of familiar lips on his cheek. Smells the distinctive light floral perfume. Joyce. "Wha . . .?"

"You're in the hospital, Ellis."

He blinks. His vision clears enough to see his wife's face. "How?"

"You had a heart attack, honey." Her voice comes out strange and cracked like a vinyl record scratched from years of play.

"When?"

"I will give you all the details soon. I promise. The doctor will be by on rounds later. For now, try to rest."

A flash of memory appears in his mind. A circle of animal faces, their round eyes trained on him.

"Squirrels?"

Joyce's lips soften into a slight smile. "Those squirrels probably saved your life."

His eyebrows lift.

"I came home after work. You weren't in the house, so I figured you were just piddling around in the yard, like you do. Then I heard this big ruckus. The squirrels sounded like they were all calling out at once. You know how they do when there's a snake or hawk nearby?"

Ellis nods.

"It felt strange, so I went outside. When I neared the boat shed, I saw you, and them. You, crumpled on the ground. Them, in a circle around you."

Joyce smooths a sweat-damp hank of hair from his forehead. "If it had not been for them, I might have gone on about my business inside for a good long while before coming to see what you were doing."

She holds her husband's hand. "I am making a declaration, Ellis. The War of the Yard Rats is officially over."

27: Hold My Beer

Annabelle notices the lady the moment she enters the diner. A long-distance trucker who stops by often when she passes through. Good tipper. Polite. Got one eye that droops a little. Walks with a slight limp. Silver-streaked hair scraped into a loose ponytail then secured with a clamp. Keeps it off her neck. Important during the hot months, no matter how great your AC might be.

She grabs up the coffee carafe and heads to booth number five. The lady always chooses it if it's vacant. This time of the wee hours, most are. When the lady spots Annabelle, she flips over the heavy pottery mug. Annabelle pours.

"Must be making your run downstate," Annabelle comments. "Bet you been thinking about a tall stack of pancakes and some of our thick country bacon."

"Ah, you know me well."

"I'll put in the order. Shouldn't take long." Annabelle turns to leave.

"Sure could use someone besides myself to talk to, if you've time."

Annabelle pulls a quick search of the diner. Only one other person shares the space, a man so absorbed in tapping into a tablet that aliens could land in the parking lot and he wouldn't notice. He's already eaten one egg over easy, grits, sausage, and biscuits. "Let me check on him and turn in your order."

The manager isn't here. Just her and the cook this morning.

In moments, she slides into the booth opposite the lady.

"I come in here a lot," the lady says. "You're always so kind. Smile on your face. Don't find that often, and trust me, I've been all over."

"Reckon I like being someone folks might look forward to seeing." Annabelle feels the heat blush her cheeks and hopes the makeup hides the bruise around her left eye, easier to cover now that it's faded from blue to a shade of yellowish-orange.

"I'm going to say something to you, Annabelle. I hope you'll take it all right."

Had she not gotten an order correct last time the lady came? For a beat, she wonders how the lady knows her name. Then she reaches up to touch the faded plastic nametag and scolds herself for being stupid. Maybe Buck is right and she doesn't have the sense God gave an earthworm.

The lady glances around as if she's making dead sure no ears are close enough. She leans forward and says in a low voice, "If you need to get away, I can help."

Annabelle freezes.

"Don't think I haven't noticed. Hard not to. I've seen women like you, like *us*, before."

"I . . . uhm . . ."

"I got a way to help you, Annabelle, if you've a mind to. Helped more women than I can count on both hands and feet, with some left over."

Annabelle would speak, but the water has left her mouth. She only nods.

"If you want me to make a plan, tell me when you bring my breakfast. It isn't hard for a woman to vanish." The lady steeples her fingertips together then splays the fingers upward, as if she releases a trapped bird.

The cook taps the order-up bell. Annabelle slides from the booth. Her legs feel as if the muscles have forgotten what to do.

She slides the plate piled high with buttermilk pancakes and bacon onto the table. Then the syrup pitcher. The lady thanks Annabelle and sets to peeling the waxy paper off several packets of butter.

Annabelle checks on the other diner. Cook is nowhere to be seen. Probably out back, having a smoke. She resumes her seat opposite the lady.

The lady streams warm cane syrup in circles over the buttered pancakes. She's the type that only sections off one bite at a time in careful squares, just enough to safely fit into her open mouth. And she drops not one splatter of syrup.

Annabelle watches the lady's movements. Hard to figure who to trust. Can't say she much trusts herself either. Comes down to one sure thing. If she leaves, she might end up dumped in some distant woods. If she stays, the woods *will* be closer.

"I have two critters. Dog. Little kitty. Saved them both."

"Dogs and cats, okay. No birds. No fish. No snakes." The lady slices off pancake bites. Chews. Sips coffee.

"What do I do?" Annabelle's stomach churns a little. Nervous. Mostly excited.

"Simple is best." The lady looks up from her meal. "Tell me what I need to know."

Annabelle holds the kitten close to her heart. It's tiny, the runt from a litter of five others that didn't make it, found dead in a paper sack she spotted by the highway when she walked out to fetch the mail. Pitched out like so much garbage. Lucky it still had enough life to cry out, or it would've perished too.

It's mottled, like it couldn't decide what sort of cat to be. Gray tiger stripes mingle with patches of yellow and black across its back. The front legs resemble those of a Siamese: dirty white ending in choc-olate brown. The rear legs lean more toward calico with uneven splotches of yellow, white, and black. One eye is yellow and the other blue.

"That is about the most butt-ugly critter I've ever laid eyes on," Buck says.

"I think she's pretty, an original," Annabelle says. The kitten's ears take up half of her head. But Annabelle knows she'll grow into them in a few months. For now, she looks like a fox or maybe like Mr. Spock on that Star Trek show her mama used to love so much.

Annabelle cuddles the barely-weaned animal. It snuggles into her blouse, searching for sustenance, finding the loose folds of her neck instead.

"Quit that sucking!" Annabelle giggles. "I'll get a hickey for sure if you keep that up, Paprika-puss."

"What kind of a name is that for a cat?" Buck asks. Beer suds circle his upper lip, a foamy mustache.

Annabelle's pale lips purse into a pout. "I like the sound of it. What's it to you?"

"Stupid cat."

"You just leave us girls be." Annabelle coos to the purring kitten. "We're going to get us a little drink of milk."

"Bring me another beer when you come back."

Buck belches and picks up the remote. The sports channel features pro bass fishermen and their fancy powerboats. "One day," Buck says, "I'll have one of them glitter-painted, eighteen-footers with a hopped-up Mercury outboard that'll shoot a rooster tail fifteen feet in the air." He flaps his hands as if he's the fountain trailing the boat.

And monkeys will fly out of your butt, too, Annabelle thinks but doesn't dare say.

Annabelle moves through the kitchen and steps from the trailer's back door onto a wobbly wooden deck to holler for the dog. A skinny black Labrador-mix bounds up the steps and wags his entire backside.

"Hey, Licorice. This here is your new little sister, Paprika." She leans over and allows the two animals to touch noses. "You're such a good boy, yes you are. Unlike some of the males around this place."

Buck's bellowing call echoes through the thin walls.

Annabelle gives the dog a pat. "I'll be back out in a second and bring you a cookie. Would you like a cookie?"

Licorice slobbers on Annabelle's knees with the enthusiasm only a mutt can muster. Buck spits out a loud string of curses.

"I'm coming!" Annabelle yells as she opens the aluminum door.

The beer is dirt-cheap. Rot gut. Buck will never consider drinking anything fancy. Calls those "pansy beers." Annabelle hates it. Wouldn't drink it on a bet. Hates to taste it on Buck's mouth. Raspberry-flavored lip gloss and a quick shot of mint-burst mouthwash kill the flavor if she gets any advance warning he's not dead drunk enough to feel frisky.

Annabelle rustles in the cramped refrigerator. Behind the yellow mustard and two plastic butter tubs of leftovers, she finds the single can of beer. She'd poured four down the drain while he was in the shower, careful to smash the cans as he liked to do before pitching them into one of the outside trash bags.

Today is too important to mess up.

She slips a dog biscuit into her pocket and walks back into the living room to hand over the beer. He pops the tab, swills half the can in one long gulp.

"That goes down so good." He grins up at her. "You looking better and better to me, woman."

Annabelle forces a smile. That line used to get Buck laid every time. Between fading hormones, hot flashes, the strain of being dirt-poor, and his anger-fueled drunkenness, she'd rather take a nap than have sex. What use is it anyway? Other than that one time she'd managed to carry a baby for a few weeks until one of his rages made it flee her body in a bloody splat, sex hadn't paid off. All that heaving and sweating and skin slapping together. Give her five minutes alone with a hot romance paperback, and she can take care of herself nicely. No bruises to hide later, either.

The kitten curls into a space between her breasts, content.

"If you loved me half as much as that dadgum cat, I'd be a happy man."

Annabelle strokes the striped fur between Paprika's ears. The kitten trills and snuggles deeper. "That was your last beer."

Judging by the look on his face, the news hits Buck like gasoline ignited on a fire ant hill. "How'd you let that happen?"

"Just stupid as a stick, I reckon."

"Well hell, woman. Go git me a six. It ain't even dark yet. I got all evenin' to get through."

Annabelle considers. "Not enough gas in my car."

Buck turns his attention away from the television. "Well, Got-Dang!"

"I can take your truck."

Buck laughs so hard, beer sputters from his lips. "The hell you say."

Annabelle turns to walk away. "Suit yourself. But if you drive and get pulled over again, they'll snatch your license. Probably, you'll end up in jail this time."

She swivels to catch his reaction and can almost see the cogs twisting in his soggy brain.

Buck leans his gut to one side, digs into his shorts pocket with a grunt, and tosses a set of keys onto the floor behind her. Oh my, the plan is working like so much magic. Just like the lady said it would.

"Take it, then. But don't you put a scratch on it, or I'll wipe your dumb rear end across this county and dance on your grave. You hear? I'll sure as hell dance on your grave."

Buck chuckles at the worn comment. He always does when he says it, like thinking of dancing on her grave is the funniest thing ever. Or is it that he laughs thinking of *putting* her there?

"You hear me, woman?" he asks again.

"I hear." Annabelle scoops the keys from the floor and picks up her mostly-empty imitation alligator purse.

"Don't get to talking to nobody or you'll be there all night banging your gums." He snorts. "And I'll be hours getting my beer."

"I got to work later, 'member? I'll be there and back before you miss me."

She stops by the bathroom to dig out the battered box of tampons from the back of the under sink cabinet. He'd never look there, a fact she's counted on for years of stashing what her mama used to call *mad money*.

One last pee. Flip-flops on. Then out. The back door shuts with a tinny click behind her.

She pulls the dog biscuit from her shorts pocket and allows the drooling Lab to lap it from her extended hand. "Wanna go for a ride with Mama?" she asks in a high-pitched voice.

Licorice beats her to the dirt-pocked car and wags his tail. All four paws dance.

"No, sugar. That one." She motions to Buck's pick-up. Before she can reach the truck and let the tailgate down, the lanky canine leaps into the back.

"It'd be easier if you'd just wait on me, baby."

Annabelle scratches him behind the ears and climbs inside the cab. The kitten raises her head and mewls. Paprika is so tiny, she fits easily into the ledge of Annabelle's tank top.

"Oh, sugar. Mama'll buy you some milk real soon."

She adjusts the rearview mirror to cast one last look at the dilapidated trailer. Half the skirting hangs in strips, never repaired after the last hurricane blew past. Trash bags long overdue for the county dump piled on the rickety porch. Weeds knee-deep.

Only one stop to make. To where she stashed the packed duffle yesterday on her way home. Nobody would dare steal it behind the rotting school bus shelter, not with snakes standing silent guard in the dried grass. Keeping it simple. Like the lady told her.

Annabelle steers the bright red, Hemi-powered pickup onto the highway before cranking up the stereo. Might as well enjoy it. She won't be riding in it again. Ever. It will be deserted beside the ratty convenience store with the six-pack growing hot and flat on the passenger floorboard. And no Annabelle to be found, or the dog and kitten for that matter. Oh how tongues will wag.

Folks know Buck. There's bound to be talk. Delicious talk. Talk the police will hear.

"Hang on, Paprika-puss. You, me, and Lic are going for a ride. A long ride." It's her turn to chuckle now. "And maybe one day if *I* decide to pass through, I'll dance on *his* grave."

28: Epiphany

"Know why cannibals don't eat clowns?" Sylvester Mabry, *Sly* to his friends, cheeses a smile over a steaming, off-white mug of truck-stop coffee. The beefy hand trembles a little. He feels every bit of his sixty-nine years, some days.

"You want to bite on this one, or do I have to?" Billy Don Starnes tips his head toward his buddy Tom Watts across the booth.

"Believe you did the honors last time. My turn." Tom glances up to Sylvester, who is patiently waiting for someone, anyone, to snatch the comic bait.

Tom sighs. "Okay, Sly. Lay it on us. Why don't cannibals eat clowns?"

Sylvester takes a noisy swill of coffee and settles onto the bench seat beside Billy Don. "I figured anyone with even half a brain would know the answer to this one."

Tom rubs his eyes. "Too early for me to claim having a brain, Sly."

Sylvester savors the anticipation. The best thing about a joke is the split second before he delivers the punch line.

"Cannibals don't eat clowns," he pauses to add emphasis, "because they taste funny."

Billy Don and Tom chuckle. Aileen, the head server who has stopped by to refill their mugs, laughs too, her white-starched bosoms dancing like twin volleyballs caught in a beach net.

"Where in the pluperfect hell do you get your material, Sly?" She tops his mug with black coffee strong enough to drive railroad spikes.

"Internet, mostly. Used to rely on passed-on jokes. Now, I can get a million of 'em with one or two pushes of a button. Amazing thing, technology."

Billy Don offers, "Must be a cornpone joke site, then."

"A person can be funny without the benefit of profanity and lewd content," Sylvester says. "The cornier, the better, in my book."

"That clown joke must rate pretty high on your list, then." Aileen shakes her head and continues to make her way down the line of booths with a smile lifting her red-painted lips.

"Speaking of corn, me and Tom are heading out to the hunting camp first thing tomorrow morning. We put out corn and salt licks a couple of days ago. You want to come with us?"

Sylvester shakes his head. "Naw. Not this time. Appreciate the offer, though."

"Can I believe my ears?" Billy Don says. "Sly Mabry not going out on the first day of deer season? Dude, you taught me how to shoot a gun when I was knee-high to a grasshopper. You feeling okay, buddy?"

Sylvester shrugs. "Fine as frog hair split three ways. Just ain't ready to polish off my rifle, is all. Maybe later."

Tom frowns. In his camouflage shirt and pants, he resembles a mossy oak tree that happened to stop by for a coffee break. "Won't be right, hunting without you, Sly. I can't believe you're bailing on us. You and me been out on the first day of deer season for going on forty years now."

Billy Don adds, "My wife has already cooked up a ham for us to pack for lunches. Buttermilk biscuits, too. Sure you won't come with us?"

Sylvester takes a deep breath and blows it out. "Reckon I could work up some enthusiasm if it means so all-fired much to you boys. The granddaughter is staying with us, but I reckon the woman I answer to won't miss me for a few hours." He tilts his head toward Billy Don. "Your wife, she make any of that sour cream pound cake?"

Billy Don nods. "Already sliced and wrapped up."

"Well, heck fire. I reckon I *can* go after all."

Billy Don slaps Sly on the shoulder. "Attaboy! Time you catch sight of a big ole buck staring you in the face, you'll get your juices flowing."

Sylvester takes a sip of Aileen's refill, winces, and adds several teaspoons of sugar. "This coffee is good enough for that, and I don't even have to get up at chicken-thirty."

Billy Don pulls the battered pickup truck onto a grassy clearing and cuts the engine. It coughs and spits for a few minutes before moaning into silence.

"Dang, boy. When was the last time you got this thing tuned?" Tom asks as he steps from the cab and pulls an orange safety vest over his thick camouflage-print coat. His words come out in puffs of steam in the chilled early morning air.

"She'll outrun that new piece of foreign junk of yours hands down," Billy Don fires back. "I tune her myself. Just put a new set of plugs in last fall."

Sylvester grins. "That was only a few hundred thousand miles ago. Can't imagine why she sounds like my asthmatic grandma."

"Y'all can shut up now." Billy Don pats the fender of the faded blue Ford. "You're talking about my baby, here. Besides, I'd like to see one of you old goons do a tune-up on the fancy trucks they have out there now. There's twenty mile of wire under the hoods! Not to mention, all that computerized mess. Takes a rocket scientist to change the oil on one of them."

"You got a point," Sylvester agrees. "I'm afraid to touch mine, except to steer."

"Like I said." Billy Don coughs and spits a glob of phlegm onto the dry dirt.

"You taking the stand on the west end, Billy boy?" Tom asks.

Billy Don narrows his eyes and sniffs the wind, as if some throwback to his wild ancestors gives him an edge. "Reckon I will, if one of you don't claim it."

Tom lifts one shoulder, lets it fall. "Six of one, half dozen of the other."

"All right then," Sylvester says. "Tom, you take the east stand, I'll go south."

Sylvester suits up in an orange quilted jacket and pulls his rifle over one shoulder. "I'm going to head out down by the fork in the millpond stream and find a nice quiet place away from you both."

Billy Don slips on his safety vest. "Still say we'd get more accomplished if we ran the dogs."

"Never saw that as much of a contest myself," Sylvester says. "Not to talk bad about your hounds, Billy Don. I know you put a lot of time and energy into those dogs. I have always liked the notion of pitting myself against the deer, one on one."

"You being the one toting the gun, of course." Tom smiles.

Sylvester sticks a toothpick in his mouth and chews the end. "Suppose I do have a little better odds, at that."

Billy Don tosses thermoses filled with hot, black coffee to each of his hunting buddies. "Way you shoot, Sly, I'd say the odds are definitely in the deer's favor."

Tom and Billy Don hoot. Fact is: Sylvester has been the first to bag a kill for five years running. Seems the bucks gravitate to him, and he has a deep freezer full of venison to prove it.

"You just keep on with your foolishness, Billy Don," Sylvester says. "God don't love liars."

Billy Don checks his watch. "What say, we meet up around eleven for some of Kitty's sandwiches? By then, my breakfast will have worn slap off."

"Works for me," Tom calls back over his shoulder.

Billy Don studies Sylvester for a moment. "Two quick shots if you need me, same as always, Sly."

"I'll keep that near to my heart, Billy Don. Surely will." He ambles off a few steps, then turns around to add, "Only shots you'll hear from me will be when I land a buck with so many points, you could use the rack to hang up every hat you own."

A twelve-point buck steps into the clearing, parting the morning mists that twirl in eddies at the base of a massive hickory tree. Sylvester holds his breath.

The deer twitches, scenting the air for danger. His ears tip forward and backward. The trickle of one of the natural springs feeding the millpond echoes in the silence.

Trained as a hunter from a young age, Sylvester knows the importance of utter stillness.

The buck looks back over his shoulder before stepping forward and bending his long neck to nibble from the scattered yellow field corn bait. Behind him, a doe enters the clearing. In contrast to the buck's solid presence, the female seems demure, almost wraith-like.

Sylvester raises his shotgun as if the air is explosive and one jerky movement can set it off. He lines up the buck in his sights. His finger, steady, poises on the trigger.

The buck jerks his head up in the direction of the clump of bushes where Sylvester crouches. For an instant, the glistening large brown eyes gaze into his. A whisper, the slightest brush of air ripples the fine hairs at the base of Sylvester's neck.

The woods, the ground beneath him, the morning sun breaking through the autumn foliage: all fall away. Sylvester is aware of nothing but his shallow breathing and the majestic animals, their small family. Moisture gathers in the corners of his eyes. He feels the sting of tears.

Sylvester lowers the barrel. The buck's muscles twitch beneath his tawny coat. For a few moments, the pair feed, seemingly at ease with his presence.

29: Gift of Life

Standing in Sam Fisher's back yard— the same yard he and the boys have stood in for over forty years of friendship— Les pats his jacket, then moves down to fumble in his pants pockets. "Dang. Where's my lighter? It was just here. I swear, I get to where I can't keep up with nothin'."

"Here, I got one." Wayne Fred reaches into his pocket. His un-lit cigarette balances between his lips. "Well shoot. Must've laid mine down somewhere."

The two men's breath comes out in chilled puffs in the late-December night air.

"Need to quit these cancer sticks, anyway," Les says. He stares at the Lucky Strike for a moment before returning it to the pack. "Promised my son. Been smoking since we all started up, back in high school."

"Funny how we done that and played football too." Wayne Fred stuffs the spit-damp cigarette into his jacket pocket and takes a deep swill of beer. "And we was *good*, natural-born *good* at it."

"Last time this town won a state championship," Les adds. "Last time we had a QB like Sam Fisher." Les curls up the corners of his mouth. "And these," he pats his pocket, "weren't the only things we smoked."

They laugh.

"I'm quitting after the holidays," Wayne Fred remarks. "Too tough to do before that, with all the parties."

"Right. How many years have I heard you say that?" Les coughs hard.

When the two men step back into the warmth of the modest ranch-style house, the rest of their core group of friends huddle around the kitchen island, cold beers in hand. Feminine laughter echoes from the living room. Good thing the two Fisher kids are grown and off to college. No need to act all pure now. Adult-only party. About time.

"It's the offensive coordinator's fault," Gabe says. "Florida State has a killer defense. But they can't stay on the field for the whole game. Sooner or later, the offense has to show up." He lets out a resinous belch. Beer foam frosts his mustache.

"Good one," Jeff comments. "More room out than in, my dear Mama always used to say." Jeff: skinny dude. But one hell of an end receiver, back in the day.

"Your mama could out-belch and out-drink anyone in this county," Mark adds. "Matter of fact, she could take on anyone this side of the Mason-Dixon Line if you let her swig down a six-pack or two." Mark, the only one who stuck it out, got his college degree. Fat lot of good it did him. Ended up back here, working for the State.

"Don't be talking about my mama, now." Jeff sucker-punches Mark in the arm. Mark wobbles but manages to stay upright.

"Any of you dogs got a light?" Wayne Fred asks.

The men dig into shirt pockets and pants, coming up empty-handed.

"Dang it, Fish! Where are they?" Jeff swipes a finger in the general direction of the shortest member of the group.

"Me?" Sam Fisher's boyish dimples flash for a moment, the picture of little-lost-lamb innocence. He's the only one who could pass for below forty. The only one who keeps in shape. Runs ten miles a day.

"Check his pockets!" Jeff lunges.

Sam shoves a hand deep into his pants before any of the men can reach him and holds forth a palmful of assorted butane lighters and a ragged book of Blue Moon Tavern matches.

"Fish, you're a cleft-toe-maniac, son, if I've ever seen one." Jeff extracts his slender, cherry-red Bic from the bunch.

Sam Fisher spreads the remaining lighters and the matchbook on the bar counter and sweeps his fingers through the air as if he is Vanna White revealing a crucial *Wheel of Fortune* letter. "It's *klepto*maniac, idiot. And I ain't one, thank you very much."

Les picks up a dented silver Zippo with the initials LFG engraved in block letters across the front. "You missed your calling, then. You learn to lift wallets that slick, and you can hit the big time."

Wayne Fred plucks a flag-printed lighter from the display. "I've never lost a lighter in my life. Not one. Lost women. Lost a few weekends. Lost where I parked my truck once at a Garth Brooks concert. But not once, not one single solitary time, do I recall losing my Bic."

Sam shrugs. "I don't know why, but I just like the feel of a pocketful of lighters."

"And you don't even smoke, Fish." Jeff shakes his head. "Be different if you stole something you actually *use*."

"Not stealing, I told you. I was just safekeeping." Sam twists his lips. "Didn't I always lead y'all right? Even when I faked a pass, I signaled you where to head out. Besides, don't I always give them back?"

"So far." Mark slips the dog-eared matchbook into his pocket before any of his cronies, or his wife, God forbid, see the name and phone number scribbled on one side. "But, you could escalate into pilfering other things."

Wayne Fred laughs. "Lighters as a gateway to a life of larceny. Reckon they'll start throwing folks in jail over it? Hey, I know . . . We can start up some kind of charity thing for lighter-stealing dudes."

Gabe runs with it. "Yeah, we could stand up at the red light at gettin'-off time with empty boots and collect spare change." When he speaks, his graying moustache does a hoochie dance.

"Then we could use the cash to buy beer!" Jeff holds an arm heavenward like a revival preacher calling down praise. "We could print up some shirts and sell 'em." He fans his hands through the air. "I can see it now. T-shirts with *Got Light?* stamped on the front. Or maybe *Do You Know Where Your Lighter Is, Tonight?*"

Mark guffaws. "I got one! *My Bic's bigger than your Bic.*"

Jennifer Fisher swishes into the kitchen and stops next to her husband. "What y'all carrying on about in here? We can hear you laughing clean into the other room."

"Men stuff," Jeff states.

Jennifer rolls her eyes. She notices the lighters on the counter and switches her gaze toward her husband. "Sam . . . ?"

"Yes, my love?"

Her lips twitch upward and she shakes her head. She pushes past the men to the refrigerator where she removes two platters of sliced cheese and cold cuts. One, she leaves on the counter for the boys. The other, she balances expertly on one hand.

"I better not find a single lighter that doesn't belong in this house later on." She throws the lame threat back over her shoulder as she leaves the room for the company of her female friends.

"Poor woman," Jeff comments, "having to live with a lighter-stealing freak. Must be hard."

"How she's done it all these years is beyond my imagination," Wayne Fred says.

Les takes a swill of beer. "Gives her something to fuss about. Woman doesn't fuss, she'll blow up. It's all that pent-up pressure."

"Unfulfilled, that's what the magazines call it," Wayne Fred adds.

"Speak for yourself," Les fires back. "My wife fusses and she is thoroughly fulfilled."

"Not what she told me," Wayne Fred punctuates with a wink. "Let's step outside. I'm dying for a cig."

Less than two weeks later, the friends stand around the same kitchen counter.

Women's voices are barely audible from the other room. Young children of various ages huddle around a video game in the cramped den. Hard to fathom, having kids old enough to be married with kids of their own. But all of them have the next batch of little ones, except Les's.

"I still can't get my mind wrapped around it," Wayne Fred says.

"Me neither," Jeff echoes. The others shake their heads.

"Exactly how old was he, anyway?" Mark asks. "I know I was a year beneath him in school."

"He was my age. Forty-three." Gabe's eyes water. He blinks to hide the raw emotion. Even his thick mustache droops.

"My wife says we're smack dab in the middle of heart attack range," Les adds. "Scary as hell."

Wayne Fred pulls a shiny silver lighter from his pocket, engraved on one side. Hasn't had the heart to use it yet.

"I got one of those for Christmas," Jeff says. He scoops an identical lighter from his pants pocket. "Got my name on mine, too."

Les, Gabe, and Mark pull lighters from their pockets and set them on the counter.

Wayne Fred whistles. "Well, I'll be danged. I suppose you all got these from Fish?"

The friends nod.

Wayne palms his lighter, stares at it for a moment, then asks. "Ain't that a kick? Wonder why he up and gave us all these."

"So you won't use them." The voice behind them is gentle, feminine. "Same reason he kept taking the ones before."

The men turn their attention to Sam's widow. Even with the dark undereye circles, she retains her youthful beauty. The head cheer-leader that married the star QB.

Jennifer Fisher tucks a lock of frosted blonde hair behind one ear. "That's what Sam told me when he picked them out. If you haven't tried them yet, you'll find none of them work. Sam took out the wicks and drained the fluid."

"What the—" Les starts.

"So you'll all quit smoking like you've been promising for years." Jennifer lowers her voice, imitating Sam, "reckon the only way they'll stop is if they try and try and can't fire one up."

After Sam Fisher's widow leaves the kitchen, nobody speaks for a beat. Then Wayne Fred looks up, "reckon you pulled a fine Hail Mary pass after all, Fish."

30: Inheritance

Lena stares at the line of print. "You've got to be kidding." She shifts her gaze to the attorney. "You *are* kidding me, right?"

The attorney offers a slight smile. "It's no joke, Lena. Gordon left it all to you: everything he owned, land, and what money was left over after settling his affairs."

"He has family around Pensacola. I've heard him mention them before. A brother, maybe?"

He nods. "Actually, two. From what little Gordon told me, they weren't on speaking terms."

"But, why me?"

"Why not?"

Lena mentally thumbs through the handful of times she had befriended the old man over the past few years. Gordon served as the unofficial office mascot for the veterinary clinic she manages. Sure, she checked on him on the holidays. Took him a meal once or twice. Always called ahead, and he met her at the gate. She had baked him a chocolate layered cake for his birthday last year. Certainly, nothing to merit this! "What if the family contests it?"

The attorney pushes back from his mahogany desk. "Gordon was of sound mind when he made the will." His lip quivers into a half-smile. "Well, as sound of mind as the old cussing mule man could claim, anyway."

"What do I do? I mean, no one has ever left anything to me before. I got a few pieces of crystal from my grandmother's estate, some things from Mom and Dad's. But, nothing like . . . this."

"I'll be happy to assist as you wade through the paperwork. For all the times you've helped save that sniveling, nasty little ankle-biter Chihuahua of my mother-in-law's, it's the least I can do."

"That little dog isn't all bad." Lena stops herself before she adds to the lie.

"Keep spreading that around town and you'll be in my mother-in-law's will, too."

Lena hums the tune to *He's Got the Whole World in His Hands*. She finds the children's church ditty oddly comforting. She plugs in whatever worries her into the lyrics. Lately, she catches the tune running around in her head, a demented, endless-loop earworm.

She lowers the driver's side window and allows the warm, sweet air of early spring to twist her dark hair into knots.

"He's got all the mules in His hands! He's got all the burros in His hands! He's got the geese and chickens in His hands! He's got a pot-bellied pig in His hands! He's got a bunch of scruffy barn cats in His hands! He's got the whole world in His hands!"

Lena smiles. God himself would be singing reassuring tunes if He had to deal with the hot mess she was driving toward.

"Well, Lena," her husband Mickey had commented the first time they visited the farm, "looks like your kindness paid off. I've always said a good deed never goes unpunished."

Her husband fondly accuses Lena of picking up strays, animals *and* people. Whether she attracts them or vice versa, she befriends the down and out. She simply can't abide the thought of a living thing suffering, or lonely.

Mickey puts in as much time at the late mule man's farm as Lena. Since their only son left for college at University of Georgia, time has dragged, until Gordon's will and the inherited Farm from Hades.

The deal Lena and Mickey share: for every act of selfless love and aid provided to the other partner without whining, one earns points toward a prized possession. For Lena, the jewelry box at home brims with inexpensive baubles honoring hours spent dripping buckets of sweat in 100% humidity and September heat while watching Florida State football. For Mickey, the hard labor spent clearing Gordon's barn and outbuildings will undoubtedly secure some high-end power tool with all the attachments, after hours joy-roaming the aisles at a home improvement store.

Thinking of her husband, Lena shakes her head. Such a free spirit. So disorganized. Maddening, yet endearing. As a couple, they're polar opposites. Lena is petite, neat, organized, and punctual. Mickey is rumpled, tall and muscular, spontaneous, and will be late to his own funeral.

Their twenty-one-year-old son inherited the cream of both parents, thank the heavens. He has his father's good looks and steady disposition with his mother's drive for precise accountability. As an engineering student, he excels.

Lena makes the sharp turn from the state highway onto a narrow dirt road barely wide enough to accommodate a vehicle. In the two months since the previous owner's release from Earth, nature has stepped in to reclaim her rights. Wild grape vines dip like melted frosting from the low-hanging branches of shortleaf pines. Thorn-armed scrub bushes jab the flanks of her car. She hears the elongated scream of scratched paint and pledges to drive Mickey's beat-up truck on future forays into the wilds of Gadsden County.

My land. Lena wraps her mind around the astounding concept. She's never owned a scrap of property larger than their postage-stamp yard in town. Because of generous baking and a handful of kind words, she now possesses twenty-five acres of southern pine and oak forest. Also, twenty mules, three burros, four goats, three geese, a flock of the ugliest chickens she's ever seen, hosts of field mice and squirrels, rabbits, and a two-hundred pound pot-bellied pig named Elvis.

I own a pig nearly as big as my car. Lena laughs. *A freakin' pig!*

The lane widens and spills onto three acres of cleared and fenced pasture. Lena pulls the vintage VW bug parallel to a single-wide mobile home. When she kills the engine, she relishes the profound peace of the country: no barking dogs, boom boxes, or squabbling neighbors. Songbirds trill from a row of blooming hog plum trees on the periphery of the clearing. Overhead, a breeding pair of red-tailed hawks carves lazy circles in the cloudless blue sky. As soon as she opens the car door, the geese and several of the nappy chickens trundle to greet her, more from the promise of fresh seed than to offer welcome.

The chickens own their own shack behind the trailer but choose to embrace the free-range concept. In the evening, the flock returns to the coop. A lone rooster is as unattractive as the hens he guards. Lena feels somewhat inadequate; she knows only the pig by name. Surely Gordon called each creature by its given title. He seemed that sort.

Lena names the rooster *Travolta*, fitting with her notion of a backwoods tribute to Hollywood. The geese trio reminds her of dignified older women with a fair share of pizzazz and piss-and-vinegar: *The Golden Girls*. Since Mickey has graciously taken on the chore of managing the remaining farm animals, Lena hasn't become familiar enough to provide appropriate individual names. Yet.

A piece of a torn envelope flaps on the weathered post supporting the bottom of the front steps. In uneven red marker, the message reads: DID YOU LOOSE A POP BELLY PIG? SIGNED, BULLY JONES.

Elvis *is* fat enough to pop, really. And loose? The misspelled word is appropriate: Elvis is definitely loose.

"For the love of Pete, Elvis," she mutters. "Can't you stay out of trouble?"

Maybe the porker has just recently entered a life of delinquency prompted by grief over his missing owner. If Gordon had suffered from the same ill-timed jail breaks, he never mentioned it. Since Lena's inheritance, Elvis has jumped bail four times and rampaged nearby farms, raiding garbage cans, scaring the bejabbers out of guarding hound dogs, and generally spreading havoc.

Her husband pulls up beside her car in his weathered pick-up. He hops out and she hands him the note. "Don't worry, hon. I have the routine down pat," he says.

Mickey will make a couple of inquiries, ride a few backcountry roads, and manage to extradite Elvis back to the sanctity of his pen. Add a few points to Mickey's column. Maybe enough for that new grill he's eyed.

Lena digs in her purse for the set of worn keys. "Maybe Elvis just needs a girlfriend." She opens the flimsy aluminum trailer door.

"He'll have to lose a little lard and clean up a bit."

A vision of Elvis prancing on a treadmill with terry cloth sweat bands circling his feet makes her smile.

The faint scent of blooming Confederate jasmine reaches Lena's nose. How easy it would be to throw an old quilt onto the soft, new grass and bask in the breeze flowing across the pasture, more appealing than the drudgery of clearing away layers of the last forty years of a mule man's life.

Lena stands at the stained and scuffed linoleum entrance to the living room, marveling at the progress she and the team of dedicated cleaners have made. After two weeks of sorting, pitching, and swearing, the mud-brown shag carpet finally peeks through.

From the second she and Mickey entered the property that first day, they were drop-jawed at the proliferation of junk. The front gate was chained and padlocked. Who in his, or her, right mind would consider setting foot in the minefield of a yard?

Rust-infested farm implements— pieces and parts of harrows, tractors, augers, tillers, and gas tanks— languished in weed-upholstered clumps. A motorcycle rested on its side. Four automobiles in various states of decay provided condo living for scores of vermin, insects, and reptiles. Behind the single-wide trailer, rows of empty fifty-gallon drums leaned against three metal storage buildings filled with discarded furniture, mildew-powdered saddles, and sacks of horse feed. Scattered among the yard debris stood a variety of lawn chairs, most missing arms or legs.

"It's like a wacked-out theme park," Mickey commented with a slow head shake. "Rusty Metal World."

On the listing wooden deck leading to the front door, a mud-encrusted pitchfork leaned, as if the Devil had dropped by for a visit, went inside, and was never seen or heard from again. Small wonder.

Stepping inside, Lena stopped to survey what little she could see of the living room. A cleared path wide enough for one person snaked through the dimly lit room. Stacks of mail, newspapers, and magazines towered in ragged columns. A long metal rack on casters held a line of drycleaner hanging bags. Lena walked over and took a quick visual count: seven pairs of professionally laundered, blue jean overalls, ten flannel shirts, seven white T-shirts, and one black dress jacket.

In one corner, a mound of empty feed bags poured over onto a wooden table holding a big screen television. The only piece of furniture visible beneath the rubble was a sleeper sofa, its bedding tucked military straight.

Lena dropped the bucket of assorted cleaning supplies and sighed.

Mickey stepped up behind her and whistled low. "I think we'd better look into renting one of those dumpsters."

"Uh-huh."

"You think this is bad? You should see the sheds and barn."

On the third trip, Lena attacks the cramped galley kitchen. Lena's coworker and best friend Candace volunteers to help.

"There's no food in here." Candace backs away from the opened refrigerator. "Three cans of cheap beer and a carton of soured milk. Didn't Gordon eat?"

Lena points to the cast iron skillet filled with murky grease. The stove top is dull with layers of dried oil. "If he did, he fried it."

Candace picks up a quart jar of lumpy, amber-brown preserves. "Wonder how old these are? Wonder *what* they are?"

Lena shrugs. "Toxic waste, at this point."

Candace pulls on a pair of heavy rubber gloves. "Might as well get to it."

Lena smiles. "You are a true friend."

"Couldn't let you do this alone. Besides, it's like a treasure hunt. There's really no telling what all we'll find."

"Same way I feel every time I open one of those big military crates, the ones with *Do Not Remove From Ship* printed on the side. It may be a million dollars. It may be a dead body."

By the fifth trip, the aging trailer resembles a dog bone with the marrow sucked out. Only one uncharted area remains. Mickey moves two heavy metal foot lockers blocking the master bedroom door.

Lena steps into the biggest surprise yet.

The master bedroom overflows with cabbage rose-printed chintz from the ruffled bedspread to the pleated café curtains. Other than a fine, undisturbed film of dust on the bureau and bedside tables, the room is tidy.

"What you reckon?" Mickey asks.

Lena opens the mirrored closet door. Rows of women's dresses, pants, and shirts hang between ribbon-suspended lavender sachets. On the floor stands a line of pumps and flats in varied colors and styles.

"Gordon had a lady friend?" Mickey opens the bureau drawers, revealing neat layers of gowns, undergarments, socks, and T-shirts. "It's like one of those Anasazi Indian Cliff Dwellings out west. You know, where they just walked out."

Lena picks up a carved bone brush and comb set, then lifts one of six jewel tone perfume decanters.

"Wonder who she was," Mickey ponders aloud.

"I didn't find any pictures of women, or family, anywhere in the house. She must've been loved . . . or hated. Looks like Gordon closed off this room and forgot it existed."

"A preservation room," Mickey states.

"Huh?"

Mickey waves one hand. "Like in a historical house where everything is left exactly like it was when someone lived in it. Frozen in time."

Lena glances around the room. Other than the dust and a slight closed-off scent, the room appears neat and ready for its occupant. No pilfered military metal boxes jammed with postcards, no used tires, no mule paraphernalia, and no teetering stack of Gordon's life flotsam.

Lena backs from the room, gently guiding her husband. She closes the door.

"What—?" Mickey begins.

"I don't know. Doesn't seem right, just yet."

"We have to clean it out, babe. We want to be able to sell this place."

She sighs. "I know. I know. You're right. Could we give it a couple more nights? I mean, obviously whoever she was, she meant a great deal to Gordon at one time."

Mickey plops down beside Lena in the tall Bahia grass. The day's work is behind them. "You okay?"

Lena wipes a tear from one cheek. "Yeah."

"It's done. Can you believe it? Waste Management will send a truck to haul off the dumpster tomorrow. We're all set to call the Realtor and put this place up for sale."

Lena picks at a long, seeded stem of grass. The last of the morning dew shivers on the thin stalk. "I don't know how I feel about all that."

"Sifting through the old mule man's stuff bothered you, didn't it?"

Lena stares across the pasture. Two burros remain from the equine herd. The mules and goats have relocated to the country home of a Quincy veterinarian, Travolta and his harem of unsightly chickens to a nearby farm, and Elvis to a kindly old woman in Gretna with a penchant for pot-bellied pigs. The barn cats come and go with little notice of the changes around them. The Golden Girls remain, trundling idly about the grounds, honking and looking a bit lost.

"It's the first time it really hit me, how you can't take it with you." She gestures toward the trailer. "Gordon's life was in there. Years of military service, work, relationships, such as they were. In the end, it all came down to this. Ninety percent is dumped. The other ten percent gets recycled or moves on to someone else."

Mickey nods. "About sums it up." He reaches over and massages the tight muscles of her neck.

Lena closes her eyes. Collective weariness and sadness threaten to wash over her. She wishes she could curl into a tight ball and cry. "I don't think I can part with this place, Mickey."

"I suppose having the land could count as an investment. Prices are going up in the Panhandle, what with all the south Florida folks escaping the crowds. Taxes can't be that high. We could afford to pay them, I think. Given a couple of years, you could turn it around for more of a profit."

"No. I mean, what if *we* live here?"

Mickey gathers his wife into his arms and nestles the nape of her neck. "Why the change of heart?"

Lena hesitates before she answers. "Everything I've ever done, everything *we've* ever done, has been for someone else. Work, work, work, to get money to raise our son and put him through college. Time spent taking care of our parents until they passed. We've both done without for so long. You know, I can't even remember the last time I had anything brand new."

"You saying you're dissatisfied, babe?"

Lena studies her husband's sun-weathered face. The creases around his eyes. The gray hair feathering his temples. "I wouldn't have lived my life any other way. I love our life." She shifts her gaze back to the acres of open pasture. "But I feel something here, Mickey. Something I've never felt in that little house in town. This land is mine . . . it's *ours*. We don't have to share it with some bank for years and years. Because of the generosity of a lonely mule man, we have a place to build the house we've always dreamed of."

"It would mean a lot of work. I don't think we can afford to live in two places."

"Then we can sell the house in town and move into the trailer while we build. We can take our time. Do most of the work ourselves. What do you think?"

Mickey smiles. "I think you must want this pretty darn bad, is what I think."

"We've lived in worse places."

"Can't argue with that." Mickey's eyes sparkle. "I'll agree whole-heartedly, work my tail off, live in that run-down, but now clean, trailer under one condition."

Lena tilts her head. "What, a permanent paid pass to the hardware store of your choosing?"

"Nope. Better'n that." He leans in, brushes her lips with a kiss. "You don't beg for another *pop*-bellied pig. *Ever.*"

31: Generation Gap

Judy looks forward to missing her mother. When Lorene Dougherty no longer haunts the earth, the bad memories will sink, maybe, and allow the few good ones to rise to the surface.

Each time the thought pops to mind, a gush of guilt pours in and lodges between Judy's heart and stomach. Wishing one's parents dead during teenage angst is somewhat acceptable, if not expected. For a fifty-four-year-old woman— wife of a respected internist, president of the garden club, and mother of three successful children— the wish seems ghastly.

No one sees Lorene Dougherty through her only daughter's eyes.

Judy grabs a mug from a line of custom pickled oak cabinets. The cup is ugly, chipped on one side, and stained by years of coffee and tea. Her family thinks it horrid. Several times, Judy saved it from the trash. A gift to her maternal grandmother Ada, the yellowed mug's design shows cartoon cats in overlapping poses. At first glance, the animals seem cute, but a closer examination reveals their nature. The felines smile from various coital positions.

Judy recalls the Christmas the mug made its way into her grandmother's delicate, gnarled hands.

Jeff, her youngest child, picked up the mug in a quirky little shop, the type Judy loved to peruse for unusual gifts.

"Look, Mom. Can I get this for Grammy? She loves cats!"

Judy glanced toward the mug in her five-year-old's hands. "Sure, honey. If that's what you'd like to give her, I know she'll like it."

The mug was trussed in green tissue and nestled into a glossy white box by a bored college-age clerk. One less thing to wrap. Good.

On Christmas Eve, her grandmother beamed when Jeff handed over his offering.

"I picked it out all by myself, Grammy."

Her grandmother sifted through the layers of tissue and lifted up the mug. Her eyes widened. "Oh, very nice, baby boy. You knew just what your old Grammy would like, didn't you?"

She discreetly stored the mug in its box and pushed it beneath her chair with one foot when her grandson wasn't looking.

Later, when the dinner dishes stood by the sink in gravy-slimed piles, her grandmother tapped Judy on the shoulder.

"Judy, dear. Did you happen to notice the mug your son gave me?"

She glanced up from the steaming hot water to her grandmother's amused face. "Sure, Grammy. He picked it out, but I paid for it. Don't you like it?"

Her grandmother grinned. "I love it. Of course, I love it. But I may not be able to sip coffee from it on a Sunday if the preacher comes to call."

Judy shook the water from her soap-reddened hands and dried them on a kitchen towel. "What, he doesn't like cats or something?"

Her grandmother opened the box, carefully extracted the mug, and handed it over. "Take a close look, dear. It might be my old eyes playing tricks, but I do believe these cats are enjoying themselves a bit much."

Judy's lips parted. "Oh my."

Her grandmother stifled a giggle. "You see?"

"Grammy. I am so sorry. I never in a million years. We'll take it back."

Her grandmother snatched the mug from her and secured it back in its nest of green tissue. "You will do nothing of the sort. My great-grandson picked it out, and I will proudly drink my coffee from it until the day I leave this old world." She smiled. "Besides, it fits, don't you think? All my years of helping babies enter this world. I should have a mug that celebrates how they got here to start with."

Judy's eyes water slightly, remembering. Grammy used the mug every day. When she died, her favorite granddaughter inherited it, though no one offered any objection except Lorene Dougherty.

"Why in the world you want to keep that vulgar cup is beyond me, Judy," her mother commented on one of the many Sundays Judy brought her from the assisted living facility for dinner with the family. "You're just like your grandmother. She never had a sense of propriety either."

Judy bit the insides of her cheek. She did that a lot when she was around her mother. She wanted to retort that Grammy had more propriety in her little finger than Lorene has in her entire body. Compassion oozed from Grammy like warm tupelo honey. At least Grammy had some humor in her life, no matter how hardscrabble it was. And Grammy wasn't mean as a cut snake.

The only person Lorene Dougherty communes peacefully with is Judy's daughter Lily. While the rest of Judy's small family is headed straight to Hell in a hand basket in her mother's estimation, Lily shines forth white and pure, the picture of grace, love, and all things worthy. Judy marvels at the relationship between the two. From birth, Lorene heaped affection on her granddaughter; affection denied Judy. When Lily misbehaved, Lorene coddled. When Judy disciplined, Lorene offered solace and a cookie or three.

Now when Judy needs help with some mother-related agenda, Lily is called into service. The same words uttered from Judy's lips, labeled as dictatorial, come as welcomed advice from Lorene's grand-daughter. Judy learns quickly, there's no need to approach the matriarch head-on. Coming in from an unlocked side door is safer and could add years to her own life, or at least not necessitate increasing the dosage of her antidepressant.

Judy fills the fornicating-feline mug with strong coffee, adds a dollop of reduced fat milk and a packet of artificial sweetener. She walks toward the front porch. On the way, she stops to pick up a small ornate frame with a faded black and white picture of an old woman holding a baby. The woman is Grammy. The identity of the child is a mystery. It could've been one of hundreds of infants her grandmother helped usher into the world. Behind her grandmother's rocking chair, a section of white porch railing shows. Unlike the simple, two-bedroom frame house behind it, the woodwork is ornate, with fancy cutout scrollwork in the shape of hearts.

Judy smiles, thinking of the many times spent on Grammy's porch. Lazy, summer-sweet afternoons shelling peas in the deep shade. The swoosh of cars passing on the avenue. Nobody in a hurry. People stopping at the curb to call a few words from a rolled-down window. Neighbors taking one of the vacant rockers to sit and fan sweat and comment on life.

Judy returns the picture to its spot on the marble top foyer table and opens the front door. Other than its size, her porch is a close replica of Grammy's.

"It'll cost you to put this kind of railing on your front porch," the builder had warned.

"I don't care. If we have to cut back somewhere else to make it look like my grandmother's, so be it."

Judy and her husband have lived in three houses; each, built to others' specifications. They have remodeled and made do. Now she had a chance to finally own a home to her liking, and she'd have Grammy's porch across the front, by golly.

"People just don't sit on porches like they used to in the South," Judy often comments. "You would be amazed at how much I get downright stared at when I'm sitting out here in the mornings."

"Porches are mostly for show," one of her closest friends says. "I think people in bigger cities are afraid to sit out front. Drive-by shootings, you know. It's much more private, and safer, to sit out back on a patio. You live in a city, Judy. Not like at your grandmother's house. I doubt three cars drove by her house in an hour."

"I don't suppose I'll make the kind of enemies who would shoot me from a car window. And if my neighbors think me nuts, so be it."

Her husband understands. Sometimes in the late evening when he returns from a wearying shift at the emergency room, he joins her with a glass of wine. They sit on the wicker porch swing and talk about anything and nothing. The kids are grown now. Jeff lives across town in his first townhouse, fresh out of law school and building a life. Lily, a registered nurse, works for one of the local Hospice organizations. The only bird to fly farther than the Florida Georgia line, Leanne, lives in Atlanta with her husband and their first grandchild, a sweet baby girl named Savannah, the love of Judy's life. Unless Judy and Robert invite activity, peace generally reins. Other than the jangle of the phone signaling her mother's latest real or imagined crisis, the two enjoy the absence of turmoil.

The early afternoon is warm, one of North Florida's deceptive winter Sundays. By the next day, it could easily dip into the mid-thirties and cast a layer of hoar frost over the early Japanese magnolia blooms. Judy settles onto the porch swing opposite the rocking chairs holding her quilt-swaddled mother, her son Jeff, and daughter Lily. Robert is at work, but their two children provide ample cover against her mother's tongue. The meal went smoothly. Her mother was delighted with the spaghetti, salad, and garlic rolls. Since Judy learned to attribute all of the cooking to Lily, the family meals flow without Lorene's snide comments. Lily plays along with the farce, though she seldom cooks.

"Isn't it a nice day?" Judy comments.

"Too cool to sit out on this porch." Lorene's features crease into the accustomed disapproving frown.

"Oh no, Grandma. It's wonderful to be outside." Lily reaches over and straightens her grandmother's quilt. "The fresh air is good for you."

Lorene's expression brightens. "You're right. You always know what's best, you being a nurse and all. You work too hard, Lily. Too hard. You should take a lesson from your mother. She has never worked a day in her life."

The statement jabs Judy in the gut. Her children glance her way, their eyes wide.

"I'll go bring out some hot tea." Judy jumps up and rushes into the safety of the house. She leans against the kitchen counter and stares idly from the window over the sink. She can no longer feel the bitter anger that fueled her childhood, adolescence, and most of her young married life. A weary resignation takes its place.

Jeff walks in and rests a hand on his mother's shoulder. "I'm sorry, Mom."

Judy dabs at a single, unbidden tear. "It's all right, Jeff."

"No, it's not all right. How can she say things like that? You haven't worked? Are you kidding me?"

"In her eyes, I suppose all the years I held down menial jobs after Daddy died don't count. Nor the ones I had to put myself, and later your father and you kids, through college. Being your father's office manager doesn't count either, me being the doctor's wife and all."

Jeff's brown eyebrows knit together. "I don't know why you even have her over here anymore, Mom. She's so hateful to you."

"She's my mother."

"Still." He shakes his head. "I suppose you're assuring your place in Heaven."

Judy offers a weak smile. "With the thoughts I have, I'm not aiming for Heaven anymore. I'll be happy for a cooler layer of Hell."

Judy joins her son in laughter.

Jeff wraps his arm across his mother's shoulders. "If it makes you feel any better, Grandma doesn't like me either."

"She loves you kids."

"Hate to burst your bubble, but no. She loves Lily. She likes Leanne okay. She tolerates me."

"Oh that can't be true."

Jeff grabs water from the refrigerator. "It's fine, Mom. Really. All of us know it. We've talked about it from time to time."

"She never mistreated you, I hope."

"Not physically, no. But she was Hell on wheels when it came to psychological torture. I remember this one time when I was little.

You were at the office working, and I stayed with her after some school thing. Don't know where Lily was. Anyway, she told me the reason I had to stay with her was that you didn't want me. I believe her exact words were *your mama dumped you off with me because she doesn't love you.*"

Judy slumps against the counter and closes her eyes. "Naturally you being a child, you believed her. And, you never told me this."

"Nope. I didn't. I always knew Grandma was full of crap. You and Dad never *ever* made me, or any of us, feel like we weren't wanted."

Judy sighs. "I don't know what I did to deserve her wrath. Honestly."

"It's a good case for karma. You know, like maybe you were this horrible plantation owner in a past life and Grandma was your slave. She's just getting even in this life."

"To that reasoning, I would have gladly freed her and sent her packing with bags full of money and plenty of food." Judy shrugs.

"It's not too late." Her son grins.

The teapot squeals. Judy removes a tray from a top shelf while Jeff puts loose tea into two fobs.

"No tea for you?" Judy loads the tea service pieces and cups onto the tray.

"Nah. I'll have coffee. Like you."

She stretches up and pecks her tall, handsome son on the cheek. "Thank you, Jeff."

"What'd I do?"

"Just being your wonderful, sensitive self. One day, you'll make some deserving person an amazing husband."

Jeff shudders. "Let me get my practice up and running first, Mom."

He carries the loaded tray to the foyer. His cell phone dings and he sets the tray onto a table by the front door. "Can you get this? I really need to return a couple of calls. I'll join you guys in a few minutes, okay?"

"Chicken."

"You bet." Jeff slips his cell phone from his pocket and walks toward the front parlor.

Through the screened storm door, Lorene's stern voice sounds. "I detest this porch!"

Judy hesitates, hates herself for eavesdropping, but does it all the same. Instead of picking up the tray, she hovers in the shadowy foyer.

Lily's voice, soft: "You cold, Grandma?"

"How could I be cold? I have on a quilt *and* a shawl!"

"Why do you hate the porch? It's really nice out here."

Judy hears her mother's labored sigh.

"Too much like my mother's. I hated that porch, too. I can't believe Judy copied it down to these nauseating little heart cutouts. It looks silly and out of place on this house."

Judy leans forward, eager to catch the conversation. Though she is quick to scold or offer caustic comments, Lorene seldom speaks of her feelings.

"Why, Grandma? What makes you dislike it so much?"

"My mother practically lived on that horrid porch, unless it was too cold or blowing rain. There was always someone with her, never just me and Daddy. Some woman who was expecting a baby or one from the hordes she had helped through delivery. Always my mother held a baby on her lap."

Judy can tell by the tone of her mother's voice that a scowl is ruining her face.

"Don't you like babies, Grandma?"

"They're a necessary evil. My mother loved those babies, any baby, more than her own daughter."

Judy hears the sharp intake of breath from Lily. "Why do you say that, Grandma? I'm sure Grammy loved you, too."

Lorene harrumphs. "From the time I was old enough, my mother tasked me to do the housework so she could trail off to anyone who called her. No matter what time of day or night, or if me or Daddy needed her, she would run off to help someone else."

"So you resented the babies?"

"I hated anything having to do with them. The way they clung and cooed. The way they messed their diapers. The way everyone made over them like they were precious gems. No mind to me. No sir. No mind to the little girl who slaved away with no reward."

"Gee, Grandma."

Judy starts to pick up the tray, intent on rescuing Lily, but her daughter's next question stops her.

"Is that why you are kind of mean to my mother, Grandma?"

Judy strains to hear her mother's reply. For a few moments, the rhythmic rasp of a porch rocker is the only sound.

"If a woman is easy on her children, they will turn out bad."

Lily's voice quivers slightly. "Mama is a good person, Grandma. The way you talk to her hurts her sometimes."

Judy can't believe Lily is brave enough to swap blows with Lorene. No one else would dream of such.

"Your tone is fresh, Lily. You've never spoken to me in such a manner."

"I'm sorry, Grandma. I don't intend to be disrespectful."

"Your mother was too easy on you, growing up."

Judy is surprised to hear her daughter's easy laughter. "No, not really. She expected a lot from me. From all of us."

Jeff appears beside her. "What are you doing, Mom?" he asks in a whisper.

"Waiting to see if I need to bring bandages for your sister." Judy holds a finger across her lips and points outside. "Listen."

"Grandma, I love you. You know I do. So does Mama. And I ask for you not to speak so harshly to her anymore. Would you do that for me?"

Jeff exchanges surprised glances with Judy.

Lorene heaves a breath and sighs again. Some days, her mother can suck all the oxygen from the air.

"I'll try, Lily dear. I'll try."

Jeff leans down and whispers in his mother's ear. "You might want to check for a star in the east and three wise men."

Judy stifles a giggle. "Why?"

"Last time there was a miracle this huge, the heavens opened up and a chorus of angels sang out."

32: Kite

"My, how I love the scent of fresh earth," George says, his nose tilted to the sky. "Used to rush to get out here and work this field in my younger days."

Denise pushes the wheelchair across the packed dirt at the edge of the newly plowed field. A few dried cornstalks punctuate the rich, turned soil like scattered pick-up sticks. She studies the tips of the loblolly pines framing the ten-acre garden. "Not much of a breeze today, Grandpa."

"Be patient. Doesn't take as much to lift one of my special kites, young'un." He winks with the same blue eyes his long-deceased wife fell for nearly seventy years back. He's a hundred and four. How did that happen? His wispy white hair, once as brilliantly red as his great-granddaughter's, stirs with a lick from the autumn wind. "The right gust will come. Person my age knows these things."

"If you say so, Grandpa." Denise sets the brake on the wheelchair, then adjusts the hand-crocheted throw around his bent shoulders.

"You're getting as good at making one of these as your daddy was when he was your age. I recall him flying kites with you kids when you were little. Reckon he's gotten too involved with all his other doings to take the time now."

George taps the place where his wristwatch once lived. "That's the fine thing about being with me, you see. I've got all the time in the world, and I don't have one thing I'd rather be doing than flying a kite with you."

He studies the sealed seams holding the newspaper kite to its crosswood frame. "In my day, we used the straightest oak limbs we could find, deadfall branches that were dried out so as to be lighter in weight." He picked at one edge of the paper. "Didn't have store-bought glue neither, back then. Made a paste from flour and water. It held just fine, as long as you let it dry for a spell."

"I used Elmer's. Sorry." His great-granddaughter offers a shrug.

George swishes a bony hand through the air. "No mind, child. Folks these days don't have the time to take on making everything from scratch. Always busy, busy, busy!"

He digs in the paper bag in his lap. Like a magician streaming strands of colored handkerchiefs from a black top hat, he pulls out strips of an old, flower-print bed sheet tied in three-foot lengths. "Fasten this on the bottom, sugar. We may have to shorten it a yard or two, depending on the strength of the wind."

He studies the kite, comical by modern standards, fashioned by hand in a day of precision plastics. "Wish I could run it for you. Could, if this chair was one of them new-fangled electric ones."

Denise squints into the sun. The pine boughs behind him whisper secrets. As George predicted, the air currents have accelerated.

"Why don't you hold it, Grandpa. I'll let out some string before I take off."

George agrees and cradles the kite gently in his extended arms, careful not to trap the long tail.

After a few yards, Denise signals and jets off in a fast sprint, kicking puffs of dust in her wake. George releases the kite at the precise moment a blast of wind pushes through the trees. The kite lifts in fits and starts.

He tilts his head back and raises his arms. "Keep going, gal!"

Denise runs, funneling lengths of string through her fingers until the kite has gained sufficient altitude to sustain flight. She walks back toward George, a wide smile gathering the sides of her face into deep dimples.

"Fine takeoff, young'un. Finest I believe I've ever seen." George claps twice, careful not to strike hard enough to bruise the thin skin.

Denise hands the spool of string to him. "I can't take all the credit. I learned everything I know from a real pro."

The kite surfs the air. The knotted tail whips in its wake. George senses the tether tugging the spool.

"Always admired the wind." George tents one hand over his eyes to block the sun. "It can be playful as a kitten, or purely evil. I used to be quite a sailor when I was a young man too. Loved to feel the power of something unseen moving me along." He pauses. "When I pass on, I want to be a part of the wind."

"Don't talk about that, Grandpa. I can't stand it."

"Lawd, honey. I'm going on a century plus five! I've been blessed with many a year on this old earth." He chuckles. "That flu last winter dang near took me out of the fireworks, but other than that, I'm holding up well for a feller my age. I only take a half a blood pressure pill a day."

"I can't think about you not being here. That's all." Water gathers at the corners of her eyes. She's always been the sensitive one, his heart of hearts' grandchild.

"Don't tune up and cry, now. Save those tears for another day."

For a few minutes, they share the silence, caught up in the magic of flying a kite on a brilliant fall day.

"I'll make you a deal," he says in a soft voice. "After I shuffle off this mortal coil, if there's a time you wonder if I'm still watching over you, just feel for the wind." He reaches up and taps her on the tip of the nose with a crooked index finger. "I'll send a breeze to kiss you right on the face."

33: Sister Strangers

Stormy Gale Adams never met a stranger. Says so right on her grave marker, a smooth rose-colored marble monument streaked with faint lines of pale gray. Pastel, a perfect match for my sister's personality. Next to it stands my parents' ebony headstone: George Wilson Adams, beloved father and husband, with adequate space to add my mother's name and dates. They will etch those on now.

Gray marble would better suit me, Sunny Blue Adams. What would my epitaph read? I'd met plenty of strangers in my life, counseled many of them. Then again, the gods had granted me thirty years longer than my twin sister. Funny where my mind goes when I am beyond exhaustion.

Gennelle Wren Adams, our mother, told the anecdote about our names many times. How she'd cradled the two swaddled pink bundles in her arms. My proud father looked on, unlit pipe dangling from one corner of his mouth. He always kept it there, even when it wasn't in use.

"I've the perfect names for the girls, Wilson," my mother said. "Stormy Gale and Sunny Blue."

Mother fancied herself a poet. Loved words. Took the English language out and played with it like a child with a cherished toy.

"Which is whom?" Dad asked. I could just see him cocking his head like he did when considering a thing.

"You pick. There're identical. Doesn't seem it would matter much."

Poor Dad. He forever shouldered the responsibility for the discrepancy between our names and dispositions. Too bad they didn't take us home and live with us a few months before assigning titles. Like pets. Wait and see how we turned out.

The crowd of mourners thins around the Memory Gardens tent. Mother's pearl-colored coffin rests above the turned ground, draped with a thick blanket of white and yellow roses.

"You want to stay a while longer, Blue?" my brother asks.

A faint breeze plays with my brother's cowlick. Despite his age, the single spike of defiant hair and a faint dusting of freckles across the bridge of his nose and cheeks remind me of the little boy I'd loved to torment.

I shake my head. "We can go on to the house. Mother would want us to be there. Do the right thing. People will start to come. You know how it goes."

Three days pass. The casserole-laden visitors have ceased ringing the front doorbell at regular intervals. The pantry is full of homemade cakes and pies. Two refrigerators bulge with uneaten food, and the tedious process of cleaning out the vestiges of a half-century of married life begins.

"Jeez, Mom. Now I know you come by it honestly," my eldest daughter Katie says, pitching another plastic butter container into the recycle bin. "Grandma G was as bad as you are about keeping stuff."

"She lived through the Depression, Katie. Didn't throw anything away. She never knew if she'd need it later on." I hand her a tall stack of used aluminum foil, neatly folded. "Seems a shame to throw this out, but I have plenty at home, and you girls probably "

"Don't need it." Katie peers into the back of the kitchen cabinet. "This one's finished. Thank God."

"There are seven more just like it, and that's not even scratching the surface. Then, there are nine closets and the pantry." I close my burning, swollen eyes. Why hadn't I insisted that Mother start this procedure after Dad died?

Katie rests a hand on my shoulder. "Jen and I will help you as much as we can, Mom."

The next cabinet holds row upon row of empty glass condiment jars. I sigh so long, it amazes me.

Each morning brings a renewed commitment to finish. Save the meaningful and valuable. Sort the belongings to pass on. Bag the remainder destined for the landfill.

I sit in the third upstairs bedroom. A floral-print loveseat, maple cabinet sewing machine with matching ladder-back chair, layout table, and ironing board are spaced along the pristine white walls. The windows have blinds only, no curtains.

Who would know, looking at it now, that this had once been the hallowed mausoleum for a fallen hero? Unchanged for years. Door opened only for infrequent dusting and vacuuming. I slipped silently in at night. Sat in the middle of the ruffled canopy bed amidst mounds of stuffed bears. Secretly touched my sister's prized possessions. Sometimes wore the delicate frilly clothes. I needed to feel close to the one person who was the other half of me.

Once my brother was born, we had moved into a house with enough rooms to accommodate the expanded family. Stormy's and my personalities clashed on such a regular basis, sharing a bedroom would have been unthinkable. Mother Teresa and Attila the Hun as roommates. Yin and Yang with a dotted dividing line drawn down the middle of the room. Pastel, peaceful shades and lacy frou-frou on one side. Earth tones and gathering thunderhead clouds on the other.

The change to this room had come suddenly, a few years after Stormy died. I arrived home from college one weekend to find my sister deleted from the upstairs room. My mother had finally decided to reclaim the space for the living. No matter. My memory held a preserved picture of the space Stormy Gale had occupied. Over the years, my lair evolved, changing with current interests and whims, but my twin's teenage room remained frozen in time.

When I close my eyes, I can recall the exact moment when Stormy left. The football field. Noise cluttering the cool night air. Dressed in monotone gray and black, I sat on the bleachers behind my parents. On the sidelines, Stormy hopped around, blonde-haired beauty teen queen in her cheerleader outfit.

"You look like you have a pogo stick stuck up your butt," I told her every chance I got. Stormy disliked it when I said that. "How can you be a *cheer*leader? It's such a waste of perfectly good energy."

"Poor, poor Sunny." She'd smile and pat my head. "If you'd crawl out of the books for even a second, you'd see how much fun you're missing."

I saw her pitch forward on the field. Thought she was pulling some sort of joke. Stormy wouldn't just trip and fall. Not with her grace and style. The squad gathered around her, laughing. What was she up to? That Stormy!

She didn't move. I saw one dark-haired girl shake my twin's shoulder and gesture toward the others. Adults were called over. My parents stood, unconcerned at first, then bounded down the bleachers toward the tight cluster surrounding their fallen daughter. Bradley and I held hands, unsure of what to do, until he tugged me from the spot where I was rooted.

A weak blood vessel in her brain, they told us later. A blister. A bubble bursting. Instantly, Stormy Gale Adams was no more. Just like that. Poof.

I insisted on being called by my second name after that. People didn't really understand. I was part of a broken set. Stormy and Sunny. Salt and Pepper. Night and Day.

Blue suits me better, anyway. Not the blue of clear, sunny skies as my mother had intended. Instead, the deep blue of murky hurricane seas. Full of hidden rocks and danger. Moody, yet strong and eternal. Able to withstand any onslaught.

Bradley pokes his head in the door. "You coming along in here, Sis?"

"Good as it gets. At least the girls were with me to finish the kitchen. That was a chore. They're making a charity drop-off run before they have to leave for the airport."

"Jack and I are almost done with Dad's shop and the storeroom. I wish now that Mom had let us tackle it after he died. It wouldn't have left so much to do now."

"Had that same thought. Guess it made her feel good having it out there. Like she did with this room for a few years."

He nods. "How long are you and Jack planning on staying?"

"Another day or so. My patients are covered, but it would be nice to have some time at home to regroup before I dive back in. Jack has plenty of annual leave with the State, so he's in no urgent rush. Still, I'd like to finish packing up so that the house will be ready to go on the market. The more we do now, the less we have to come back for later on."

"I'll call Stacey and tell her I'll be staying on, then. Between the three of us, we should be able to knock it out by the weekend."

Bradley blows a kiss across the room and I catch it in midair and pat it onto my cheek.

"Nice catch for an old broad," he throws over his shoulder on the way down the stairs. Too bad I don't have a pillow to pitch at him.

An hour later, I near the bottom of the closet, having peeled layers of boxes from the endless stacks. One cracked leather suitcase remains. A pink satin ribbon ties it together. I tug and grunt to hoist it from the floor, and drag it into the center of the sewing room. *Stormy Gale Adams* is written in black marker across the side in my mother's careful script.

When a person is lost to you, you never forget them. My sister lurks just under my skin, a filmy dreamlike layer beneath my epidermis. She comes to mind often in my mental health practice. I unconsciously label new patients as *SGs* or *non-SGs*.

Over the years, I had seen plenty of tormented SGs (Stormy Gales), my private nomenclature for people with too much starry positivity for their own good. Being a realist by nature, I can't imagine a life with a constant *Rebecca of Sunnybrook Farm* outlook. Sensing the dark underbelly of human existence, I had somehow managed to avoid the pitfalls of blind optimism. The SGs I counseled crashed earthward when the world around them failed to comply.

Bad things happen. Also, good things. Best to live somewhere between with a healthy respect for both.

If Stormy had survived to tackle adulthood, would she have continued to bounce along in her oblivious happiness? Would she have been yet another clinically depressed woman in search of answers to unfathomable riddles?

Had she ever, once, had a moment of doubt?

I remove the frayed pink ribbon and unlatch the clasp. I take a deep breath and open the suitcase. A delicate aroma, a faint trace of honeysuckle cologne, washes over me, as if the angel of my dead sister floats overhead. I close my eyes.

"Mom, you okay?" My youngest daughter Jennifer steps into the room.

I open my eyes. Swipe moisture from the corners. "Sure."

"You're kind of pale. Why don't you stop for a while? Katie and I picked up some burgers from that little restaurant on the corner uptown. Maybe you need to eat."

"You bought food with all we'll have to throw out, anyway?"

Jennifer wrinkles her nose. "Really. I can't eat another bite of that stuff."

"It *is* a bit over the top Southern, isn't it?" I pause. "Mr. Bill does make some great cheeseburgers." Heaven knows, I had eaten my share over the years. No matter how far we moved from my hometown, city eateries were no match for a fresh-ground, Angus real beef, hand-slammed grease-burger. And those *fries*. Don't forget those spicy fries oozing with chili and cheese.

My daughter leans forward. "What you got there?"

I pull the suitcase toward me. "Just some things your grandmother packed up."

Jennifer shrugs. "Sure you don't want Katie and me to stay on and drive back with you and Dad?"

"No, honey. You need to get home before you miss any more work. We only have a few more things to go through."

"Well, okay. Listen. Take a break. Seriously, Mom. You should eat."

Is this where it starts, the subtle shift of power?

"You go on down, Jen. I'll sift through this one last case, then I'll join you. Save me some chili cheese fries. If not, your father will eat them all."

Pictures fill the suitcase. Stormy in her cheerleader outfit, hundred-watt smile beaming at the camera. Stormy and me beside the azalea bush in the front yard, dressed in Easter finery. Stormy showing every tooth in her head. My face, granite. Memories flood faster than I can contain. Tears blur my vision.

At the bottom, I find a diary. Pale pink and seafoam green with a tarnished silver clasp. Unlocked, open and unguarded, like my sister. Feeling as if I'm invading her private realm but unable to stop, I open the diary to the last page. Stormy didn't get that about me.

"Read the entire book, Sunny! Don't just skip to the final chapter. You'll miss the good parts!"

In my way of thinking, the last page told me whether or not I wanted to bother with the rest.

"Let's see if *this* is worth the time," I mutter to Stormy's spirit.

The final entry is dated October 3, 1972. The day she died. My pulse stutters. The moisture leaves my mouth.

Sometimes, the curly script reads, *I wish I could be more like Sunny.*

34: Perspective

From where I stand
Looking up
The rainbow is a swipe of Red Orange Yellow Green
Blue Indigo Violet.
The ends rest on faded lore of little people and pots of gold.

From where you stand
Looking down
The rainbow is a solid path beneath your feet.
The ends rest on pinpoints as concrete as bridge piers.

From where I stand
Looking up
The rainbow is an illusion,
Flecks of water bending light.

From where you stand
Looking down
I am an illusion,
Spirit woven into the remembered shape of a friend.

I lift my hand, trusting you can see.
You lift your hand, trusting I can see.
And the rainbow shines for us both.

35: Still, Wonder

Dan Davis hobbles to his secret place. The uneven terrain and steep downhill slope make his descent difficult. In one hand, he grasps a walking stick of weathered oak. He resists using a cane; that would make him feel officially old. But a good, sturdy walking stick is another matter; every woodsman requires a little extra balance from time to time.

One of the loyal mutts, a mixed breed named Spam, forges ahead, his shaggy reddish-golden tail held high, nose to the ground. Frequently, he jerks to one side or the other following pools of scent.

Dan slowly lowers to a section of fallen oak tree, a remnant of a several seasons' past hurricane. The wood accepts his weight without complaint.

A few feet farther down, a small natural spring bubbles, its brand of tinkling music adding to the whisper of fall breezes through the canopy of oak, sycamore, pine, and hickory. Dan lifts his nose to sniff the mix of musty earth and the blended perfume of the trees.

"When I die," he announces, "I'm going to lift straight away from my old, worn out body and fly into the deep green of the nearest forest."

Spam trots up, licks one of his extended hands, and sits at his feet. The two stare straight ahead for a moment.

"You realize, don't you boy, I know the names of every tree on this property."

The yellow dog tilts his head to study him.

"Take that one there." He motions to a shortleaf pine tree whose circumference would exceed the grasp of two grown men. "George. That tree is named George."

He leans back his head and laughs. Spam stands, tail wagging.

"I used to love to pull that one on Hattie when she was little. She fell for it every time."

Dan remembers his baby daughter, now grown and living forty miles away in Tallahassee. Daddy's little girl. Hattie thought her father knew everything there was to know, especially when it came to the land.

Once on a family vacation, he told her that the mountain cows had legs shorter on one side than the other to keep them from falling over while they grazed the hillside. His wife, Tillie, had jabbed him hard in the side, shaking her head. Then he proceeded to further educate his child. Those same cows had to walk clean around the hill they were on to return home to the barn in the evenings. Couldn't they just turn around? Oh no! The two longer legs would be in the wrong place, and they would surely topple over and over until they reached the bottom of the hill.

Pity that children had to grow up and realize their father wasn't all-knowing, all-seeing. Now his daughter and son often correct him, respectfully, when he repeats a story too many times to consider it accidental. He is the bumbling, uncertain child since his stroke. Even fully recovered, he is clucked over as if he were the bad offspring in a clutch of biddies. Tillie and the two children hover around him, watchful for any pain or indication of impending trouble. It is love. But often he feels the confinement of such love. His spirit is tired. Oh so tired. More and more, he longs for the freedom of release.

Dan gazes into the overhead canopy, then outward through the dense old-growth forest. Above all the living things on his acreage, he holds the trees in highest regard. Even in death, trees serve a purpose: nesting sites for woodpeckers, hunting perches for red-tailed hawks. The tall hardwoods felled by high winds or weakened by disease or lightning strikes provide horizontal shelter and food for beetles, worms, and armies of insects. Their desiccated hulls offer shade for rattlesnakes seeking relief from the sun and a smooth sitting place for an old woodsman.

No need to worry about snakes today. The recent late October cold snap sends them slithering into underground burrows, often shared with gopher turtles. Necessity makes for odd roommates.

The woods provide solace, broken only by the occasional snap of a twig or the wind song through the branches.

Dan thinks about purpose.

Does he have one at this point? Seventy-nine years old, ten years past his father's age at death.

He has loved one woman for nearly fifty-six years, raised two children to successful adulthood, suffered the loss of a middle child, owned a small business, run a farm, and overseen the Davis land. He has built a farm house, an in-ground pool, a workshop, and a smoke-house: all with his two once-strong hands and without the aid of written blueprints. He fashioned a riverboat cruiser from bare lumber and nails, where he and the young family spent many summers on the Apalachicola River and Inland Waterway from Apalachicola to Panama City, Florida. Later when the Davis clan entered the camping craze, Dan built a small box trailer base for a canvas tent, long before the commercial world imagined pop-up tent campers.

"A rich man buys ready-made," Dan repeats his motto, "A poor man invents and makes do with what he has available to him."

Because of this, the family has seldom gone lacking.

All along, Dan Davis serves the purpose of provider, husband and lover, father, and friend. Since the stroke and subsequent heart issues, he wonders what purpose is left.

Dan recalls the night of his stroke. Tillie reclined on the couch in the den, pretending to watch the evening news. Her eyes were closed, and her breathing deep and even. Dan sat in his favorite brown chair, his feet propped on an ottoman, the remote in one hand.

The left side of his head near the crown felt odd, like when one of the kids faked breaking a raw egg over his head. A pop, then the broken yolk running down his scalp. He willed his breathing to stay calm.

"Tillie?"

The word came out molasses-slow, twisted, and garbled.

His wife, a light sleeper, sat up, her eyebrows knit together. "Dan?"

The sentences were there, but his brain refused to force his mouth to form words. A fine line of saliva slid from the sagging right corner of his open lips. His right arm went heavy and numb.

Tillie grabbed the phone headset and dialed Margie, the nearest neighbor, a retired nurse. Within minutes, Margie and her husband John rushed into the den.

"You need to phone the ambulance, Tillie." Margie's trained voice was calm. "Dan may be having a stroke."

A hospital stay. The discovery of an underlying heart condition. Months of slow, agonizing recuperation at home.

The right side— arm, leg, mouth— refused to obey without coaxing. Tillie sewed an oversized adult bib to capture the food and liquid he dropped as he relearned how to guide his hand to his mouth. Often, he choked on the smallest portions. Mealtime stretched out. No more dash and run. Dan laughed at his feeble attempts and poked fun to hide the embarrassment.

"Your daddy is weaker," Dan overheard Tillie whisper to Hattie one evening in the kitchen. "He's going downhill fast. I live with him. I see it more and more each day."

"He seems to be walking better, Mama."

"Yes, but he can't drive. He really wants to, so badly. I let him a couple of times on the way home from town when there were no cars around. He steers to the right. We've run off the shoulder each time. He lets me do all the driving now. Scared him. Scared me!"

"It's going to get better, Mama. Daddy's so determined."

Dan heard Tillie sigh. The sound told him that tears gathered at the corner of her blue eyes. He hated Tillie's tears and lived to avoid them, especially the ones he caused.

Now six months after the stroke, his speech is almost normal, he can eat without a full body drape, and he drives the ATV to the fishpond, then farther into the woods to his secret spot. Clipped to his shirt pocket is a walkie-talkie. Tillie insists. If she calls to no reply, she will rush in his old pick-up to find him. The electronic tether is at once comforting and annoying.

Dan is pleased with the slow progress, but his life holds no more surprises. No more delight. In His infinite wisdom, perhaps God has decided that Dan Davis is sliding toward Home with such momentum, he's beyond expending any more divine consideration.

Spam stands, his ears flexed forward. The tip of his nose twitches and the nostrils flare.

"What do you see, boy?" Dan whispers.

A bobcat steps from a thicket of underbrush no more than thirty feet in the distance. Freezes. Its piercing eyes study the human and canine with keen interest.

Dan inhales sharply. In all of the years he has wandered these familiar woods, he has never seen one of the elusive wild felines. The cat is lanky, lean, and taller than the domesticated house variety. Dan does not think *cute and cuddly*, looking at the wiry animal.

"Easy, boy." Dan rests a hand on the dog's flank. Spam's muscles tremble beneath his touch.

As quickly as it appears, the bobcat vanishes back into the magical realm from whence it came.

A tingle lifts deep within Dan's spirit and spreads through his worn body. For the first time in months, he feels fully alive.

36: Gift of Flowers

Suspended on a blue grosgrain ribbon from the front glass door of the Blossoms Flower Shop, a brass bell trills. Lucy Gray glances up from the Get-Well arrangement on the workbench in front of her.

Standing before her is the scrawniest young black girl she has ever seen.

"May I help you?" Lucy's voice: professional, friendly.

"Yes 'um. I hope you can."

Lucy wipes the dampness from her hands onto a blue-checkered apron. "You need to order an arrangement? Or I have some nice daisies in fresh today, if what you need is a little bouquet."

The girl's features contort into a frown, then ease back into a smile. "No 'um. I don't need flowers. Thank you all the same."

Lucy notes the thin cotton dress, neatly pressed, but faded and worn wisp-thin in spots. She can't be that old, fourteen or fifteen at the most.

"What I need, Ma'am, is a job." When the girl smiles, her face sends off rays of shine that urge Lucy to smile in return.

"Well now. I don't know . . ."

"I can do anything," the girl adds. "Clean, run errands, take out the garbage. You just say the word."

"What is your name, first of all?"

"Minnie Mae. I just moved here from near Chipley. My sister cleans houses. She moved here a while back."

"Well, Minnie Mae. I'm Lucy, Lucy Gray. Pleased to make your acquaintance."

Minnie Mae tries to keep shock from jumping all over her face. Most white folks, especially the ladies in this town, aren't altogether friendly, not in a real type of way. Some are polite enough, but not like it came from anyplace deep. Others are downright hostile, or worse, ignore her like she is lower than the dirt beneath their feet.

"Pleased to meet you, too." Minnie Mae flashes the high wattage smile again.

"Here's my problem, Minnie Mae . . . or do you prefer just Minnie?"

Imagine that! Someone asking her what she prefers. Minnie Mae pinches herself on the arm to see if she is dreaming. "Minnie Mae. Mama always said it made me not sound so plain, with the two names together."

Lucy Gray bites back a laugh. The child certainly has spunk, especially to march into a white business establishment and ask for employment. Lucky for Minnie Mae, Lucy doesn't share the basic dislike and distrust of some of her fellow merchants.

"As I was saying, here's my problem. I don't require any help at the moment." She gestures to the cramped florist shop. Most of the room is taken up with ceiling-high coolers. The rest is crammed with pots, shelves of glassware, wire candelabras, and metal filing cabinets. Other than faded flower posters, a 1948 calendar is the only wall decoration.

"It's just me, here. But if I did need a person, I would be happy to consider your offer, Minnie Mae."

The girl's expression fades, reminding Lucy of the way funeral roses droop in the relentless summer sun.

"That's all right. Thank you, anyway, Miz Lucy."

For several days, the image of Minnie Mae's sweet smile stays with Lucy like the vague memory of spring flower scent: pleasant, soft, and lingering.

Can I afford to hire help? Do I really need anyone here, just yet?

The answers to both questions is no, absolutely not.

Do I want someone to share the increasing load of orders? Wouldn't it be nice to have someone nearby to talk to, someone to lean on just a bit?

The answers to these questions is yes, without a smidgen of doubt.

Lucy's husband, there's another story. Once jovial, robust, and leaning a bit toward pudgy around the midsection, Paul Gray is sickly and requires more and more. Lucy struggles with the role of caretaker.

No siblings can show up to help her. No family will rush in to assume part of the yoke of illness. Simply, there is no one but her and her husband. Soon Paul will require a sitter during the hours she spends in the cheerful company of flowers and ferns.

Lucy finally understands her mother's words, though she doesn't necessarily endorse them: *life has a way of beating you down.*

Instead Lucy imagines herself as a strong-stemmed black-eyed Susan, its yellow face turned to the light. A heavy downpour can hammer the plant to the ground. With a little time and the gentle warmth of the sun, the stem rebounds, and the bloom, though tattered, seeks the heavens.

She always bounces back, too. Lately, a bit slower.

"Will you look there!" Lucy extends a shaky arm and points up. The summer cloudburst has passed, leaving blue laundered skies with a scattering of cottony cumulus clouds.

Minnie Mae shifts forward. The worn willow seat of the porch rocker protests as she leans to see the sky beyond the roof's deep overhang. A perfect rainbow glistens overhead.

"It's a full arch, too." The smile lines around Minnie Mae's mouth deepen. "You don't often see a whole one like that."

Lucy studies her old friend. The familiar face, now etched with telltale signs of a life fully felt, still offers the same brilliant smile of the sassy fifteen-year-old of years past.

"What do you suppose it means?" Lucy tugs a crocheted wrap tighter around her shoulders. The air is warm and humid, but Lucy is often chilled.

"Means God's promise not to send another killing great flood to wipe clean the world," Minnie Mae answers.

Above her many attributes, Minnie Mae's unflinching faith shines the brightest.

Lucy chuffs. "I think there's a pot of gold at one end. Which end is it at, you suppose?"

Minnie Mae crinkles her brows together. "Never dwelt on pots of gold, Miz Lucy. Never got something for nothing in this life."

Lucy nods. "True enough. But, every now and then, magic happens."

A secret nudges at Lucy's awareness, one she has hoarded the last few years. Her attorney possesses her Last Will and Testament, a document sharing her estate between her church and Minnie Mae Blue. The sum is not great, but more than enough to help her friend's grandchildren with college and leave a small nest egg for Minnie Mae.

No other person, save for her late husband, has ever proved as true and faithful. A handful of neighbors nod good day and a few church members stop to inquire after her health. It is Minnie Mae Blue who delights her with fresh-cut flower bouquets, steaming casseroles, and hours of comfortable companionship and easy conversation.

Many in the small town would not understand how two women of different colors and backgrounds could share such a bond. Over the years, the two have laughed, cried, rejoiced over the birth of Minnie Mae's children and grandchildren, and toiled long hours side by side in the cramped florist shop. After Minnie Mae opened her own shop, Blue Moon Flowers, the two remained close, often sharing the work load on special occasions.

Lucy's sister-in-law has only recently started to hover, circling like a buzzard sniffing fresh roadkill. The woman rarely came around when Lucy's husband was alive, much less when he lay dying. Now she casually drops by, a package of store-bought cookies in hand, under the guise of family goodness and concern.

What a shock she is in for! Lucy's lips curl upward with the thought. *An ironclad will with no provisions for a stingy, self-promoting sister-in-law.*

Minnie Mae returns to the porch with two tall glasses of iced tea, hands her one, and settles back into the rocker. Lucy wonders how she missed her going inside. Anymore, life has a lot of unexplained holes.

"You sure are happy, Miz Lucy."

"You have a way of rejuvenating me, Minnie Mae."

"Glad I have such a profound effect on you." The black woman takes a long sip of tea and studies the rainbow. "I thank the Good Lawd every single day for my eyes. Just look at the colors in that 'bow, will you? God outdone hisself on that one."

"The red is the exact shade of Valentine roses, long-stemmed ones," Lucy states.

"That's zinnia orange if I've ever seen it," Minnie Mae adds.

"Daffodil is the yellow." Lucy grins. Often over the years, she and Minnie Mae have spoken the language of flowers.

"The green is leather leaf fern."

Lucy tilts her head. "Could be ivy."

"Blue . . ." Minnie Mae rests a finger on her chin. "That's a stumper." She turns to face Lucy. "Why you reckon there aren't more blue flowers, I mean *really* blue?"

Lucy's thin shoulders rise and lower. "Maybe because there's already so much blue in the heavens. Flowers would be hard-pressed to compete."

"Good a reason as any."

Lucy continues, "Indigo. There's a hard one, too. My memory for flower names is not what it was."

"Skip over it, then. We can come back. Purple. That's iris, for sure."

Lucy jabs a bony finger in the air. "Or statice. Deep, deep purple."

The two women imagine the rainbow as a line of cut flowers plugged into a ribbon arrangement stretching across the late summer sky. They rock in comfortable silence, accompanied by the occasional high-pitched screech of a cicada and the whoosh of a passing car.

"You seem in a fine mood this afternoon, Miz Lucy," Minnie Mae comments after a few moments.

"I had a revelation this morning."

Minnie Mae slaps the chair arm lightly. "Do tell!"

"I realized I'm not going to die young."

The small black woman halts the momentum of the rocker and stares over at her friend. "I suppose that's a fair statement, seeing as how you're nigh to eighty-two."

"Eighty-three. But who's counting."

Minnie Mae's laughter stirs Lucy's humor and the two chortle.

Minnie Mae dabs at the joy tears gathered in the corners of her eyes. "And was this a concern of yours?"

Lucy draws a wobbly breath. Another belly laugh threatens. "Used to be, I worried over it. But I realized it's one less thing I have to worry over now."

"You a card, Miz Lucy. You surely a card." Minnie Mae shakes her head.

Lucy notes how the once-thick ebony curls have begun to blend with traces of white. Time is reshaping and recoloring both of them. For a while, they rock and sip tea, content in easy company.

"You ever worry about dying, Minnie Mae?"

A pensive expression flits across the black woman's features. "Not so much, no. I don't have the leisure to worry over such. Too busy working my flowers and making do." Her deep brown-eyed gaze rests on her friend. "Do you?"

Lucy sweeps a hand through the air. "Not as such. I think death might be a welcomed relief, actually. No more aching bones and joints, no more sleepless nights, no more being this dang old."

Minnie Mae leans over and rests a hand over her elderly friend's. Lucy notices the difference between Minnie Mae's strong, confident fingers and her own. Hands that had once flown in circles around an arrangement, plugging in flowers and greenery with mindless speed, are now gnarled and claw-like with arthritis.

"Don't you fret, Miz Lucy. I'll be around to see you through."

Tears well in the old woman's eyes. "You always have been." Lucy's gaze falls to the wooden porch slats beneath the rockers. "I do worry, just a little, about who's going to keep my plot tidy."

Minnie Mae smiles. One thing about Lucy Gray: she loves clean and tidy. Cleanliness and organization have served her well over the years. Minnie Mae mirrors the same in her shop and in the friendship garden behind her small house.

"I 'spect it will stay picked up. Wouldn't a weed dare grow within ten feet of a sainted florist such as yourself."

Lucy waves a hand. "Goodness you do go on so!" Her gaze shifts to the sky. "The rainbow has faded. How sad. I wish it could last on and on."

Minnie Mae stands and reaches for the empty tea glasses. "It's the memory of a thing makes it last. Now, I'm going to warm you up a nice bowl of my turnip greens. I picked 'em fresh from my garden and cooked them up this morning. I brought a piece of cornbread hoecake to go along. It's bound to put a bloom on those cheeks of yours."

Minnie Mae steps through the screened door as Lucy calls over her shoulder, "What it will do is give me the toots the rest of the day and well into the night."

Minnie Mae's deep musical laughter echoes behind her, a sound as magical and pure as a rainbow.

37: Zelda Files

Sergeant Rich Burns pulls away from the curb. On his way to the call, he reminisces about the first time he met Zelda Ellen Bunch. He had been a rookie then, fresh out of the police academy off State Highway 90, east of Quincy, Florida. Why they always sent the wet-behind-the-ears officers on the crank old-lady calls was a mystery. Certainly, nothing in the academy training manuals quite prepared him for Miz Zelda.

Rich shakes his head, remembering how his fellow officers had guffawed at his carefully penned report, complete with descriptions of the purloined belongings and a pencil rendering of the alleged crime scene. When Chief Turnbull plopped a timeworn, ten-inch-thick, accordion folder onto the conference table, the room erupted into fresh fits of hearty laughter. Rich's report, by far the most detailed, was added to the police masterpiece fondly dubbed *The Zelda Files*.

He recalls vividly the first call to the white frame house on Bonita Avenue. Zelda's modest ranch-style home with its half-acre lot bordered the rear of Betsy Lou Witherspoon's expansive property. The location provided irrefutable proof, at least in Zelda's mind, of the CIA and FBI's extensive meddling in her affairs, specifically her laundry. The government was interested in the goings-on at the Witherspoon mansion, and Zelda, as the closest neighbor, bore the fallout ripples of their espionage. Maybe Betsy Lou Witherspoon was a Russian spy.

As the rookie cop stepped through Zelda Bunch's wooden screened front door into a ten by ten living room, the aroma of hot baked sweetbread filled his nose. Briefly, his long-dead maternal grandmother flashed into his consciousness. The sensation of being coddled deep in pillow-soft bosoms suspended beneath folds of a cotton flower-printed housedress. A tantalizing scent of the vanilla extract Mamaw Adams dabbed as perfume behind her fleshy earlobes.

Rich smiled, remembering.

"You caught wind of my teacakes, did you?" Zelda's voice had snapped him to the present.

She stood barely five feet tall, a squat, square woman with broad sassy hips and ample padding on her arms, legs, and bosoms. Gray-streaked mousy brown hair was piled haphazardly atop her head. In her mid-seventies, her face had taken on the slack-jowl appearance of a woman many years her senior. Vibrant blue eyes shone beneath heavy lids. Her only attempt at decoration was the plum-red rouge painted high on her cheeks.

"Bless Pete. Don't just stand there. You might as well come all the way in." She narrowed her gaze. "You're a new 'un. I can tell by the way you carry yourself, with your shoulders all squared and your legs splayed so your gun belt won't pull your pants clean off. Law enforcement hasn't dragged you down. Not just yet."

She pointed to the booklet in his left hand. "Brought your report pad, I see. Glad of that. Sometimes, you new fellers don't remember diddly if you don't put it on paper, right off."

Zelda eyed him, as if appraising a cow at auction. "You got a familiar look about you." She focused on his name tag. "You're J. B. Burn's boy, ain't you?"

"Yes Ma'am."

"Well, I've been knowing your folks many a year. Reckon you can't be all bad, cut from good cloth like you were. Come on back to the kitchen. I was about to take my cakes from the oven."

Rich sat at the aluminum and aqua Formica kitchen table as Zelda unfurled intricate theories on governmental conspiracy and international espionage. Though the lucid reasons for any federal agency requiring pilfered pieces of a North Florida woman's wardrobe escaped him, Rich dutifully recorded the details. An hour and four teacakes later, he departed with a three-page written account and a sketch of Zelda Bunch's back yard. Without a doubt, the call was the most unusual cry for public service he would experience in all of his years of police work.

How many times had he repeated the scenario? Rich had long since lost count. At first, Zelda's complaints were confined to the days of early summer when local school children with too much time and too little social conscience took pride in the midnight panty raids. As Zelda aged, so did the frequency of phone calls to the Police Department.

Sensing the old woman's gradual decline, Rich often stopped by. Always, Zelda would have "just happened" to bake a batch of homemade oatmeal cookies, a fresh fruit pie, or a multi-layered cake thick with icing. The unlikely friends would sit over sweet tea in the warm months and hot strong coffee in the cooler weather, discussing local affairs and world events.

The alien invasion is a recent spin. The first time the aliens visited her back yard, all Zelda Bunch witnessed was the aftermath evidence: tiny marks in the dew-damp dirt beneath the twin wire clotheslines stretched like taut guitar strings between a sweetgum and oak tree, and three missing pairs of size twelve ladies Fruit of The Loom underdrawers.

Rich leans back and pats his belly. "So Miz Zelda. You've gotten my curiosity aroused. You've explained a hundred times in the past twenty-four years why the government is interested in you, or were . . . but, aliens? How did you reach this conclusion?" He dabs a few stray coconut flakes from the corners of his mustache.

Zelda grins. "And you a police man!" She tisks. "This is one you ought to be able to figure."

Rich raises one eyebrow and cocks his head to the side. "Enlighten me. Please." He opens his notepad and clicks his pen. Zelda won't settle until he records what she calls *proper investigatory quotes.*

"No human footprints in the sand beneath the clothesline. Just . . ." She whips a fleshy hand through the air. "Whoosh! Clothes disappearing off my line like magic!"

He suppresses a chuckle. "What did they take this time?"

"One Playtex Cross Your Heart brassiere, size 48 double-D, two of my best slips, one white and one powder blue, and a pair of pink nylon lace-trimmed panties, my Sunday best."

"What you figure aliens want with your undergarments?"

"That," she points a finger in the air, "is as plain as the nose on your face, young Richard. They're getting ready to appear amongst us."

"You've lost me."

"I've seen drawings of them on the TV shows about folks that have been taken up into their ships, poked and prodded and what all. They're bug-eyed with big ole heads. Ain't no way in Hades they'd pass for one of us."

She leans forward and narrows her eyes. "They're using my underwear, and God knows how many other folks' pilfered clothes, to figure out ways to make a costume they can wear so as to blend in with human beings."

Rich closes his eyes, inhales, exhales, and hesitates a beat before opening them and responding. "Another conspiracy, then? Suppose they have a pair of my boxer shorts, too?"

"You can wipe that smirk right off your mug, Mister. How many folks keep a good accounting of their private garments? Do you? Can you tell me, to the last pair, how many socks and drawers you own? Or your wife Carol, for that matter. Reckon she knows?"

"Never thought to take a census, Miz Zelda."

She huffs and props crossed arms over her ample belly. "There! You see? They could be stealing your family's belongings right from under your very nose."

Rich smiles. "Certainly would explain why socks go missing every time Carol does a load of laundry."

Zelda pushes up from the table with a grunt and shuffles over to pick up the coffee carafe. "Warm up for you?"

Rich slides the half-full cup across the kitchen table. "Sure."

After she tops off both mugs and returns the carafe to its warmer, Zelda slides into her chair with another grunt. "Let me ask you something."

Rich takes a loud swill of the fragrant black coffee. So much better than the burned mess back at the station. "Sure."

"What lights you up?"

"Beg pardon?"

199

"What lights you up? You know, what just grabs you up and makes your heart beat faster?" She clenches both fists and does a little full-body wiggle.

He shrugs. "I'da know."

She flat-palms the table. "Oh come on now. You gotta have something that puts a sparkle in your eyes."

"Carol? The twins?"

"Why you asking me? You act like you ain't so sure."

Rich glances at his watch, closes the pad, and slips it and the pen into his uniform chest pocket. "I really have to get on to the station here in a minute or two."

The old woman reaches across the table to place a hand on his muscular forearm. "This is important stuff."

He settles back into the chair. "All right. I'm listening."

"When you get to be my age, Richard, you finally figure things out. What's important, and what's not. Here's how I see it. If you have even one thing that makes your imagination quicken, that takes you away from all the everyday worries." She winks. "Alters your reality, as they say on Star Trek. That is what will keep you satisfied while you're on this side of the dirt."

"Good theory, Miz Zelda. So, what's this *thing* for you?"

"Mystery." She spreads her arms wide. "Even thinking for one teeny tiny second that there's still mystery left in this tired old world we live in."

"Is that why thinking about the connection between aliens and underwear gets you going?"

Zelda tilts back her head and laughs hard. "That and watching you trying to put it all down in police words."

38: Jeremiah is a Watchdog

The mailman got it yesterday. Yep, Jeremiah bit him on the butt. Right. On. The. Butt. Didn't so much as shred those gosh-awful Bermuda shorts he takes to wearing come summertime. Nope, but he shore drew blood, Jeremiah did. Uh-huh. Did. Reckon I'll get sued over it, or at least have to pony up for a new pair of shorts.

Last week it was that sweet old lady that don't have all her marbles and the ones she has left bounce up against each other, or maybe her dentures ain't fittin' right and that's what I hear clacking. That '72 Buick of hers gets dragged into my impound yard at least once a month. She only goes to the grocery store and back, but she pulls up wherever she takes a mind to, leaves it behind, and then I get the call to go get the car.

I got to where I don't charge her a thin dime. Nope. We all gonna get old one day. Except Jeremiah. That dang dog's goin' on fourteen, half deaf, can't see out one eye and blind in the other. He nipped the old gal on the knee. Sure did. Man, did it bleed! I wanted to call the doc, but she said no, that her son would learn of how the car had ended up at the Go!-Or-Tow! again, and that he'd take it away, or worse, he'd put her in one of them old folks homes. She'd surely die there, I do believe. I patched her up with near half a box of bandages.

But back to Jeremiah.

I figured him being a mutt, he'd make a good watchdog, keep the crackheads off my lot, right? Oh hell no. He's done made friends with them. I caught it on those video cameras I had to break down and buy. They slip him a dog bone and he goes from growling to wagging his tail and following them around like they was kin.

And let's talk about that Tomcat that sprays all over the place and struts around like he's boss of the yard. You'd think Jeremiah'd bare what's left of his teeth at least. No siree Bob. The cat backed right up to that speckled pup and pissed a stream. It smelled worse than a skunk for near 'bout three weeks afore it wore off.

I tried everything: a can of Lysol spray, half a bottle of my Old Spice. I even took the old woman's advice and poured tomato juice all over him. All I got was a cat-piss-smelling orange dog for that bit of business.

Still, he's company of sorts, even if he ain't diddly for a watchdog. We sorta took to each other over the years. And I reckon we suit each other. I ain't much to look at anymore either.

39: Precisely When

She doesn't know precisely when the takers vanished
and jewel tone friends sifted through.
From people who called on a flu-fevered evening
to drone without once asking why her voice
crackled like a three-pack smoker's,
To people who listen and kindly offer to kick her behind
when everything sucks and she threatens to give up her dreams.

Or when the questionable lovers evaporated.
From people who delighted in conquest
and whispered intrigue and drama,
To one Beloved who feeds her before she grows cranky
and sits for hours in a faux leather chair while she whines after surgery.
One Beloved who loves both her *and* her evil twin.

Or when her body and mind shifted
and a different person took its place.
From a perky chest, high and round
and tanned lean legs,
To crow's feet and thigh dimples and gravity's hard pull.
To walls lined with sticky notes, forgotten faces and names,
and a phone smarter than she's ever been.

She lifted to a higher orbit.
Adopted a mantle of bemused wisdom
Gleaned the value of having less and laughing more
Embraced a life to enjoy, to exalt.
She doesn't know precisely when.

40: Moving On

Juanita "Nita" Johnson can't exactly recall how or when she started to collect wind chimes. Her faulty memory is the problem, not so much for her, but for everyone else it seems. Her only son, Jeremy, is coming much sooner than she wants to think about. Coming to cart her and a handful of belongings off to south Florida. To one of those retirement homes. Just one room and a bathroom. In God-forsaken south Florida, nothing but miles of highways crammed to the gills!

When Jeremy caught wind of his mother's last lapse, he had put his foot down. Hard. Said she didn't need to be driving anymore or even parking, for that matter.

"You're going to end up hurting yourself or someone else, Mama! It's high time you were down here near me."

Wasn't like she had been going far. Just a few miles into town for errands. And what could parking her car and not recalling where the heck it was end up bad for anyone else but herself? Worst case, she could beg a ride home with someone and figure out about the car later. Yes the police had gotten involved this last time, but only for a few minutes. It wasn't like it took up a lot of their time or gas. The officers weren't busy anyway, not in a town the size of hers. Most times, the nice fella who runs the tow service lets her know to come get it and doesn't charge her for the trouble.

"Please, please, dear Lord, if you're listening," she prays daily, "find a way to keep me from having to move away from here."

The old rickety wooden house isn't much, but it's hers. One corner in the second bedroom has termites so bad, she almost fell through the floor. Nita had solved that problem by sliding an empty chest of drawers over the weak spot. If you didn't notice that the chest listed a bit to one side, you'd never realize the peril. Besides it's only her now, what with Bud being dead for five years and Jeremy off in that hell-hole down south.

The worst part, the part she worries over until her head feels sore: her wind chimes can't make the move with her. Last time she counted, there were over fifty, all different shapes and sizes. Most are store-bought, the type made from lengths of metal tubing hung to ring just so. Bud had built one set with his own tools from leftover sections of pipe. Takes a strong wind to get that one to clanging. When it does, the crows rise from her vegetable patch in a frenzied black cloud. At one time, Nita could name off who had given each set to her. What does it matter, really, having to keep up? So much of life is tiring detail.

Some sets are decorated with cutouts of dragonflies, bumble-bees, and frogs. One is attached to a tall garden stake and rings out like the devil busting loose in a stiff breeze. Two are made from some type of pottery and sound like sunbleached bones when they tap together.

Fall is the best time to enjoy the chimes. Dry, cool masses pushing down from the north stir the thick humid air and send it dancing through the treetops. Otherwise, Nita has to set up a pole fan and hang up a few sets in a row on the back porch, just to hear them sing.

No doubt, God will have passels of wind chimes in Heaven. Nita can close her eyes and imagine being lifted up, high above the slow-moving, pillowed clouds. Angels singing on high couldn't possibly sound more beautiful.

Nita's second love is the Weather Channel. Whether she is sitting in the threadbare recliner or making a meager lunch in the tiny kitchen, the small color television is tuned to the latest forecast.

This weekend, the Sunshine State shudders in anticipation of the third hurricane of the season, Ivan. Wasn't Ivan some really bad fellow in history? Yes, Ivan the Terrible. She can't resurrect the historical details. Her failing memory, again. But there has to be some good reason he was called *the terrible*. Certainly, a man didn't get that name by kissing babies, building churches, or sowing goodwill.

Folks question the reason why this year's season seems so intense. One wave of disturbed tropical air after another pours from the coast of Africa, taking dead aim at Florida. The best comment Nita has heard concerns God's punishment for Florida's crazy politicians. Nita highly doubts the Almighty dabbles in such.

This latest hurricane's going to be a humdinger, from what the Weather Channel folks report. Nita can always tell when something big is coming. The commentators' voices go up a couple of pitches and they start calling it "a weather event." Sounds to Nita like something you'd need a ticket to attend. Ivan lingers in the Gulf, churning and debating exactly where he will do his dirty business. Most projections have him making a beeline straight for the Panhandle.

"Pack up and go into town to stay at the shelter," her son orders. "I can't leave to come get you, Mama, until after the storm. We're still cleaning up down here from the last one. Under no circumstances, whatsoever, are you to stay in that house!"

Nita huffs. This little country farm house has stood up to storms before, why not now? That last one, Francis, had practically sailed into North Florida right over her head. Still, here she sits.

She wraps her arms across her chest and giggles like a schoolgirl. The wind is going to be delicious!

The day before Hurricane Ivan is to make landfall, Nita awakens well before dawn. She rescues three cardboard boxes from the second bedroom closet and unwraps stored chimes from sheets of yellowing newspaper. Normally only a dozen sets hang from rusty nails around the backyard. In honor of Ivan the Terrible, Nita plans to go all out.

By midmorning, when she finally halts her labors to eat a cold ham biscuit, Nita has located spots for every set of wind chimes she owns. They remind Nita of the icicle garland she used to hang in careful strips on the Christmas trees when Jeremy was a boy. All around the back yard, from the tips of oak limbs to the clothesline poles to the eaves of the house, the chimes hang ready. If breezes can be summoned by sheer will, nature will send a few her way.

She packs the remainder of her clothes in a cracked leather suitcase. No use to put it off any longer. Jeremy will arrive after the storm to cart her away. Prayers had been sent up to Heaven, but to no avail. She should have climbed the ladder in the barn and stood on the roof. Perhaps prayers of such magnitude and passion need to be closer to the sky.

Nita is on the toilet when she hears the roaring commotion. After pulling up her panties and flushing, she trundles to the back screened porch. The sky is an angry purple-gray with rows of thick roiling clouds. The jangle of wind chimes starts at the rear of her property and ripples to the house.

She grabs an aluminum folding chair with a few intact webbed lattices and pushes the back screened door open. It bangs against the side of the house. Nita fights the gale to position her seat in the middle of the yard.

No finer concert has ever been played. Baritone humming echoes from the suspended lead pipes, accompanied by the midrange and high pitches of the smaller chimes. The wind increases. The pace quickens. Nita closes her eyes. She reaches up and releases the tight hair bun and allows her long silver hair to dance wild. When the wind screams, she keeps her eyelids squeezed tight. The chimes sing. Nita Johnson spreads her arms like angel wings.

The tornado from Ivan's feeder bands dips down, sparing the farm house. One massive live oak tree loses its grip and thunders to the earth. The grass fills with tangles of wind chimes.

When Ivan's fury is spent, Ned Turner, two miles south, finds Nita Johnston draped like a clump of fallen Spanish moss across his back-forty fence. An audience of cows stands in a semicircle around her, chewing grass and eyeing the lifeless adornment.

41: The Lurkies

The thing to worry about is the nights.

Daylight pushes away the lurkies. They're still there, hibernating between the shower tiles, like black mold. Got no cure.

Oh for sure.

Everyone calls him Doo-Wop 'cause he dances and sings a bit. Name was Dan Dumont, years back. Dan died when the lurkies got 'im.

Bleach kills the lurkies sometimes. He's seen them curl up like salted garden slugs.

Oh for sure.

Halfway down West Washington Street, Doo-Wop stops and pats his coat pocket. Pill bottle with a splash of bleach, still there, in case he gets caught out. Good. It's two hours before the gloaming time when the lurkies come awake. He'll be long checked back into Unit 13 by then. They give town privileges to those like him, ones not intent on evil. Doesn't mean evil doesn't stalk him.

Oh for sure.

Lurkies don't follow Doo-Wop into the state hospital. The beat of collected unwell scares them off, except in the shower stalls where they still hide, the reason why he bathes in the morning before he checks out for the day. Not like the other patients in there in the evenings. No sir. Not with those lurkies about.

The bleach bottle bumps his leg, weighing down the coat on that side. A man passes by. "Afternoon, Doo-Wop," he says. Doo-Wop dances a step. Pulls a twirl. Takes a bow. Same as he does for anyone who will say his name above a nervous whisper.

Too bad he doesn't have a dog. Like Mr. Bojangles. Someone might write a snappy tune about Doo-Wop, too.

Oh for sure.

Didn't that dog die in that Bojangles' song? Believe so. Guess it's best he doesn't have a dog. Wouldn't want one to die on his account, just to live on in a song. Dogs like Doo-Wop and he likes them. He feeds them treats from the non-bleach pocket.

Lurkies won't come around if a dog licks his hands. Don't know why. Dog slobber ain't bleach.

A woman rushes past, a little girl ahold of her hand. Doo-Wop drops his gaze to the sidewalk like he's studying the cracks for lurkies. The woman herds the sunshine-haired child. Reckon she's scared *he* is a lurkie.

Pity. He would've danced an extra step or two for them, to hear that sparkly girl giggle. All they had to do was say *Doo-Wop*.

Oh for sure.

42: Angel Kisses

Iris enters the assisted living facility's lobby. An elderly woman shoves a fire engine-red, wheeled walker as if she plows a row in muddy Georgia clay. Iris smiles and nods. Many of the residents of Magnolia Manor are familiar. Not this one.

The woman stops. "Well, now. If you don't have the prettiest set of dimples I've ever seen, I'll pay for lying."

"Ma'am?" Iris asks.

"Your dimples. They light up your whole face when you smile. Bet you were a real boy-charmer when you were a young girl."

Iris stops opposite the old woman. "Not really. But thank you for the compliment."

"Marigold Brady." She sticks out a thin, liver-spotted hand. "But everyone calls me Miz Marigold."

"Iris Hampton." She shakes the elderly woman's hand, careful not to squeeze. That, she learned from her grandmother. Arthritic joints aren't made for hearty, bone-crushing grasps.

"Isn't that something? Our mothers both named us after pretty flowers. *Iris* suits you. It's a happy-sounding sort of name. I wouldn't expect someone with those dimples to be named Prudence."

When Miz Marigold smiles, her blue eyes twinkle. With each minor movement, the butterfly pins decorating her denim shirt flash. Several vibrate. "Are you visiting someone here?"

Iris nods. "My grandmother."

"Do I know her?"

"Wilma Gayle Doyle?"

"Ah, yes. Believe she goes by Willie if I'm remembering right. I moved in a little over a month back, so I'm not so sure of names, just yet." Miz Marigold taps her temple. "She's from, is it, Sycamore?"

"Yes, Ma'am. That's my Nana."

"If I'd looked at you a few minutes longer, I could've picked it out. You favor Willie around the eyes. She doesn't have those dimples, though. You must've gotten them from the angels."

"Maybe." Iris likes the idea. No one has ever remotely connected her with angels.

"That, and freckles. Freckles are angel kisses, you know."

Iris nods. "Guess I'd better get to Nana's room. It was nice meeting you, Miz Marigold."

"You bet, honey."

By the time Iris reaches the end of the hall and turns back, the old woman has stopped to talk with another passer-by.

"There's my dimple gal!" Miz Marigold wears a pale blue sweatshirt dotted with a swarm of butterfly pins.

Iris stops in front of the elevator doors. "Good morning, Miz Marigold. How are you today?"

The old woman shrugs. "Best as I can be at my age, I suppose. How's Willie? I haven't seen her down in the dining hall the past couple of days."

"She has some sort of sinus thing," Iris supplies. "I'm bringing her some juice and extra tissues."

When Miz Marigold nods, wings flit in time on her shirt. "Sure hate to hear she's ailing. Give her my regards. I'll add her to my prayer list. Always something going around, this time of year. The weather is changeable. Makes for colds and flu and such."

Iris shifts the packages hanging from the crook of her arm. "I guess. She told me some lady was coughing at the table next to hers. Said that was where she picked it up."

Miz Marigold swishes one thin hand through the air. "Laying blame won't make it go away any faster. Still, I know how she feels. Sometimes I think they should quarantine sick residents. Save the rest of us from it. Old folks have no resistance. Just like babies, we are, for the most part."

Iris reaches for the elevator call button, then pauses. "Miz Marigold, may I ask you something?"

"Sure. If I don't have a good answer, I can make one up." She winks.

"I can't help but notice all of your butterfly pins. Seems like it must get awfully cumbersome, wearing all of them like that. Why don't you wear one or two at a time?"

"Why, honey," the old woman glances down, "I couldn't possibly choose between them. I love them all. Each one holds a memory of the friend who thought enough of me to give it."

"I see. I wasn't trying to tell you what to do. It seems like they might be a bit heavy after a little while."

Miz Marigold pats Iris's forearm. "When you get to be my age, I'm going on ninety-six, you've learned that something you love could never be a burden. Even if it is, you gladly bare it."

Iris finds no words to compete with Miz Marigold's logic. She hits the elevator button.

The old woman rounds the corner from the spacious front parlor as Iris passes by in the hallway.

"Iris! Haven't seen you or your grandmother for a couple of days. Least, I think it's been a couple of days. They tend to run together for me, anymore. Everything okay, is it?"

Iris takes a breath, sighs it out. "Nana is in the hospital, Miz Marigold."

The old woman's lips form a thin line. "Oh, I do hate to hear of it. She's bad off, then? Has to be, to be taken to the hospital."

"Pneumonia."

"The old folks' friend." Miz Marigold mumbles, her gaze far away.

"I don't follow, Miz Marigold. How could pneumonia be a friend?"

Miz Marigold pushes the walker and closes the distance between them. "On account of, it usually is the thing that takes us out of

212

our misery. Know that sounds a bit brash, but it's true, all the same. Old lungs are tired. Can't keep up. Nature finds a way to help us to cross over. So pneumonia becomes a friend."

Iris studies the old woman. Could she have been wrong about her? She always seemed so empathetic.

Miz Marigold reaches over and brushes Iris's arm. "Oh dear. I've offended you. I can tell. Since I've been in my nineties, things don't always come out the way I intend. Never would I wish illness on a person. And certainly not one as lovely as Willie."

"It's okay, Miz Marigold. Really."

Miz Marigold's expression remains troubled.

"It's been nice talking to you, but I really do have to pick up Nana's things and head on back to the hospital." Iris tucks her purse beneath her arm.

"Of course, dear. You go right ahead. You can talk to me any old time. I'm here. Not like I'm going to hop a bus to Vegas."

Miz Marigold sits on the front porch in a pool of sun. The wicker chair protests when Iris plops down beside the old woman.

"You look tired around the eyes," Miz Marigold says.

"I am." Iris drops her purse onto the concrete porch and allows her shoulders to slump. "Seems all I do is race between work, class, the hospital, and Magnolia Manor."

"I was just taking up for you." Miz Marigold points to the cluster of residents beside her. "They say you drive like you have a heavy foot. I told them you have important places to be."

"I do tend to be a bit hurried, most of the time."

"It's just that little car of yours. It's zippy."

"Must be it. Couldn't be the driver." Iris reaches over and pats the old woman's hand. "You look pretty today."

Miz Marigold smooths her white curls with the tips of her fingers. "I'm upright. That's what I can say. But thanks for the high praise." She leans closer to Iris and asks, "What's that pin on your lapel? Is it a butterfly?"

Iris touches her collar. "It's a dragonfly. My best friend gave it to me last year for my birthday."

"What do dragonflies do?"

"Fly around. Eat bugs, I guess."

Miz Marigold glances down at the sea of pins on her cotton blouse. "I prefer butterflies. They're put on earth to do nothing other than be pretty, service the flowers, and make folks smile. How many things can lay claim to that? If I could die and come back as any of God's creations, it would be a butterfly, a bright yellow one, or maybe a tiger-striped swallowtail. I just know that Heaven is full of butterflies, hundreds of them." She raises her hands and flutters the fingers. "I imagine myself— if I end up there, mind you— surrounded by every color and size imaginable. That would be *my* Heaven."

Bird calls echo from the copse of trees at the edge of the parking lot, as if the mere mention of Heaven makes them sing.

"How's your grandmother today, honey?"

"Not so good, Miz Marigold." Iris blinks back tears. "I don't know if she's going to come back to Magnolia Manor, to be honest."

"You've talked this over with your folks?"

"There's just me. My parents died when I was little. Car crash. Nana raised me from the time I was eight."

Miz Marigold nods. "Oh I see. Willie was your mother, then. In all the ways that matter, eh?"

Words form in Iris's mind but can't make it past the constriction in her throat.

"You must have been a comfort to her. To have a granddaughter to share one's later years. What a blessing."

Iris turns to face her. "I wasn't such a good kid. And I was a horrible teenager. Don't know how much comfort I was. Mostly, I gave her grief and gray hair."

"You're here for her now. That's what matters."

"It's like . . . she's just giving up."

"Would you like my take on things?"

"Sure."

"I've lost a lot of friends and family, honey. Many, younger than me when they passed over. Even at its best, living can be tiresome." Miz Marigold's voice grows soft. "When a person's body or mind constantly pains them and their spirit grows weary, it's not giving up so much as waiting for release."

Miz Marigold winces and shifts position. The butterflies quiver. "Somebody like Willie, with a life filled with giving and kindness and the joy of seeing a youngster grow and thrive, might see the one that appears to take her to a place of peace and rest not as a Grim Reaper, but rather as a guiding angel."

43: Similar Snakes

Lizette hates the garden that spans the cleared acre behind the farm-house. Everything about it. She hates the long, dusty rows of powdery brown soil that grinds into her shoes and wedges in the tender flesh between her toes. She despises the biting gnats and mosquitoes that hover menacingly, awaiting a piece of her flesh. Most of all, she dislikes the glare of the early morning sun and the salty trickles of sweat that burn her eyes.

"Go get under the hose, Lizzy," her father says when she complains of the sticky Southern humidity. "Cool off, then it will be easier."

She stomps to the faucet next to the feed shed and gives the metal handle an angry twist.

When there are chilled rows of perfectly pruned vegetables in the IGA uptown, why should she have to toil in the field? It would be so easy to carry them home in those crisp brown grocery bags. She watches rivulets of dirt trail down her arms, then splashes the cool well water across her blistered face. She could stay right here and let the water soothe her tormented body. Fall should come with its first frost and kill the garden. If only she was the child of wealthy parents who wouldn't dream of planting vegetables, much less harvesting them.

There had to be a law, some child labor thing, that her father was breaking. How could you submit a poor eight-year-old girl to the punishment of weeding?

Lizette heaves a sigh heavy enough to crush the squash hills to yellow and green sludge. Her eyes focus on a slender brown rat snake lying half-hidden in the mint patch by the spigot. She kneels and clasps it gently behind the head and holds it up so that she and the snake are eye to eye.

"Things are looking up," she whispers. Snakes are fun, at least the ones that won't kill you. Daddy taught her about their identifying markings, and which ones to leave way alone.

Cradling the snake in her hands, she walks deliberately to where her six-year-old sister Lisa Anne sits cross-legged, transferring tomatoes from a small pail into a larger plastic bucket.

"Lizzy? Stop right there!" Her father plops a bucket laden with lemon-yellow summer squash onto the ground and stares down at her. "Let me see what you have there, young'un."

Lizette shrugs and opens her hands.

"That's what I thought. What exactly are you intending to do with that little snake?"

At the sight of the reptile, Lisa Anne's eyes grow wide. She jumps up and scuttles for cover behind her father. Her sister is such a wiener. She won't touch a lizard, bug, frog, or snake, not if her life depended on it.

Lizette's gaze falls to her feet.

"You weren't planning on scaring your baby sister, now were you? Cause that would not be such a wise notion."

"No Sir."

"Don't let the devil sitting on your shoulder tell you what's what. Listen to the angel on the other shoulder. Always. Go put that snake down where it can go on about its business. The sooner we finish our chores, the sooner we can hook up the boat and head to the river."

Lizette's mood brightens. The river! Long sand bars. The cool water. Watermelon chilling in one of the small fresh springs feeding into the wide Apalachicola.

"Can I try to ski again today?" she asks.

"Don't see why not."

Her father picks up an empty five-gallon bucket and turns toward the cucumber patch. "We can play this afternoon. Come tomorrow, we'll have to help your mother can some of these tomatoes so they don't go to waste. We'll need to put up pickles, too. Go wash your hands after handling that snake, Lizzy."

Lizette releases the little snake and watches it slither away.

Like Daddy insisted, she returns to the faucet to scrub. Then she snatches up a pail and trudges to one of two long rows of okra plants; their spiked tips point like gladiator spears toward the cloudless sky.

Cutting okra pods is serious business, and Lisa Anne isn't allowed to attempt the chore. Lizette pulls on a faded pair of dirt-stained cloth gloves. The material is thick and hot and her hands sweat. Without protection, the prickly fuzz on the plants' stems would bite into her skin. Using a small pocket knife, she snips the okra pods and drops them one by one into the pail. After a few minutes, one row is complete and she moves to the second. She dreams of cooked okra, the dark green pods boiled, salted, and slimy. Or sliced, floured, and fried brown and crisp. Or stewed with homegrown tomatoes.

"All this work is making me hungry," Lizette calls out in the direction of the cucumber patch.

Her father looks up from where he kneels amongst the low, leafy vines, cropping the elongated vegetables from their stems. "We'll have a picnic on the river sandbar."

Lizette smiles. She imagines thick slices of pineapple between bread wet with mayonnaise. Or bologna and cheese with dill pickles and yellow mustard. Cheese curls and sweet tea. Chocolate chip cookies or gooey, half-melted Milky Way bars for dessert.

Sunday dinner, a meal served just past noon after church adjourns, brings the family together around the country kitchen's oblong pine table. Lisa Anne arranges the woven placemats, plates, glasses, napkins, and utensils while Lizette helps her mother bring heaping bowls and platters to the table. Lizette's mouth waters from the blended aroma of beef pot roast cooked with onions, potatoes and carrots, hot buttered rolls, and warm pear cobbler.

Her father sits down and motions for the family to join him. They hold hands as he says a brief blessing.

"Do you realize something, ladies?" her father asks. He spears several thick, scarlet tomato slices. "Everything on this table with the exception of the rolls and roast, we grew here on our land and harvested with our own hands."

Lizette glances around the table. Tomatoes, potatoes, carrots, creamed sweet corn, onions, white acre peas, okra: she has helped with it all. The pears for the cobbler are last summer's bounty, sliced, cooked and preserved in one-quart glass jars neatly labeled and stacked in the pantry. The bread and butter pickles with their crisp, tart sweetness come from cucumbers gathered from the previous year's garden.

"Wow!" Lizette says.

Her father talks around a mouthful of roast, though Mama is giving him the stink eye for doing it. "Yeah, wow." He gestures with a fork, jabbing the air. "When your mother and I were growing up, we didn't have big grocery stores where we could buy everything. Didn't have the money to buy it with, even if we could. As long as we had a garden, we could eat."

He winks at her mother and glances first at Lisa Anne, then at Lizette. "Remember this well: a garden not only feeds the caretaker, but it also feeds the spirit and holds the family together."

Lizette stands at the edge of the overgrown field. Clumps of broom sedge dot the high weeds, nature's comment on man's need to tame and control.

"Hard to believe it's been so many years since we helped Daddy out here." Her sister kicks a mound of dirt with the tip of her dress shoe. Black, proper funeral wear.

"Not hot as Hell's fury today like it was then."

"I loved it. Every minute. I mean, my garden at home is nothing like this one used to be. Three raised beds. I'm lucky to make enough tomatoes and cukes to have a few decent salads."

"You're doing better than me. I ride to a local small farm to buy mine. I make sure to fill up the freezer. No canning though. Had enough of all of that when we used to help Mama."

"I remember sitting on the front porch shelling peas until my fingernails turned green." Lisa Anne dabs fresh tears. "I am so going to miss this place."

Lizette rests an arm around her sister's shoulders. Though she's cried more than her norm, she can't let loose around Lisa Anne. Once her little sister gets started, it's hard to stop her.

"Reckon snakes still live in here?" Lizette gives the shoulder a quick squeeze. "Bet I could find one for you if I look."

"Don't you dare!" Lisa Anne's tearful expression shifts. She play-slugs Lizette. "You are such a twit, you know?"

"And proud of it."

"Guess we should get back to the house. People are coming in droves. I'd forgotten how they show up with food. What will we do with it all?"

"Eat what we can, I suppose. It'll take us a few days to clean out the house and outbuildings."

Though their mother had donated Daddy's clothes and tools two years back after he passed away, every closet, nook, and cranny holds years' worth of mementos. Their parents' generation never threw away anything. No telling what treasures hide amidst the trifles.

Each time Lizette had flown home for a visit, she returned to her own house and went on a pitch-it rampage. Lisa Anne inherited Mama's tendency to hang onto every paper clip. Not Lizette. But even a minimalist has to war against clutter.

"You coming?" Lisa Anne asks, turning toward the house.

"Be in shortly."

Maybe she should plant a small garden, come spring. A few tomatoes, squash, and cukes. Would it kill her to do that? When her grandkids visit, she'd get them involved. Buy them some little gloves. Their own set of tools. Kids like to dig in the dirt. And it will keep them from staring at some video screen for hours.

Alone, Lizette allows her gaze to do what Daddy called *going wide*: staring slightly off-focus to allow her eyes to pick up on subtle movement. Best way to spot wildlife. Or maintain vigilance on crowded expressways. The method often helped her detect possible sketchy drivers before one did something stupid and killed her.

A rustle in the autumn-browned grass draws her attention and she sees the creature responsible. Stepping closer, Lizette studies the scale pattern and shape of its eyes. A young rat snake. Not full of venom like a pigmy rattler or cottonmouth. She crouches and scoops it into her hands. Oh if only Lisa Anne were here.

She lowers and releases her gentle grip. The snake remains in place, tongue licking the air. Then it eases deep into cover.

44: Paint-by-Numbers Club

The very first time Piddie Davis Longman held the pink-handled gen-u-wine horsehair fine-tipped brush in her hand, she knew she was a natural. All she had to do was have sense enough to match up the color numbers with the little plastic pots of paint and stay within the lines, and she'd have a masterpiece to hang on the wall in no time flat.

"Grab her hand, Sissy!" Piddie motions toward Betsy Lou Witherspoon. "She's at it again."

Betsy Lou's delicate features squeeze into the picture of puzzlement. "What?"

Sissy Pridgeon sighs, rests her brush on the edge of the plastic palate in her lap, and snatches the red-tipped paint brush from Betsy Lou's petite hand. "That's not green, Betsy Lou. I keep telling you to double-check the numbers."

Betsy Lou's coral lips purse into a pout. "Looks green enough to me."

Sissy snorts. "Trust me. It's not. See that number four on the leaves? Four's this here shade of lime green."

Piddie swishes her brush in a mason jar, turning the rinse water swamp brown. "Don't crawl all over her so bad, Sissy. We all know she's colorblind as a cross-eyed mule. Just help her find the right pot."

"Then you sit next to her! She's wearing me out." Sissy overloads the tip of her brush. A glob of forest green oozes over the faint purple guideline onto a section of sky. "Dang it!"

Piddie jabs her finger in the air. "See there. God don't love ugly, Sissy Pridgeon. You're supposed to help out your neighbor and love them like yourself."

Elvina Houston pushes a sweat-damp hank of Lady Clairol brown-tinted hair from her forehead. "Hardly think the Almighty hands out His just desserts at a paint-by-numbers party." Her crisply starched, ruffled cabbage-rose print apron is accented with smudges of red and yellow.

"Ain't up to us to decide when the judgment's eked out, 'Vina." Piddie sticks a clean brush in the beehive tower of curls atop her head.

Elvina shakes her head. "Lordy, Piddie. I wish you wouldn't stuff your hair with brushes like that. You look like one of those Japanese ladies."

Piddie's fine-line plucked eyebrows shoot up. "And you look like a short order cook who had a fistfight with a pair of catsup and mustard bottles, Elvina Houston. Reckon it's in your dress's favor that you wear that apron."

"Lay-dees!" Betsy Lou tilts her head and allows a drawn-out sigh to sing through her lips.

The triple-tone trill of the front doorbell squelches the impending hissing contest.

"You going to get that, or do I have to?" Piddie asks Betsy Lou.

"It is *her* house, Piddie, after all." Elvina waves a yellow-tipped brush in the air.

Betsy Witherspoon stands, straightens her red polka-dot dress, and starts toward the door to the mansion's expansive front parlor. "Y'all would fight with the Archangel Gabriel over air space." The doorbell sings out again. "Who in Sam Hill could it be anyway? Every one worth knowing is here already!"

"Maybe it's Angelina. She's been wanting to join the group for some time now. I told her to come on over." Sissy shrugs. "She probably doesn't have time, what with taking care of her family."

"She's a hard worker, that's one thing for sure. Can't fault her that. And every single solitary one of them kids what's old enough has after-school jobs," Elvina says.

"I'd sure like to get her in with us," Piddie adds. "She makes the best dang spaghetti sauce I ever laid my lips to. Reckon she'd give up the recipe?"

"Wouldn't do you any good to have it," Sissy says. "You ain't Italian, Piddie."

"Ain't from above the Mason-Dixon Line, neither. Still, I can cook a mean Yankee pot roast."

Sissy tucks a stray strand of blonde hair underneath her checked bandana. "Sometimes, you just need to have that special thing in your blood to cook things like they're supposed to be done. Like Chinese food. Needs all sorts of special spices and pans, and such."

Piddie pats her massive beehive hairdo until she locates a fan-shaped brush. "That's pure bull malarkey. You give me one good iron skillet and I could cook up the Devil hisself if he landed in it."

Betsy Lou reenters the room. A short, middle-aged man dressed in an outdated tweed suit with high-water-level pants follows in her wake, a worn felt hat clutched in his hands. The three women pause to study the new arrival.

Betsy Lou's lips quiver in an attempt to squelch a smile. "Ladies, this is Mr. . . . ." She glances over her shoulder.

"Lars. Lars Gunuetsen." The man tips his head.

"Mr. Gunuetsen." Betsy Lou nods. "He's come highly recommended to us, it seems. And he wants to join up with our Ladies' Painting Circle."

Sissy Pridgeon ducks her head. The tissue she holds over her mouth barely snuffles the giggle-turned-cough.

Piddie Longman jumps to her feet. "Here, take my seat. I was about to go for a fresh cup of coffee anyhow. C'mon Betsy Lou, let's get this man a cup of joe."

In the kitchen, Betsy Lou pulls a delicate china cup and saucer from the glass-front kitchen cabinet and pours from a highly polished stainless steel percolator. "Third one we've had in less than five months," she says in a low voice.

"Must be hiring on at the dam, then." Piddie refreshes her cup. "All the veteran construction workers know better than to get caught up in the gag." Piddie chuckles. "Lawd help, if those two women who used to run that house of ill repute off Washington Street a few years back knew how famous their *ladies' sewing circle* was going to become, they'd of branched out. Don't know quite how those men picked our paint-by-numbers club as a shoo-in, but I reckon it makes a pretty funny joke on the fella who's dumb enough to fall for it."

Piddie takes a loud swill of coffee. "Whew! This brews a mite strong, Betsy Lou. You must have knocked your elbow when you was measuring out the grounds."

Betsy Lou positions the rose-patterned cup and saucer on a silver serving tray along with creamer and a sugar dish. "Better for you like that. Gets your circulation going."

"The way my heart's a-beating, I'll finish my painting and start another this very afternoon." Piddie's blue eyes twinkle. "Maybe we should make some extra spending money like the sewing circle ladies used to."

"Right. First of all, I don't need the money. And secondly, Piddie Longman, would you actually prostitute yourself? I can't fathom it."

Piddie lifts one shoulder and lets it fall. "Been a while since I laid with a man. Even Egghead Jones is starting to look good to me."

Betsy Lou Witherspoon clucks her tongue. "Listen to you! And you a church-going woman, at that!"

"Ain't a thing wrong with desires, Betsy Lou. Long as they don't grab you by the short hairs." Piddie pauses. "Don't know who I'm kidding, though. I've only lain with one man, Carlton Longman. Can't see myself ever lovin' another good as him."

"We best get on back in there. Poor man, we left him alone with Sissy and Elvina. He might have given up and took off by now."

When they enter the sitting room, Elvina and Sissy perch on either side of the male caller. Hemmed between the two women, Lars's face holds the bewildered expression of a homecoming queen at a hog-calling contest: out of place and off-kilter.

Betsy Lou eases the silver tray onto a mahogany side table. "One lump or two?"

Lars's eyebrows lift. "Lump?"

Betsy Lou pats Lars on his shoulder. "Sugar. You want sugar in your coffee?"

"No Ma'am. Black is just fine."

"You like it like I do," Sissy says with a wink.

Piddie picks through a tall stack of small cardboard boxes. "You like landscape pictures, Mr. Gutter-man? Or do you fancy flowers? We have all kinds to choose from."

The impish little man shifts slightly in his seat, balancing the china cup and saucer on one knee. A faint sheen of perspiration shines along his thinning hair line. "That's Gunuetsen. Please, you may call me Lars. I know my last name is hard to say."

Piddie hands him a box with a mountain scene printed on the top. "Here you go, Lars. Believe you'll like this one. It ain't too difficult for your first try at art. Only has six colors, not counting the black and white here and there."

The puzzled expression on the man's face as he takes the proffered paint-by-numbers kit sets Sissy to giggling again.

Elvina shoots Sissy a hard look before smiling in Lars's direction. "Don't mind Sissy, Lars. She's prone to fits. Most of the time, they're controlled by medication. Reckon the shelf life on her last prescription has worn off."

Piddie sets a mason jar of water on the end table closest to Lars. "Now you have your own rinse jar. Mind, if it gets to looking too much like swamp water, it needs to be changed out or your colors will all start to look the same."

Lars opens the box as if it holds a poisonous snake. Inside is an eight by ten rectangular canvas printed with the faint outline of the mountain scene.

"Those teensy numbers," Piddie points to the canvas, "are to show you which one of the pots to pull your paint from. The set comes with one brush, but we've got plenty more. Some of these itsy-bitsy spots, like the ones on this tree in the front, you're gonna need a fine-tipped brush. You try to use the one they give you, and you'll run all across the borders and into another part. We've found that fact out the hard way. You might as well benefit from our hours of painting experience."

"You got any more of that baby blue color, Piddie?" Sissy asks. "Mine's got lime green mixed in it."

"Sometimes, you don't have the good sense of a dog turd." Piddie shakes her head. "How many times have I got to tell you, Sissy? Rinse your dang brush out before you take on a different shade!"

Sissy bats her eyelashes and smiles at Lars. "I tend to forget sometimes."

For a few moments, the paint-by-numbers club members and guest grow silent, except for the occasional swish of a brush in a mason jar.

Elvina grows restless. "So . . . Lars. How'd you catch wind of our little club meeting?" She winks in Piddie's direction.

Lars glances up from his canvas. "The boys I've been working with at the dam told me."

"I see." Elvina chews thoughtfully on the edge of her ruby-red painted lower lip. "Had you been particularly wanting to take up," she pauses, "art?"

Lars's shoulders creep up to his earlobes. He resembles a startled box turtle returning to the safety of its shell. "Some of the boys thought this, uh, club, might do me good."

"I see." Elvina shoots a help-me-out look toward Piddie.

Piddie grabs up the game ball. "You got a wife, Lars? I mean, back home somewhere?"

Lars frowns. He hangs his head. "No Ma'am."

Sissy Pridgeon wiggles. "So, you're a single man then?"

The four widowed women lean forward like hungry wolf spiders that feel the faint panicked vibrations of trapped lunch on their communal web.

Lars seems to curl in on himself. "My wife. My wife, Estelle. She passed on last year." He glances up into the direct gaze of Sissy Pridgeon.

Sissy rests her hand on his. "I'm so sorry. We didn't mean to pry into your private affairs. It's just . . . ."

Betsy Lou dives in. "We don't often have the pleasure of *quality* gentleman callers. That's all."

"We're out of practice," Piddie adds.

"And just plain-out rude, to boot." Elvina snorts. "Reckon you just as well write us all off and head on out the door, the way we've picked and pried."

Lars's thin lips lift into a faint smile. "I'm enjoying the company." His gaze drops to the floor. "This reminds me of Estelle and me. We used to sit in the evening. Having a cup of tea. Talking over the little things that had happened during the day."

He focuses on Sissy Pridgeon. "You remind me a little of her. Estelle had a quiet way about her, like you do. We could sit and talk, or not say much of anything, and it was all right." Lars's expression brightens. "Estelle always had something in her hands. Mending, knitting, her fingers doing some business of their own as we sat together."

He lets go of a long exhalation. "Listen to me. I didn't really mean to say all that. It's just . . . I haven't had an evening since she passed when I've felt so . . . at home."

Silence cloaks the fancy parlor. Betsy Lou finally speaks. "We're having a pot of Piddie's beef stew for supper, Lars. We would be honored if you would join us after the painting party."

Later that evening when Lars stands at the mansion's double front doors with his completed masterpiece in hand, the paint-by-numbers ladies bid him good night. Piddie hands over a paper bag with a container of beef stew and two homemade Cathead biscuits wrapped in a napkin. He thanks them one by one, then disappears into the balmy late spring evening.

Betsy Lou Witherspoon is the first to speak. "Wasn't he the nicest man? I thought we were in for another of those crude hired labor construction types."

"Wonders never cease," Piddie says.

"No, they don't." A sly smile plays across Sissy's lips. "I invited him to my house for dinner Saturday night."

45: Lil' Ladybug

The morning mists curl in ethereal eddies around the dormant mountain laurel bushes in front of the Ladybug Inn. Come spring, the woody shrubs will erupt into showy clusters of pastel pink against the backdrop of deep green leaves. Now, they step back to allow the pignut hickory, beech, yellow poplar, sassafras, sweetgum, birch, and red maple trees to gain center stage. Though the leaves are showy, Bev knows they are about ten days from peak.

Soon lines of sloth-like leaf-peepers will snake though the back road switchbacks, and Heaven help the poor local who dares venture onto the Blue Ridge Parkway. Bev is by birth a lowlander. After four years, she is officially one of the half-crazed mountain drivers who keel around the pitching roads with little thought to the sheer drop-offs. Bev makes her living from the visitors, she often reminds herself when she's trapped for endless miles behind a moss-gathering, out-of-state driver.

As soon as she steps from the inn's wide wooden plank front porch, two canines bound to meet her, an aging female Springer spaniel and a massive Labrador retriever the color of milk chocolate. The dogs are all wagging tales and wet hand-kisses. Bev reaches into the pocket of her blue jean jacket and offers a handful of treats.

"Let's go, kids!" She claps her hands.

The Labrador leads, his massive head held low to the ground. The spaniel is content to plod along at her side. One protector and one companion. Everyone should be so lucky.

The downhill trek to the mailbox takes ten minutes, longer if the dogs key into a particularly fascinating scent pool. Bev's hiking boots grip the dew-wet asphalt. In a few weeks, the first frost will make the trip more challenging. She digs her bare hands into her jeans pockets. Her exhalations come in staccato ghost-puffs.

Bev allows her mind to dip into the day's concerns. Two sets of guests leaving, two more arriving in the early afternoon. Town for groceries later. Man from the landscaping supply coming with another delivery of stone for the waterfall and pond planned for the side yard, adjacent to her private quarters. She looks forward to drifting into sleep with the music of falling water washing her dreams with peace.

Her thoughts stray to her father's upcoming visit, the first time in almost twenty years she has seen the man responsible for half of her DNA. She presses two fingers to smooth the worry crease between her brows, the sole wrinkle on an otherwise smooth, younger than forty-one-year-old face. If she had to name the line, it would be labeled with her father's initials.

When Bev thinks of the relationship between her and her father, a medieval labyrinth comes to mind, full of twists, turns, and blind alleys, with no true direct route to its heart. Though she can see him in the misty distance, lodged in the center, she is forced to orbit in slow arcs like a jet circling a crowded metro airport.

"You must try, Beverly," her beloved Aunt CeeCee urged. "When J.W. is gone, there won't be another chance to heal your broken bonds. I know he's done wrong. He knows it, too. He's paying the ultimate price for the years of drinking. Please, please consider my words."

Does Aunt CeeCee know the details of the years she and her mother spent with her older brother? Surely Bev's mother has fed bits and pieces to Aunt CeeCee. Can she fathom the delicate balance Bev and her mother had maintained between the loving man who called Bev *his little ladybug* and the maniac whose violent rages filled first the weekends then the weekdays with fear? Does her aunt know how long her mother struggled with two or three jobs to keep a roof overhead and food on the table, while her father drank his way into near-bankruptcy and unemployment?

The final blow came when Bev was thirteen. The tiny galley kitchen of their house brimmed with the scent of roasting turkey. Dinged pots piped with steam on the gas stove.

"I'm going down to the basement and fetch some potatoes," her mother said. "Keep an eye on those greens. When they start to boil, turn the heat to a low simmer and put the lid on."

Bev hovered over the stove, eyes trained on the greens pot. She'd always heard *a watched pot never boils,* and it fascinated her to no end to defy the old saying.

Her father entered the kitchen. Grumbled. Opened the small refrigerator and grabbed a beer.

She should have seen the warning signs. The reddened eyes. The half-stumble gait. Should have paid attention to the fine hairs standing erect on the nape of her neck.

Now years later, she can't recall the exact words she spoke that had sent her father into blind fury.

When her mother entered the kitchen, the front of her worn apron pregnant with potatoes, J.W. had Bev pinned against the counter, his massive working-man's hands wrapped around her petite neck. Her mother screamed. Potatoes thudded to the linoleum floor. When her mother managed to disengage the killing hands, his fury turned on her instead. As Bev struggled for air through a half-crushed windpipe, her mother received the first of several blows that would leave her nose permanently crooked and two teeth missing in front.

That night, after the carefully prepared Thanksgiving meal, after her father finally passed out on the couch in front of the television, Bev and her mother slipped away.

From that point, life was a struggle. But never again was Bev afraid to come home. No matter where home was, often meager, it was safe. She joined her mother in making enough money to get by. Still, the remainder of her early years were happy and secure.

The cool dampness of Ethel's nose bumping her palm brings her back to the present. Unlike Hershey, who only worries when the food bowl is barren, the senior, black-and-white-spackled spaniel possesses an uncanny instinct when it comes to reading Bev's moods.

Today her father arrives at the Ladybug. Bev's stomach pitches. The therapy sessions and life lessons gleaned over the years can't prepare her for his presence.

To visitors, Bev might appear to be a rich city dweller who opened an inn on a whim. The three-story Victorian house offers every carefully thought-out amenity from thick down-topped mattresses,

Jacuzzi tubs, luxurious sheets, and themed décor, to gourmet breakfasts and specialty coffees and teas. The type of place for special celebrations: honeymoons, anniversaries, birthdays, lovers' trysts.

What visitors don't see is a woman who has worked for everything, and who takes great pains to offer the kind of comfort and homey hospitality she now shares with her husband. One thing her deceased mother's constant love taught her: the more pain wallows out your soul, the more beauty and compassion it can hold.

She hears the truck minutes before it pulls into the gravel-paved parking lot in front of the inn. The engine sputters and kicks, then dies. Bev stands in the shade of the porch overhang, hands propped on her hips, waiting. Must be her father's. The guests drive late model SUVs or rental cars. She knows the vehicles of the local workers who occasionally come calling.

The faded red pick-up's door screeches as it opens, a raspy siren song. Will it actually manage the trip back to whence it came? And, how in the name of Pete did it make it from south Alabama without completely melting down beside the highway?

A stooped man pulls himself from the driver's side. Slowly. As if each movement requires prior permission. Bev tries to equate the old man ambling her way to the massive, omnipotent demon of memory.

It wasn't all bad, was it? Not in her early childhood. She dimly recalls a warm, dry hand on her forehead. A kiss to her cheek. The deep whisper in her ear. *Sleep tight, my little ladybug. Don't let the bedbugs bite.*

Until recently, she thought bedbugs were some kind of make-believe thing adults said to children. As an inn owner, she's heard horror stories of infested hotel rooms and even high-end establishments battling the snarky little insects. The Ladybug Inn has, so far, avoided infestation. Bev, the queen of neat and clean, keeps a vigilant eye.

The man pauses at the threshold to the front garden. He takes in the expansive home with its rocking chair-studded front porch. "Beverly?"

She steps down the short stack of stairs. Her voice fails her.

He removes a sweat-stained John Deere cap and holds it in front of him, as if entering a church sanctuary. "CeeCee told me this was quite a showplace, but I had no notion of," he sweeps a hand through the air, "all of this."

"Mark and I have put a lot of work into it."

What in the world can she find to talk about with this stranger? Once she covers the weather and a smattering of national affairs, what will be left to say? Are you still crawling inside the bottle; I'm sorry you're dying? No, that would be false. She wasn't sorry. She really wasn't much of anything.

The shaky old man standing in front of her awaiting some kind of signal flag could be any down-on-his-luck bum begging for wine money at a street corner.

Her manners take over where her emotions fail. "You must be exhausted. Come on in. I'll show you to your room in case you'd like to freshen up a bit. I have some chicken salad made . . ."

Claire, Bev's assistant chef and innkeeper, pushes through the swinging door separating the kitchen and the guest breakfast room. She carries an empty coffee carafe. "Your father's down."

Bev glances up from dusting powdered sugar onto plates of the morning's special: Belgium waffles with thick strawberry and blueberry compote. "Did he order?"

When Claire smiles, twin dimples dot her cheeks. No matter how hectic her private life is at the time, her expression reflects compassion and interest, the two qualities Bev finds most attractive about her employee and friend.

"He said to tell you that anything would be fine with him. He can find no fault with your cooking."

Bev feels a flush of pride. At what point does an adult stop yearning for approval from a parent? "He likes orange juice. Please take him a glass while I make a fresh stack of waffles."

Claire pours the juice and scoops up two finished plates for the couple at table three. Bev admires the way she balances a full load while back-tapping the swinging doors without dropping a thing.

For the past three days, Bev has driven her father to view the changing foliage, introduced him to numerous town acquaintances, eaten lunch at nearby small cafés, and walked the property with him hobbling beside her and the dogs. He has studied scrapbooks filled with pictures and construction details of the inn and followed her and Claire as they went through daily routines.

Her father soaks up details of her life, a warm buttermilk biscuit taking up red-eye gravy. He has pored over the notes on funny incidents since the inn's opening: the first winter when she and Mark had to park the truck at the base of the iced-over driveway and hike down to drive into town for supplies; stories of numerous famous guests seated on the wide porch swing with the dogs posing alongside; and the time a disgruntled mama bear took up residence in one of the outbuildings.

Bev notes his sickness-ravaged body. The only part holding weight is his distended stomach, testament to a destroyed liver. A faint yellow tinge paints his skin and the whites of his eyes.

"When's that husband of yours coming home?" her father asks when she slides the warmed plate of waffles in front of him.

She offers refills of coffee to the newlywed couple from south Florida before returning to his table. The other guests have eaten and vacated with maps in hand.

Bev eases into the wooden chair opposite her father. "His flight is coming in day after tomorrow to an airport about an hour from here."

"Too bad I won't be able to stay to meet him."

"You're leaving, then?"

He takes a sip of coffee and nods. "I have a doctor's appointment to get back to. Figure to head out in the morning after another of your wonderful breakfasts. It'll take me a couple of days to get home. I like to break up the trip."

Bev cares more than she would like. "You could come back sometime . . . for a visit."

His rheumy eyes search hers. "Wouldn't want to wear out my welcome. You sure?"

Bev nods. "Maybe in the spring. May. The mountain laurels and rhododendrons are spectacular. There's one place off the Parkway called the Pink Beds where there are so many growing in clusters, it looks like clouds."

"Sounds like Heaven. We'll plan on it." He reaches out a thin hand and rests it over Bev's. The touch brings moisture to her eyes.

The last morning, Bev and her father stand by the pick-up. She lifts his worn, Army-green duffle bag into the back and slides a Styrofoam cooler onto the seat. Both dogs, now friendly with the old man, offer farewell licks and tail wags.

"Claire packed sandwiches for you. In case you get hungry. I put in some bottled water and a couple of soft drinks. There's a plastic bag with homemade oatmeal cookies, too."

"You've spoiled me, Beverly."

Bev stretches for words and comes up empty.

He shifts his gaze from her to the inn. "One thing I've been wondering about . . ."

"Yes?"

"The name of your place. Ladybug."

Bev offers a slight smile. "You called me that when I was a little girl. Guess it stuck with me."

He combs his fingers through his thinning hair. "Well . . ."

Her father snatches the door open and slides inside. The engine starts after three protests. Bev steps back. Waves as the wheels turn.

He shifts the truck into reverse. Stops. The window lowers. "You are one thing in my life I did right, my lil' ladybug."

Bev watches the pick-up until the mountain mists swallow the tail lights.

Tears trickle down her cheeks. Some things can't be forgotten. Perhaps they can be forgiven.

Ethel pushes her cold wet nose into Bev's hand and she ruffles the spaniel's silky ears. "It's okay, baby girl. *I'm* okay."

46: Ordinary

The lighting in the Burger Barn is harsh, the colors garish and jarring. Fast food joints plan it such, so that customers won't be prone to linger too long, taking up space.

Sandra slides onto a hard plastic orange bench and swipes another diner's crumbs onto the floor with a folded napkin. When she unwraps her discount burger, the bun is shiny with oil and dry-crisp around the edges. The sheaf of lettuce looks more like limp tissue paper than anything once alive. Even the soft drink tastes strange, the mix of carbonation and syrup incorrect.

Just as she digs a clump of limp, salty fries into a smear of cat-sup, a man appears by her table. When she glances up, her mouth falls open slightly.

His voice is low and creamy. "Hey, aren't you . . . well, I can't remember your name, but I think you went to school with me."

"Sandra Brown." Her voice is high and squeaky like a mouse with its toes stuck to a glue trap.

"Yeah. Right."

Sandra's fries drip catsup onto the wax paper burger wrapping.

"You don't mind if I join you, do you?" He doesn't wait for an answer before sliding into the booth opposite her and extracting the contents of his Burger Barn bag onto the table.

"Uhm . . . no, I guess . . ."

"Of course, you *do* know me." He flashes a grin that's a cross between baby-kissing politician and back lot car salesman.

If she manages to engage in conversation, she won't be able to eat and swallow. Sandra pushes a sweaty strand of dishwater blonde hair from her eyes. Even if she wasn't in rumpled green scrubs, she wouldn't consider herself in any way attractive. Ordinary. Her mother always said she was just so terribly *ordinary*.

"You used to drive a yellow Mustang." She instantly chides herself. How lame!

The too-tanned skin crinkles around his brown bedroom eyes. "Gosh, I loved that car."

His gaze darts from his food, to scanning the room, to his watch, and back to his food. Maybe two quick flicks toward her. Sandra notes the fine dusting of gray hair at his temples. Other than a slight paunch around the midsection, the man has changed little from his boyish heartthrob years.

What female within a ten-mile radius wouldn't give her firstborn to be seated across from *the* Jonathan Lovegood? Sandra remembers how she and her gaggle of friends— all, pimpled and date-less— used to loll around during one of their many sleepovers, making up romantic interlude tales about him.

All of the stories were variations on a theme. Girl walks alone on a sidewalk. Hears the shush of a car pull alongside. Glances over to gasp at the mustard-yellow muscle car growling beside the curb. The door pops open slightly. An invitation. Girl looks both ways nervously before disappearing into the dark and cool interior. Fade to vague, heated fumbling encounter masquerading as true love lasting for a lifetime.

Through her junior and high school years and beyond, the fantasy morphs, but the tall, dark, and handsome boy stays the same. Jonathan Lovegood. *The* Jonathan Lovegood.

Sandra jerks back to now, embarrassed for her lapse in attention. Jonathan carries on a one-sided conversation about his amazing job and glorious life. He could just as well be seated across from a pigeon-pocked statue of St. Francis or bowl of strawberry gelatin.

Her burger is cold. The salt clings to the French fry casings. Sandra manages a few sips of flat cola.

Jonathan dabs the corners of his lips with a crumpled napkin and crams his trash back into the bag. "Well, Sally. It surely has been good to share lunch with you. I hate to eat alone."

He stands, palm-smooths the wrinkles from his slacks, and walks away. He flips the bag of trash into a bin and pushes through the glass door in one fluid motion. Jonathan moves like warm cane syrup oozing across buttermilk pancakes. Always has.

"It's Sandra," she mutters. "My name is Sandra."

She watches through the plate-glass windows as Jonathan Lovegood ambles to his car, a late model sedan, and drives away. No one she knows, and no one who cares, bears witness to the fact that she shared lunch with him. Had it been twenty-four years ago, she would have called everyone she remotely knew to share every embellished detail.

By the time a person gets what she wants, she probably doesn't want it anymore. Or it's too late to matter much.

She shoves the uneaten, cold fast food into the trash.

Maybe the random encounter is a sign from the Gods. Today she will email yet another slew of inquiries into the prospective agent/publisher void. If the universe allows her to finally have more than five seconds worth of Jonathan Lovegood, then magic can still happen. Even for someone as dull and ordinary as her.

As she steers the half-mile back to the state hospital, Sandra drifts into a worn daydream. Famous New York agent drops what she is doing when she reads the first few lines of *Serendipity Singing*. The phone rings. *Yes, I would love to sign a contract!* The agent lands her novel with a huge publishing house. The editor barely makes any changes. It is perfect. Amazing. This book will be a bestseller! The novel is released to critical acclaim unequaled in recent history. Calls come in from talk shows and there's mention of a movie deal. No more medical aide, Sandra Brown. You have hit the big time, girl.

Back at work, the second heavy metal door slams shut behind her. One more separation between her dull, ordinary life and the community of criminally insane who people the Forensic Ward. Sandra taps her chest to assure the state ID tag is secure. In the five years she has worked with the deranged menagerie, Sandra has tamed her initial fear. She treats them with the kindness and respect every living thing deserves. For the most part, the inmate patients like her, or at least, she falls shy of their evil-intent radar.

A tall woman stands in front of the drink machine, her fists clenched.

"What's the matter, Miz Eliza?" Sandra keeps her voice even.

"What is wrong with me! Why won't it give me my drink!"

The prickle of downy hair at the nape of Sandra's neck alerts her to intrinsic danger. Before she can offer a solution, the patient reaches into a pocket and drives a crude shiv into her own neck, crumbles to her knees, then falls.

Sandra raises her voice to yell for help. Aides pour into the corridor.

"It's all right, easy now, you're going to be all right," Sandra coos in a soft tone, both hands clamped over the ruptured artery. Before the patient loses consciousness, Sandra stares into the fevered eyes of a woman whose life is anything but dull and comprehends the true value of being ordinary.

47: Reunion

Theresa settles into a recliner, leans in to gather the conversation rolling around her. No lack of jabber in her family of origin. For sure.

"I remember my days as a nurse back during the second world war," her younger sister Dorothy says. Dorothy's white hair forms a fluffy halo around her petite face. "I was so new to it all, so green. And scared witless. I would wake up every day before I went to work at the hospital and wonder, *will I kill anyone today?*"

A ripple of laughter sounds from the audience of kinfolk. Theresa shakes her head.

"Heavens to Betsy, Sister," their baby brother Charles says, "I'm glad I never ended up in your ward."

Theresa smiles. At eighty-eight, she is the eldest of the remaining Gibson siblings. Two others— one brother and one sister— have already gone to glory. The other two call her Terri. "You always are such a comedian, Dorothy." She fingers the lace on one of her cuffs. "I surely hope we get out to the homeplace while we're all together. At our ages, this might be the last time."

"The old farmhouse is still standing," Charles says. "Pauline and I rode out there a while back. They were redoing the siding. The dairy barn is gone. Nothing left but the concrete slab."

"I always wanted to go back and look for the meteorite." Theresa holds her hands together like she's praying. Times like this, her mother would've said her blue eyes sparkled like sapphires, to support whatever she was asking for. All of her siblings have those same blue eyes, but hers are the brightest. So she has been told.

"What meteorite, Mama?" Theresa's son James asks.

"Right by one of the fencerows," she answers. "Papa used to have to plow around it so as not to break the blade."

Charles's lips turn down. "I don't recall such, Terri."

"It was a story passed down from Grandpa's day." Theresa warms to the retelling. "Sometime around the turn of the century, it came soaring down from the heavens and buried itself in the dirt. Boom!" She flays her crooked fingers to illustrate. "Only a part of it was visible. Rest was underground. That's how blasted hard it hit."

Dorothy nods. "Seems I dimly recall the old folks talking about that. Could be just a silly tale they made up."

"If it's a true meteorite, it would be worth a bundle." Charles rubs his palms together. "I would be willing to mortgage this house and buy back the family farm if it was true."

James nods. "Piece of a meteorite no bigger than your hand sells for, oh, several hundred dollars. *If* that is what it is." And her son would know. He used to work for the space center, back when NASA was in its heyday.

"We could ride out there and see if we could locate it," Charles says.

His wife, Pauline, walks from the kitchen and joins the group. "What are we supposed to do, Charles? Ride up in some stranger's yard and ask to plunder on his property?"

"We could say we were there to visit the old family dairy farm," James says. "Not exactly a lie. And how there was this rock where our grandfather etched his initials. What harm could it do to ask if we could try to find it?"

Dorothy studies her nephew with her lips drawn thin. "But how would we know if it's real or not? I never saw such. Might not even exist. You know, Terri is prone to exaggeration."

Theresa fires the stink eye at Dorothy.

James taps his chin. "While you and the others keep the owner distracted, Uncle Charles and I will search for the meteorite."

"Then what?" Theresa asks.

James winks at his uncle Charles. "Leave that up to us."

Helene, the youngest of Theresa's three children, enters the room from the kitchen, a cup of coffee in hand. Surely hope it's decaf. The gal has always been a bit excitable.

"I can't believe what I'm hearing," Helene says. "Don't tell me y'all are already scheming. No wonder we don't get together more often. We'd probably end up in jail."

Theresa points a finger. "Don't get smarty. Besides, who's going to arrest a bunch of kindly senior citizens?"

"When shall we go?" Dorothy jiggles and her dangling earrings do a dance. "We have the reunion dinner tomorrow, and then everyone will be leaving. I have a plane to catch back home to Pennsylvania on Sunday."

"No better time than the present." Charles rises. He winces, favoring his bad hip. "The old homeplace is only about fifteen miles from here. We have plenty of time before all of my kids come in for dinner."

Theresa taps her gold watch. "Let's wait until Melinda drives in from Nashville, Charles. She should be here any minute now. I'd hate for her to arrive to an empty house. Besides, she might like to see where I grew up, too." Theresa looks toward Helene. "James's been there once, but you've not seen it either."

"Who did you say you are?" The stately, gray-haired man asks. He peers past Charles. The family stands on the porch in a tight wad, a herd of hopeful, similar-featured people.

"I told you we should have stayed in the van until after a couple of us went to the door," Helene whispers to her older sister Melinda. "We look like some militant mob, pulling up into a stranger's yard and piling out in a bunch."

"Shush!" James holds a finger to his lips.

"You ought to keep Mama from going in, at least." Helene motions toward Theresa. "She's so honest, she'll announce straight out, what we're here for."

James shakes his head. "I'll take care of it."

"I promise you she will spill the beans." Helene shrugs. "But whatever."

"I said we're the Gibsons," Charles says in a loud voice to the man standing at the threshold. Clearly, the elderly gentleman holding the door ajar is as hard of hearing as the majority of his visitors.

Dorothy steps forward. "Our father once owned this farm. He was a dairyman. Back before the depression."

"That right?" The homeowner's features relax a bit.

"You can still see the slab where the dairy barn used to sit." Pauline nudges past her husband and points. "It's been a while since we rode out here."

"We got to talking about the old place, me and the wife." Charles motions toward Pauline. "We live in town, about fifteen minutes east of here."

"We're having a little family reunion," Dorothy adds. "I flew down, all the way from Pennsylvania."

"Rest of us are in from all over. Florida, Tennessee." James leans in. "What we kindly ask is for my mama," he tips his head toward Theresa, "and her siblings to look around the old place. With your permission, of course."

"Suppose that would be all right. Come on in." The man steps back and sweeps a thin hand through the air. "Place is actually my daughter and her husband's. They bought it about five years back and fixed it up for an investment. Finally convinced me to move in. I was skeptical at first, being so far out from town. Love it now. Peaceful out here."

Dorothy is the first to step into the front parlor. She has always been the leader. "Isn't it beautiful? Charles? Terri? Do you see how they've redone the old place?"

Theresa shuffles inside. "Look, the original hearth!"

James motions to the group. "Why don't y'all stand in front of the fireplace and I'll take your picture?"

"Would that be okay with you, Mister . . .?" Theresa asks.

"William Morrison, Ma'am, and it's fine by me."

The elder Gibsons shift into position and practice smiling while James fiddles with the digital camera. "Ok, say cheese!"

Theresa walks around the room afterward, studying the old photographs. Dorothy thumbs through an album documenting the renovations. Charles remarks on the military memorabilia.

"Navy, were you, William?" Charles asks. "I was a Navy man, myself, during the war."

Theresa joins the conversation. "What we *really* came for is to see the meteorite."

Helene shoots her brother an *I-told-you-so* look.

"Meteorite?" William Morrison seems slightly more confused about the announcement of space debris than he had about the slew of Gibsons showing up on his porch.

Charles dismisses his sister's statement with the swish of a hand and a chuckle. "Just some rock my father carved his initials on, that's all. My sister believes it was from outer space."

"It's what I was told!" Theresa juts out her chin. "It was at the end of the fencerow near the road. It fell from the night sky. Sure as I'm standing here."

James nudges Theresa gently in the direction of the front door. "We'll be going now. Leave you to your peace and quiet."

"We do thank you, William." Charles shakes the old man's hand. "Do you mind if we walk about the place a bit?"

"Ah, no. Not at all. Take all the time you wish."

"Way to cover, Mama," Helene says when they gather at the bottom of the concrete stairs.

Melinda cradles Theresa's elbow and helps her transverse the uneven lawn. "Leave her be. You know lying goes against her grain."

James pulls a pick ax and small shovel from the rear of the van.

Pauline glances back over her shoulder. "We'll be lucky if Mr. Morrison doesn't look out the window and call the law if he sees the likes of that."

James scuttles ahead, the implements held close to his body. Charles walks in his limping gait a few steps behind. The group edges along the fence line for the next quarter-mile until a second fence designates the border of the adjacent farm.

"Someone has stolen our meteorite!" Theresa stands with her hands on her hips. The summer sun bores into her head.

Helene leans against a worn wooden post, her face flushed red. "First of all, it's not *ours* anymore. Second, we don't even know if it *was* a meteorite."

"Probably the road crew dug it up and hauled it away when they were paving the highway," Pauline says.

Dorothy holds a hand to her chest, takes several deep breaths before she can ask, "How do we go about getting our rock back?"

James, pick ax in one hand, shovel propped against one leg, wipes sweat from his eyes. "Could always call someone up and ask if they found a big rock when they were excavating the shoulders for the right of way."

"Lots of rocks around here," Melinda says. "Doubt you'll ever locate that *one*. I think we need to get on back into town before one of us has a heat stroke."

"Thank God for my sister, the voice of reason," Helene mumbles.

The suitcases sit in the back of the Florida-bound minivan. James slams the rear hatch, checks to make sure the lock is secure.

"Surely glad y'all could come up for the reunion." Pauline hands a bag of wrapped baked goods and bottled water to Theresa. "We should all get together more often."

"At least we don't have as long of a drive home as Melinda," Theresa says. She hugs her sister-in-law first, then her brother. "It'll take her a good seven hours to get back to Nashville. Only takes us about four to North Florida."

"She left early, so she'll be home long before good dark, Mama. Don't worry." James helps his mother into the van's front captain's chair and straps her in.

Helene slips into the back seat after her own round of hugs. "Tell Aunt Dorothy we said goodbye."

Pauline smiles. "You know Dorothy doesn't get up 'til almost noon. Don't take it to heart."

The van's engine roars to life. Doors slam. The van starts to move, then brakes. Theresa toggles the switch to lower her window. "Charles?" Theresa calls out.

Charles moves to her window.

"Remember what I told you, now. Don't let me down."

"Yes, Terri. I will do my best." He leans in, pecks her cheek with a kiss.

A few miles down the Interstate, Helene asks, "Mama, what was all that about with Uncle Charles?"

Theresa grins. No doubt her blue eyes are sparkling again. "I put my baby brother on a mission. An important mission."

James flicks a quick glance from the three stacked lines of end-of-weekend traffic. "What's that, Mama?"

"I told him to be an angel and find that meteorite. I won't rest easy until he does."

Charles waits until everyone but the immediate family vacates the mortuary tent. Theresa's memorial was no sappy tear-jerker. She would've haunted them, had that happened.

"James, help me with something," he directs to Theresa's son.

James tags behind his uncle to the back of the SUV with the Georgia tags. "I had help to get this in here. You'll need to lift it. We'll use the dolly to roll it over to her marker."

"Is this—?"

"Not what you're thinking. I went back to the homestead four more times and looked. Even got my new friend William involved. This isn't her rock *exactly*, but it's from the land. I keep my promises and maybe my sister can properly rest with it holding down her plot."

It never works to go against any Gibson. Especially when they're doing the work of angels. James pulls out the dolly.

48: Just Fun and Games

"I'da know, Beck." Stanley regards his image in the fancy full-length cheval mirror. "Feels kind of . . . weirdly wrong."

Rebecca gives him a playful slap on the upper arm. "You can be such a fuddy-duddy sometimes. Not a thing wrong with two old married folks playing a bit. Where is your sense of adventure?"

Somebody in the family needs to be the gatekeeper, he wants to inform his wife. But he has to admit that if not for her, he wouldn't have tried half the things they've done over thirty years of marriage. Rock climbing. White water rafting. Zip lining. Scuba diving. The list boggles his brain.

Rebecca urges him to face her. She has to stand on her tiptoes to slide the headband over his graying hair. "There." She whirls him back around to view the completed costume. "See? Now you're perfect."

If only his chest was muscled like when they first married and his belly didn't flop over the top of the stretchy pants. Stanley reaches up to touch the tip of one red-glittered horn. "It's a little tight."

"Don't whine. It was made for a child. Of course it's tight on that big head of yours." When she grins, mischief glimmers in her eyes. Hopefully, he won't end up in a cast like he had after the downhill skiing mishap. Adventure has its drawbacks.

"If I have to wear this, where's your outfit?"

"You'll see. I want it to be a surprise."

Stanley dislikes surprises more than adventures. A lot. Beck knows this but chooses to ignore it. He holds out his arms and flaps. "The cape is okay, I suppose. But do I have to wear the tights?"

"It's all about the look, babe. Role-playing is fun. And this is classic good versus evil. Work with me, will you?" She points to their four-poster bed. "Lie down so I can set the scene."

The bedroom window is open and a cool early spring breeze lifts the sheer curtains. He hears the whir of the next-door neighbor's weed trimmer.

Rebecca uses two of her scarves to lash his wrists to the headboard. "Don't look so worried, Stanley. I'm not planning on breaking out a bullwhip or tying down your legs. This is a fun role-play, not some kinky business."

Good dang thing they're in the privacy of their own home, away from someone who might record this with their phone. How would he ever explain that? What would their two kids think? Sure, they're grown and gone, but he doubts they'd appreciate their mother's role-playing business.

If this doesn't prove how much he loves Beck, nothing can.

Rebecca leaves the room. He waits forever until he finally hears the swish of material.

"Close your eyes, babe."

Stanley obeys.

"Okay. Open them and behold the Essence of Good!"

When Stanley lifts his eyelids, it's not Beck. It's a vision! She wears a shimmery white gown. Her silver hair hangs long and curled, topped with a halo of stars. But it's the billowy wings that make him feel as if a representative of the heavens has descended into the room.

The apparition masquerading as Rebecca glides toward the captive devil.

Then stops.

She glances toward the cherry cabinet they'd found at a vintage store. In their old house, it would've been overpowering. But this new custom-built home they'd purchased after both kids graduated from college has lofty ceilings.

Rebecca hikes up the gown and secures it with a quick tuck. Then his adventurous wife/angel drags an upholstered chair into place and uses it to help her ascend to the top of the chifforobe. She loosens the gown's skirt and it falls into place.

"Beck, I don't think you should . . ."

His wife holds a shush-finger to her peach-painted lips. Before Stanley can list the many reasons why she shouldn't do what she's thinking of doing, Rebecca launches toward where her captive devil husband awaits the classic good versus evil showdown.

He must be in Heaven and not lashed to a bed, dressed up as a devil. The female falling in slow motion toward him, hair waffling like sails caught in the wind, is the most beautiful thing Stanley has ever beheld. More awe-inspiring than when he had stood at the rim of the Grand Canyon. His eyes water.

She floats, sailing down, until . . .

The ceiling fan blade snags one of her wings.

"Beck!"

"I'm okay. It's okay!"

He watches her flail arms, doing her best to reach behind her. Stanley jerks his own arms. The scarves hold firm. He tries snatching. Squirming. Lifting both unbound legs to paw at the bindings. His belly keeps his toes from remotely reaching far enough.

His wife's not heavy, but the brace seems to be holding steady. "Good thing we sprung for that expensive fan."

Far above, Rebecca hangs. "At least it's not turned on. That would *not* be a good thing."

The two of them look at each other. The bound devil. The lovely angel dangling high above.

Rebecca squeaks out a tiny giggle. Then she's full-on laughing. He's never been immune to his wife's merriment. Especially when she does that weird hiccupping grunt like now. Stanley joins in, until both of them guffaw. He can't remember the last time they've laughed so hard. Finally, it winds down to tiny snorts, whistles, and exhaled puffs of air.

"What'll we do now?" Stanley manages.

"Call for help."

He pivots his head. His cell phone is on the dresser. No telling where her phone is. And neither of them wanted to have some listening tech device in their bedroom.

The whir of the weed trimmer stops next door. Stanley shakes his head. No way around it. At least the neighbor on this side of the house is a private sort. Unlike the biddy on the other side who would tell everyone in the subdivision. Probably call the local news. Or splash it on social media.

"Hey, Hey!" Stanley yells in his loudest voice. "Help! We could use a little help! Hey! Hey!"

Rebecca joins in. Until a female voice answers. Through the sheers, Stanley makes out the silhouette.

"Are you hurt? Do you need me to call 911!?"

"No. No!" Stanley's brain whirs.

"We're okay, we just need a little assistance." The dangling angel takes over. "Do you remember where we hide our spare key?"

"Uhm. Yeah."

"Okay, so let yourself in and come to the master bedroom."

"Sure."

The dangling angel starts to giggle again. "But before you do, please withhold judgement for what you're going to see."

49: One Who Tends

Speck Hardy's seen some strange things in his time as the overseer of Mount Hope Cemetery. Yes sir, every manner of human emotion, greed, and corruption clawing straight up from those sealed crypts into the world of the living.

Widows driving away in stretch limousines before the new sod catches ahold of the turned soil. Suited men picking dried grass from between the gravel. Grown children sitting on benches, pantomiming heated conversations with long-dead parents. An occasional visitor cursing, kicking dirt, and spitting on the spot he or she imagines the deceased's face to rest.

Speck fiddles with the throttle until the cranky engine sputters in staccato bursts. The old riding lawn mower wheezes, like Speck. Maybe it, and him, will last another year. Maybe not.

His job is to keep the grounds looking clean, to keep the grass mowed between the graves and prune back the volunteer vines and weeds that threaten to edge in from the woods. Folks ride by on the main highway and pitch trash out all the time. Not a day goes by that he doesn't gather a bag full of beer cans, used baby diapers, and fast food bags. It's a shame the way some people treat the outdoors, like it's their personal garbage can.

He wipes his neck with a damp rag. Have to get up early to mow. Might be a bad season for humans, but the summer makes the grass and ditch weeds sprout tall between the plots. Can't have that. No sir. Not on his watch.

No need to give conscious thought to this part of his job. Speck plays the same game each time he mows: passing the graves, thinking back on things he's witnessed over the years. He steers in front of one marker that always makes him reminisce. The images play out in his brain like a favorite movie scene.

Several months past the fellow's graveside service, a woman pulled up in one of those fancy, flashy little foreign convertibles.

Hair as red as the car she was driving. She had a cat with her. On a leash, of all things. Had a black lab too, only she let it loose to run a little bit. Believe it peed on a good number of headstones, but the rain would wash that off and the dead didn't much care anyway.

Something about that woman reminded Speck of the mousy little waitress that used to work at the truck stop diner out by the Interstate: the same height, about the same build, except that gal was a brunette.

That waitress was one of those women who was sweet as butter cream, the kind of woman some men take pleasure in lording over. She was one heck of a server. Never had to send her as much as a needful glance to get more coffee. Speck made sure to leave her a good tip when he was there.

After she went missing, they found her boyfriend's pick-up parked back of a convenience store, keys under the mat. The police questioned the no-account boyfriend. Thought maybe he killed her and set it up to look like she just up and decided to take off. I mulled it over, sitting in that same diner. Wouldn't have surprised anyone if he had murdered her. Many times, I noticed bruises on her arms and once or twice, a black eye she tried to paint over with make-up.

Rumor had it, Buck Jones drank himself into his grave. His liver just gave out, Speck reckons.

Speck revs the mower's engine, allowing it to get used to running, and returns to the memory. That red-headed woman had hung out for a bit by the grave. She put the cat down and it stayed beside her pretty as you please. Just like it was a dog. The black lab ran around and did its business, then sat by the car. At least someone was grieving for Buck Jones. He hardly had nobody show up for his service. Then the woman started to hop around. Speck figured maybe she had stepped into an ant bed, the way she was carrying on. But no. That lady was dancing a jig. Right on top of Buck Jones's grave.

Engine exhaust billows. The mower burns oil, more than it used to. Speck supposes he could ride to that fancy showroom and price a new one. Loyalty has to count for something. He'll fix this one until it can't be fixed no more.

The July heat will build as soon as the sun comes up good. By afternoon, thundershowers bloom and lightning feathers toward the earth. It's struck a good number of the tall pines on the periphery of the cemetery, searing their bark in long, ragged scars. Speck would rather not go out that way, in a violent blaze of ozone and burned flesh. No thank you.

"All right, my darling. Let's knock this chore out."

Helps to talk to machines. They have feelings too. The old gal's been with him for going on fifty years. Lasted longer than most marriages, including his. Heck, she's bettered half the people lying beneath the dirt around him.

Too bad there's not a burial ground for machines. The mower deserves more than ending up in some landfill. "How's that for a kick in the trousers, old gal? You've spent years making sure the dead don't have dandelions and broom sedge sprouting from their final piece of property."

Perhaps he'll tow her to the edge of the woods and park her when she gives up the ghost, let her rust and rest in a peaceful spot.

Speck lowers the mower's deck until the blades hover inches above the grass. Not too close to scrape bald spots, not too far away to make his job harder. Tomorrow, he can come back with the weed whacker for the places the mower can't reach.

If you're going to do a job, do it right.

He motors at a solid speed, for an old man on an old machine. Up one row, down the next. East to west first. An hour later, he switches direction north to south. Speck thinks of it as weaving the graves together, until the cemetery is one tidy quilt of clipped green and slabs of gray, and the occasional pink dashes of rose granite. Wonder how it looks from above? Is that what the spirits see? Perhaps they float up there, smiling down at Speck's careful tending.

Last row. Last plot. The choicest spot in Mount Hope Cemetery, in Speck's way of thinking. And it belongs to him. Years of scraping and saving to pay it off. The funeral's paid off, too, and the gravestone. Even told the funeral director what to etch into the gray marble below his name and dates. *The One Who Tends.*

Nobody crowds in from two of the edges. An old live oak spreads a roof of gnarled arms. Thick beards of Spanish moss swing. The shade from the tree keeps the blistering sun from curling the grass in the summer and lessens the hoar frost in the winter.

Speck pulls the mower beside the plot. Raises the cutting deck. Kills the engine.

"Time to take a break, old gal."

He looks around. Nothing but dragonflies zigzag in the thick air. Other living things have already taken to the shadows. Forget humans. They dash from one air-conditioned cubicle to the next this time of year, unless forced to come to Mount Hope to plant someone.

He hobbles onto the vacant plot. Wonders what it will feel like to rest here.

Speck lowers himself to the ground. Sits. Lies back.

Above, the moss quivers with air movements so slight they don't reach him. Patches of Heaven peek through the leaves. A few clouds hang in the sky — blue now, but it will bleach out to nearly white by noon. Sorrow paces around a cemetery. No doubt about that. But so do peace and beauty.

An ant crawls across his forearm, on its way to somewhere else.

Will anyone remember his story?

Speck feels a comforting hand slip into his. He closes his eyes.

50: When I Am Old and Curled

When I am old and curled,
I will look steadily down
And see all I missed when I was young and hurried.

When I am old and curled,
I will see white grass-stars spared by blades
And tiny purple lilies showing off for no one but themselves.

When I am old and curled,
I will see crosshatched patterns etched in the sidewalk
And "AR + HP" and "Jenna" with a smiley face.

When I am old and curled,
I will see lines of ants carrying important trade
And beetles rolling balls of dirt ten times their size.

When I am old and curled,
I will see a torn stamp, biscuit crumbs, and a key to who-knows-what
And know they are bits left behind, forgotten.

When I am old and curled,
I will lift off and leave, to see all directions spread beneath
Glad I was once young and hurried, then old and curled.

My Writer's Vow

I gather bits and pieces
To weave them with my words
Things I see. Things I sense.
Things I touch and smell.

High clouds. Blue-eyed skies.
Dog kisses. Cat purrs.
Easy mornings. Coffee rich with cream.
Birds dining and blooms shining.

Sweet rolls. Cinnamon air.
Ice cream. Layered cakes.
Tangy tomatoes. Yellow squash.
Watermelon juice and tall iced tea.

Full hugs. Deep conversations.
Children's giggles. Family tales.
Longtime friends. Solid trust.
Silly texts and taking time.

I will not cease this gifted game
Until my ashes fly.
To tell the stories. To nudge a laugh.
To share what truly matters.

Rhett DeVane 2025

About the Author

Rhett DeVane is the award-winning author of eight published mainstream fiction novels: *The Madhatter's Guide to Chocolate, Up the Devil's Belly, Mama's Comfort Food, Cathead Crazy, Suicide Supper Club, Secondhand Sister, Parade of Horribles,* and *Ditch Weed.* She authored middle grade fantasies: *Elsbeth and Sim, Dig Within,* and *The Dragon Box.* Her short fiction and poetry have appeared in numerous anthologies.

Rhett is a Florida native, originally from Chattahoochee. For over forty years, Rhett has made her home in Tallahassee, located in Florida's Big Bend area, where she splits her time between writing and thinking about writing.

To learn more about Rhett, her writing, and upcoming releases, please visit her website: www.rhettdevane.com

Rhett kindly requests: if you have a moment, find this book's page with your online vendor and leave a brief reader's review. Much appreciated!

Author photo by Lance Oliver Photography

Contents

www.ingramcontent.com/pod-product-compliance
Lightning Source LLC
Chambersburg PA
CBHW031215020726
47499CB00002B/589